Sam Galliford is a scientist who has worked in hospitals and medical schools in the UK and Australia, in the fields of child and maternal health. Growing up in Teesside, he learned a love of story-telling from a grandfather who told him rollicking tales of adventurers, navigators and explorers from the days of history. Later, when a work colleague described one of his scientific offerings as 'fiction', he recalled his story-telling roots and began writing his own short stories. The short stories grew and his first novel, *Skyfire*, was published in 2019. *Rockfall* is his second novel.

For David Copeland.

Sam Galliford

ROCKFALL

AUSTIN MACAULEY PUBLISHERS™

LONDON • CAMBRIDGE • NEW YORK • SHARJAH

A CIP catalogue record for this title is available from the British Library.

ISBN 9781528972048 (Paperback)
ISBN 9781528972840 (ePub e-book)

www.austinmacauley.com

First Published (2021)
Austin Macauley Publishers Ltd
25 Canada Square
Canary Wharf
London
E14 5LQ

To Jane Weightman, critic and friend, for her encouragement and her artwork for the cover of this book. To John Weightman, my walking mate who is also an expert on plastic. And to my wife, Anne, for putting up with me while I wrote it.

Chapter 1

"I had a great time in Vietnam," enthused Gerard, accepting the offered chocolate éclair. "I had intended spending only three months at Ban Long, but as soon as I got to the dig site, Professor Nguyn and his students began unearthing some fascinating finds. There were burials with exotic pots and metallic artefacts, mostly bronze but also two pieces of iron, which were a big surprise."

Great-aunt Gwendoline smiled contentedly back at him. She was delighted to have him home again and she always enjoyed hearing about his archaeological adventures in far-flung places, even as she refused to admit she never stopped worrying about him while he was away. She often despaired whether it was really necessary for him to go into such bandit-ridden locations as Indochina in order to study long-dead civilisations when there were still so many Roman and Saxon ruins much closer to home.

"When we put the two pieces of iron together, they looked astonishingly like they were parts of the same knife blade," Gerard breezed on. "Even more exciting, the Anthropology Department at Adelaide University has dated the charcoal we found alongside them to around 1000 BCE. That is about the time the Zhou dynasty first started smelting iron in China, so is very early for that part of the world."

She looked down at Rani, sitting close by her feet and noted that the dog seemed rapt in Gerard's recounting. It was more that she was able to be. She was not feeling the brightest of sparks seeing that her sleep over the past few nights had been continuously interrupted by a recurring dream.

"But I must tell you about Dr Andy Tan and his albatrosses," Gerard continued.

Her attention snapped back to her grand-nephew.

"Don't tell me you found those in Vietnam, too?" she asked.

"Not at all," he grinned. "The Australian National University is helping fund the dig at Ban Long, so I called in at Canberra on my way back from Vietnam to update them on its progress. It was there that I met Andy Tan."

"So, these albatrosses have nothing to do with archaeology?" she queried, noting that Rani's attention had not wavered.

"Not in the least," he confirmed. "Andy is studying the albatrosses on Heard Island in the Southern Ocean and he told me that these majestic, soaring birds mistake bits of plastic food wrap floating around the surface of the ocean for their usual fish prey. They swoop on it, swallow it, cannot digest it and as a result, they choke and die. He tells me the leatherback turtles in the Pacific make the same mistake, thinking floating plastic bags are the jellyfish upon which they normally feed. The populations of both these animals have fallen dramatically in recent years."

"It does sound most damaging for both creatures," Aunt Gwendoline agreed, quietly concluding that swimming with benign reptiles in a warm Pacific atoll sounded a lot safer than going into wild, green, south-east Asian, jungly places in order to dig up bits of broken pottery, no matter how skilled the ancient potter might have been.

"But perhaps the damage is about to get less," Gerard continued gleefully. "After Canberra, I flew to South Australia and Adelaide University where coincidentally, I met Dr Christopher Fadden, a visiting academic from Scotland."

Aunt Gwendoline again focussed hard on her grand-nephew.

"My dear boy," she interrupted. "Your story is becoming rather convoluted. Are you sure you know where it is going?"

He laughed and helped himself to the second chocolate éclair. "Always, Aunt Gwendoline, as you will see," he replied.

Chapter 2

Try as she might, she could not stop her attention from wandering. The dream that had been disturbing her sleep kept pushing itself forward in her mind, distracting her from what Gerard was saying. It was seemingly nothing more than the recalling of an old memory, and she was the first to admit she had accumulated more than a full store of those, but its persistence puzzled her.

She was a young girl in Low Felderby, and the village men were coming up the road on their way to work the next shift at Felderby Pit. She could hear the grit grinding beneath their boots as they dropped into the steady, synchronised tread that men unconsciously adopt when they walk together in a body.

"Come inside and shut the door," Mother called.

She closed the door quickly. It was bad luck for a man to see a woman on his way to work. If he did, he would stop and turn around and go home again, otherwise, it was certain there would be an accident at the Pit and someone, maybe even himself, might be injured or killed. She was only a girl, not a woman, but mother judged her close enough. She leaned against the door with all her weight and looked away while they passed.

The men's footfalls faded, and following them she heard a different tread. It was one of the Cleveland Bays that pulled the wagons of iron ore down in the Pit. She liked the pit horses. Her dad often showed them to her. They were big, strong animals that could frighten you with their size but were also gentle, and she loved their warmth when you got close to them and the feel of their soft noses when you fed them a carrot. She cautiously pulled a curtain aside so she could catch a glimpse of it as it passed by the window.

She dropped the curtain in surprise. She recognised the horse. There had been a rockfall in the Pit. The big jed, the huge hole under the ground that was left after the men had mined out the iron ore, had finally caved in and the horse had been caught in the collapse. It had been badly injured and its handler had brought it up to Pit Entrance and daylight, but it should not be going back to work. Even if it healed, its nerve would be gone. There were men like that in Low Felderby, men who had been below ground miners all their lives but who could no longer face the work. Some found jobs above ground, but all men have their pride, and sooner or later, they left the village with their families to find work elsewhere. A horse did not have that choice.

She slipped out into the street and cautiously followed the Cleveland Bay. There was no fear in its tread or in the regular nodding of its giant head as it walked beside its handler, and she sensed the trust it had in him. She stayed well back so she should not be seen. If the man saw her, the loss of a shift's pay would be hard felt by his family, and the whole village would know it was her he had seen.

Both man and horse came to a stop a few strides inside Pit Entrance and stood half-melted in the gloom. The Pit *frightened her. It was big and dark, and she did not like to think of the horse going down into it. She was grateful to the daylight for holding her back, and she watched anxiously in case the man should turn around and see her, but he showed no sign that he was aware of her presence. He fixed a blindfold across the horse's eyes then sat down and lit the candle in his lamp while his eyes too adjusted to the blackness within the mine.*

After a while, he stood up and tugged at the horse's reins. She stayed watching as their sinking shapes began to disappear down into the shadows of the drift. Unconsciously she mouthed "goodbye" to the horse and as if in response, the man turned around and cast a last backwards glance in her direction. She jumped in fright and quickly tried to hide. She prayed he had not seen her. She knew she should not be there, but it was more than the fear of him seeing her at Pit Entrance that jolted her. Momentarily as he turned, the light of his candle lamp threw his profile into silhouette. It was Gerard.

Aunt Gwendoline blinked back to the present and to what her grand-nephew was saying. It was something about albatrosses and plastic pollution in the oceans, and Rani still seemed intensely interested in it. She focussed once again.

Chapter 3

"Chris Fadden is a microbiologist from Glasgow who has spent his career studying microbes in soil," Gerard explained. "I can't say he is any sort of academic heavyweight, but his name must have popped up on somebody's computer screen when the United States Environmental Protection Agency wanted an independent expert to report on how well the US plastics industry was meeting its pollution targets. So, Chris unexpectedly found himself on a 'plane to the United States and inspecting the environs of the plastics factories there. He told me the lack of pollution he found so far exceeded the legislated requirements that he, the Environmental Protection Agency and even the factory managements themselves had been surprised. And it was this last comment of his that reminded me of Andy Tan's wandering albatrosses. Those wonderful birds have been driven to the edge of extinction by the plastic rubbish floating around our oceans, and now the plastics factories in the United States have cleaned up their act far better than expected. The result might just be less plastic pollution in the environment and more albatrosses. I have written to Andy to tell him to look out for Chris' report."

Gerard stopped and looked at his elderly aunt. He realised he was being garrulous, and he was pleased to see her, but he was concerned about the absence of her usual sparkle. He wondered whether he was tiring her. It was not unreasonable that in the autumn of her very long life, her inner clockwork should begin to run down and all he could do is hope it would not be in too much of a hurry to do so.

"Andy Tan is back on Heard Island as we speak, undoubtedly freezing cold and uncomfortable and trying to find a way to teach the parent birds to stop feeding their chicks plastic bags," he ended more easily. "That is the only idea he has at present to help them survive. But you never know, my trip to Vietnam might have produced some benefits to albatrosses as well as to archaeology."

"And to Pacific Ocean turtles too," Aunt Gwendoline answered distractedly.

Gerard stirred himself.

"I must be going," he smiled. "I have reports to write and papers to prepare, and I must send an email to Chris Fadden to let Andy have a copy of his report."

Rani jumped to attention and stood sniffing the wind as if trying to locate the source of a scent.

"You would like Chris Fadden, Aunt Gwendoline," Gerard continued. "He's an interesting fellow, a big, brawny Scot as strong as an ox but underneath as soft as a kitten. He reminds me of one of those big Cleveland Bays that used to work the ironstone mines in the Cleveland Hills all those years ago."

"A Cleveland Bay?" she echoed.

"Yes. Magnificent, huge, gentle beasts if I remember them correctly," he confirmed. "You took me to see some once when I was a child, the few that remained from the time when Felderby Pit was still working. Whenever I walk beside

Chris, I feel as though I am walking next to one. He is a big fellow, so it is probably not such a strange comparison."

He shrugged himself into his coat and gave his great-aunt a hug.

"It is good to be back, Aunt Gwendoline. I have missed our Wednesday afternoon chats, particularly the chocolate éclairs. The one thing I missed at Ban Long was chocolate."

"It's good to have you home again," she smiled in return.

She acknowledged his farewell, closed her front door and wandered pensively back to her sitting room.

"He is glad to be back, isn't he Rani?" she commented as she re-seated herself in her favourite, carved rosewood chair. "He was certainly all of a bubble to the point where we were scarcely able to get a word in edgeways."

Rani looked up at her mistress and wagged her tail stump hesitantly across the carpet. She seemed unusually tense.

"Yes, I know," Aunt Gwendoline frowned in reply. "You feel it too, don't you? Something is wrong."

The sense of disquiet that had been growing in her over recent days had not been dispelled by Gerard's wittering on about Ban Long and albatrosses and plastics factories, and his reference to a Cleveland Bay had jolted her.

"What are you up to, Mother?" she challenged the aspidistra in its decorated pot sitting on its Edwardian inlaid table in the corner. "I know it is you disturbing my sleep, but as usual, you are not going to be any help and give me an explanation for it, are you?"

The plant declined to communicate, and Aunt Gwendoline sighed. Why she had bothered rescuing it after mother died was a question she had often asked herself. Her only answer was that it had been mother's aspidistra, and apart from her father's oak cased grandfather clock that stood in the hallway, it was the only item worth keeping from her parents' home, although the value of a potted aspidistra would have to be open to some debate.

"Gerard leading a pit horse, one of the Cleveland Bays, to work down Felderby Pit is not right," she summarised. "The horse should not be going back to work. It would never have recovered from its injuries, and Felderby Pit was closed over a generation ago. Gerard would not be going down into it."

A shudder of trepidation washed through her. In her heart, she knew it was the family gift that was disturbing her. The family gift, or at least, that is what mother had called it. It was like having another sense, beyond hearing or touch, a sense of presence or of something being out of place, or of events moving before there was any evidence of them doing so in the tangible world. It ran through the family, sometimes through the male line and sometimes through the female. Mother had it and she had inherited it in her turn, and it was her innocent, childhood utterance that 'Sister Lizzie would not make old bones' that revealed its presence in her. Younger sister Lizzie was barely walking at the time and mother had been unsettled ever since her birth by the distant thought that she would not have a long life, but the gift was not strong in mother, so she was able to put aside her fears and deny Lizzie's destiny until her middle daughter voiced the same knowledge.

"You never forgave me for that moment of insight, did you, Mother? Not all the years that you lived," she nodded to the aspidistra.

If it was a gift, then it was not an easy one to bear. It invariably forewarned of trouble stalking someone close to her, and there was no one closer to her than Gerard, younger sister Lizzie's grandson, her grand-nephew.

"I fear you are right, Rani," she answered the dog's enquiring look. "There is trouble at Pit. Trouble is sniffing around our Gerard, and I have no idea what that trouble might be."

Chapter 4

"Lost a visitor?" Aunt Gwendoline queried.

It was the last answer she had expected to her welcoming enquiry when Gerard arrived for tea the following Wednesday.

"Apparently so," he replied. "Of all the things to come home to when I arrived back in my department, I found a note from my secretary saying that a Dr Witheney had called from the airport to say he was on his way. Since then, nobody of that name has showed up and no one has seen or heard anything of him. I can't recall meeting anyone called Witheney or of inviting them to the department, but I suppose I must have done. I expect he'll turn up sometime. People don't normally disappear in a civilised country like ours."

"One would hope not," she agreed.

She poured them both a cup of Prince of Wales tea, strong and dark, not really right for the afternoon except that she felt in need of some stiffening. She scanned her house, but there was nothing out of place. Only her newly acquired Hunter clock on the sideboard was misbehaving. Walnut veneered and in fine working condition, she was pleased to have come across it in a recent, dusty, country house auction, and while it had not so far shown any sign of keeping accurate time, she had not expected it to. It would take a few days or even weeks before it settled into its new surroundings.

"On a separate topic, I had an e-mail from Chris Fadden," Gerard continued.

Rani sprang to her feet in a half point and looked straight at him.

"Chris Fadden?" Aunt Gwendoline repeated. "Is he the man who is trying to save the albatrosses?"

"Not quite," Gerard replied. "Chris is the chap I met in Adelaide who had just completed a report on the environmental cleanliness of the American plastics industry. It is Andy Tan who is working on the albatrosses, and I thought Chris' report might help him stop them dying through choking on the plastic rubbish floating around the oceans. I was pleased he got in touch. He is back from Australia and once more installed in his laboratory in Glasgow. He sounded very excited and wanted to meet for lunch."

"In Glasgow? That's a long way to go for lunch," she commented.

"Perhaps, but I caught the train up to Scotland the next day and met him at a café near the university," he replied. "He had selected a place a bit off the usual student track, presumably so we could have some quiet time to reminisce without being disturbed, and it served reasonable food. But I'd have to say he was a bit different from how I remembered him.

"In Adelaide, he was like an undergraduate who had never grown up, writing nonsense in the university staff club visitors' book such as, 'Would members of the geology department please not leave their trilobites on the forecourt where everyone can trip over them.' He was full of mischief, cheerful and carefree, especially after dinner and a few glasses of wine, but when I met him in Glasgow, he was different. He greeted me warmly and was genuinely pleased to see me, but he seemed anxious and on tenterhooks."

"Memory and circumstances colour most first impressions," Aunt Gwendoline suggested.

She saw that Rani had lain down and put her chin on her paws, and she glanced over to the aspidistra to make sure that it too was not indulging in any mischief.

"It puzzled me," Gerard continued. "I felt he rushed me inside the café with more haste than was necessary, as if he was anxious to get us off the street and out of sight. Maybe he just didn't want to be seen by any of his students or fellow university staff, and when we were offered a table in the window, he insisted on one well back in the dining area where he immediately chose the chair with its back to the wall so he could see who was coming and going. He didn't give me the impression of being afraid, just anxious like a schoolboy with a secret he is bursting to tell and wanting to make sure nobody else overheard it. He was different."

"But you had lunch," Aunt Gwendoline reminded him.

"We did," he replied. "We ordered our food and a bottle of wine, and we talked about Australia. I asked him how his report on the US plastics factories had been received, and he told me it had gone down very well. The authorities there had been delighted to find an independent expert who was prepared to give their plastics industry such a glowing bill of health, and in return, they had made a sizeable contribution to his pension pot. He told me he had sent Andy Tan a copy of his report as I had requested, and had received a warm e-mail in reply.

"On the surface, our chat was very free and friendly. I admit I was treating him a bit flippantly, remembering the fun times we had enjoyed in Adelaide, but suddenly, he took a big swallow of wine and made a great display of looking around the café to check that nobody else was within earshot. He then leaned closely across the table to me.

"'But Australia and the United States are not what I asked you to come all the way up to Glasgow to talk about,' he whispered conspiratorially.

"'They're not?' I asked.

"'Not at all,' he replied. 'There is more.'

"'Then please expound upon your more,' I invited him, trying not to giggle in the process.

"'I've found a new bug,' he answered."

Rani sat up and looked at Gerard in close attention. To her surprise, Aunt Gwendoline saw her newly acquired Hunter clock had decided to show the correct time. Given the patience she had expended fiddling with it over the past few days, she felt that was no more than her due, but she had not expected it.

Chapter 5

"I wasn't quite sure how to respond to Chris' statement," Gerard continued.

"'That's nice for you,' I replied. 'I'm not a microbiologist, only a humble archaeologist, but I assume that your discovering a new bug is the equivalent of me finding the remains of an extinct and hitherto undescribed civilisation. It is quite exciting, could be important, at a push it might change our view of the world, and it is certainly something to put in the curriculum vitae. I am very pleased for you. Cheers.'

"We both skulled a glass of wine.

"'So, what does it do, this bug?' I asked.

"'I thought at first it was just a variant of Methylococcus capsulatus,' he replied. 'It behaves in most respects like the normal soil bacterium, and I'm still checking it out, but it is different.'

"I smiled at his enthusiasm.

"'Then, you can write your new bug, *Christopherii faddenii*, into the scientific literature and invite me to the medal giving ceremony when it delivers you the recognition you so rightly deserve,' I proposed.

"'*Christopherii faddenii*,' he chuckled. 'I like that, but I don't think it is quite that unique. Maybe I will call it

Methylococcus faddenii, though. That sounds good. It is a new bug, so I should get some credit for it. But it is more than just new. It is something special.'

"'You mean there is more to your more?' I asked.

"'There most certainly is,' he replied.

"He gave another quick look round the café. It was empty except for a dawdling, romantic couple sitting at a window table. I remember thinking I hoped they were supposed to be together because if they weren't, they could not have been more visible. But they were oblivious to everything except each other, and after a second glance, Chris too dismissed them as unthreatening. He leaned across the table even more closely to me and dropped his voice.

"'Gerry, you will keep this to yourself, won't you? Lips zippered and sealed with not a word to anyone.'

"'Absolutely,' I promised.

"'If I am right, this bug could be highly significant and worth an awful lot of money.'

"'Word of honour,' I added.

"He was looking so serious I had difficulty not bursting out laughing. He is a big and amusing looking fellow at the best of times, and his hush-hush, secretive manner only exaggerated his normal, comical expression. Maybe it was the wine. We had emptied our bottle, so I ordered another one.

"'So, what makes you think your bug is special?' I asked.

"'During my visits to the plastics factories in the United States, I collected soil samples wherever I went,' he began. 'I wasn't worried about the factories. Some were so clean I was sure they had been scrubbed and vacuumed for a week prior to my visit, but there are procedures we microbiologists follow. I wasn't expecting to find anything except the usual bugs that normally inhabit healthy soil, and I was expecting only to count and classify them just to provide the data to confirm that the factories were environmentally clean and free from pollution.'

"'But you found a new one,' I finished for him.

"'When I got the samples back to my lab in Adelaide, some of the plastic bags they were in had broken,' he continued.

"I shrugged, not knowing why that was important.

"'It's the quarantine rules,' he explained. 'In order to prevent soil samples from one country contaminating another country's dirt with unwelcome crop diseases, they have to be placed inside plastic bags before being shipped, and then each bag has to be sealed inside another plastic bag just to make sure nothing escapes. The Australian authorities are even more strict, and they insisted that my entire collection had to go into yet more layers of heavy-duty plastic before they would let me bring it into the country. It was all a bit tedious and annoying, but I would have to say that on this occasion, the Aussies were right. When I unpacked my samples in Adelaide, one or both of the inner plastic bags had disintegrated in some samples, and even the outer bag had given way in one.'

"'Luggage handlers can be a bit rough if they are having a bad day,' I suggested.

"'It wasn't that,' he replied snappily. 'The bags weren't split as if jumped on by a large Australian. They had crumbled, dissolved, fallen apart. I didn't take too much notice of it at first and just regarded it as a nuisance. That was until I set about culturing my samples to see what would grow.

The next morning was a real blinder. Half of my culture dishes had fallen apart.'

"'You've lost me again, Chris,' I interjected. 'Why is that significant?'

"He looked at me with that expression we lecturers adopt when we realise we have to go back in the explanation and hope that our students will eventually catch up.

"'We grow bugs in little, round, flat dishes called Petri dishes that are partially filled with a nutrient gel,' he explained. 'The dishes are made of plastic and it was the plastic of the dishes that had fallen apart.'

"'So, you got a bad batch of them,' I replied. 'It happens, even to us archaeologists.'

"'But not to us microbiologists,' he countered. 'It took me a few days to nail the little creature and eventually, I had to grow it in glass. And when I added plastic food wrap to the nutrient mix, I got a magnificent growth of the organism responsible. The more plastic I added, the better it grew.'

"'Are you saying you've found a bug that eats plastic?' I asked.

"'I'm almost certain that's what it does,' he grinned triumphantly. 'And I think I will name it Methylococcus faddenii. It is a new bug, and I see no reason not to claim it as mine.'

"We chinked glasses once more to celebrate his discovery, then he stopped abruptly and looked quickly around the café again. The lovebirds in the window had finally decided to leave, and only the bored waitress stood behind the counter.

"'Look, Gerry,' he whispered very quietly to me. 'All this is very new and I'm not certain about any of it anyway, not really, so you won't say a word about it to anyone, will you? It's important that you don't say anything about it to anybody, nobody at all, at least not until I have got it sorted out a bit more.'

"'I've already promised,' I replied. 'It sounds quite an exciting find for you, but it's not my field of study, and I wouldn't have any idea why it is significant.'

"'It's significant,' he nodded enthusiastically. 'It's going to make me a fortune. Keep quiet about it for the moment and I'll cut you in on the deal later on.'

Chapter 6

Aunt Gwendoline looked at her grand-nephew. He had come to a knot in his story and was struggling to proceed. She glanced down at Rani, who remained watchful.

"Did Dr Fadden give you any idea why his discovery might be valuable?" she prompted.

Gerard came out of his reverie.

"None whatsoever," he smiled. "I was a bit annoyed with him when he said he would cut me in on whatever deal he was going to make with it.

"'You don't have to buy me off,' I protested. 'I already said I won't tell anyone. Other than you've discovered a new bug, I wouldn't know what or who to tell anyway.'

"Whatever his plans for it, he was very enthusiastic about it. It was only afterwards on the train home that I began wondering whether or not he was being carried away by dreams of money and glory. I don't doubt that he is sincere in his belief that he has found a new bug and it would be an amazing discovery if it is true, but he is no great academic brain, and his naturally comical appearance makes it difficult to take him seriously. And after lunch, he managed his familiar trick of not being able to find his way out of the café."

"What do you mean 'not being able to find his way'?" she asked.

"Chris doesn't have much of a sense of direction," Gerard grinned. "In fact, he doesn't have one at all, particularly after a couple of drinks. We used to have the most awful fun with him in Adelaide. After our dinners in the university staff club, which invariably included much wine and port to follow, we would deliberately misdirect him when he tried to go back to his room. We would send him into broom cupboards and toilets and get him hopelessly disoriented. We were more than a bit mischievous with him, but fortunately, he is such a good-natured fellow that he always took our pranks in good spirit. We had polished off a couple of bottles of wine with our lunch and had also enjoyed a couple of beers beforehand, so after we had finished, I was not completely surprised when he headed off the wrong way around the dining area looking for the exit. The waitress thought he was looking for the toilets and confused him even further by pointing in their direction. We did eventually make it outside."

For a moment, the image recreated itself in Aunt Gwendoline's mind of a blindfolded Cleveland Bay being led down into Felderby Pit, not knowing where it was going but with complete trust in its handler.

"Disappearing into the gloom," she muttered, then waved a hand to dismiss her grand-nephew's puzzled look.

"I hope Dr Fadden did manage to find his way home," she smiled. "It would be a shame if his novel discovery became lost in some railway siding or bus terminus never to see the light of day again."

Gerard laughed and began his move to leave.

"I'm sure he got home, although almost certainly by a circuitous route. At least, I hope he did. I've not heard from him since our lunch and having one lost soul is quite enough for me to be dealing with at the moment."

"You mean the mysterious Dr Witheney who called your office to say he was on his way and then did not arrive?" she asked.

"Exactly," he replied. "Nobody in the department seems to know anything about him, and I still cannot put a face to anyone of that name. All I have is the scribbled message left for me by my secretary before she went on holiday."

"Curiouser and curiouser," Aunt Gwendoline quoted.

Gerard grinned and shrugged himself into his coat.

"I must be going. I'll see you next Wednesday."

He gave her a last smile and hug.

"I shall be here," she called as she waved him goodbye.

She closed her front door and strolled back to her sitting room with Rani close at heel.

"Our Gerard describes his friend, Dr Fadden, as being like a Cleveland Bay and I am dreaming of such a horse being led back to work at Felderby Pit. The horse is blindfolded so it cannot know where it is going and Dr Fadden seems similarly unable to find his way out when trying to leave a restaurant," she summarised. "Not only that, but our Gerard has a visitor, a Dr Witheney, who is also lost. That is more than one too many lost individuals for me to feel comfortable about."

She glanced over to the aspidistra.

"I don't suppose you have any suggestions to make, do you, Mother?"

The plant did not move.

"I thought not," she sniffed. "But you can stop pretending. You were never that uninterested in what was going on around you even when you were alive."

She had still not forgiven it for the continued interruption of her sleep. Indeed, she had even ended up in the dark hours of one morning standing in her dressing gown in front of it.

"Why are you doing this, Mother?" she had demanded.

The plant refused to respond, which had left her even more furious.

"Useless foliage," she stormed at it. "You even used to talk to it, Mother."

She stopped when she realised she was doing the same.

"Heaven preserve me from becoming like you," she muttered.

She looked down at Rani, who patiently returned her stare.

"You are quite right, Rani," she sighed. "I am a silly old woman who talks to an aspidistra. I do worry about me sometimes, but in the meantime, we can get ourselves some supper. I am very tired and an early night would not do us any harm."

'Supper' was a word Rani recognised, so she wholeheartedly agreed, and later she settled on her blanket beside her mistress' bed, nose tucked under her front paws, listening for the steady breathing of her mistress in sleep.

Chapter 7

It was not to be a restful night.

She was in school and pencils froze in mid-letter at the sound of the accident siren at the Pit. Everyone had known for weeks that deep underground the rocks were straining. They had felt them. The talk in Low Felderby had been of little else as with increasing frequency, windows rattled, and houses creaked, doors opened with nobody there and ornaments fell off shelves, and the ground juddered beneath their feet.

"It's the big jed," they nodded to each other if they spoke of it at all.

So much ore had been taken out of the ore seam that the jed had ended up bigger than all of Low Felderby, or so the men said as they tramped off to work at the change of each shift. It was a huge hole under the ground, and it had to fall in. There was no other place for it to go and the entire village held itself in wait for the accident siren to sound.

Silence weighed heavily in the classroom. The lesson stopped and all of them, including the teacher, pressed their faces against the glass of the classroom windows to watch and wait. There was only one thought in all their minds. Whose father, uncle, brother or neighbour had been caught in the rockfall and how badly were they hurt? There were two boys who had been in school with them last year and were now working down the Pit. Strangely, she had no fear for her dad. She knew he was safe.

The uneven crunch of men's boots shuffling up the road heralded the coming of the casualties, and a sigh of relief escaped them all as they saw the stretchers being carried at hip height. "A rockfall never left a man looking bonny," her dad had told her, which was why dead men were carried at shoulder height, out of sight of their womenfolk and bairns until they could be delivered home to be cleaned up by their family and await the undertaker. Injured men were carried at hip height, also to be taken home to be cared for until the doctor came later that day or perhaps the next. No one was taken to the hospital. "You died in hospital," mother had told her. It seemed to be true. She knew only one person, a girl from school, white with fever and mad with pain, who went to the hospital and came home again, and she never walked properly afterwards.

"Gwen Penderrick, back to your desk now."

She hesitated. That was when she saw the Cleveland Bay. It was being led limping and bloody along the road, whinnying with pain as it went. Huge shreds of skin and flesh were hanging from its front leg and left shoulder and from lacerations down its side, and it had a vicious gash right through to the bone on its hind fetlock. She was amazed it could still walk, and she watched it in surprise. A horse was usually shot underground after being injured in a rockfall and only its carcase brought to the surface, but its handler must have thought it was worth saving. He too was covered in dust

34

from his cloth cap down to his boots and his gait was shaken and unsteady, and there was blood on him, although whether his or the horse's she could not tell. She sensed the bond between them and her heart began to pound.

"Gerard!" she shouted.

Aunt Gwendoline found herself sitting bolt upright, eyes staring into the darkness of her bedroom with the echoes of her call rebounding around her. She scrambled for the bedside light as she became aware of Rani standing on hind legs pounding at the side of the bed in a state of agitation.

"Just a minute, Rani."

She slumped back exhausted on her pillows as the light's glow drove away whatever shadows that might be hiding in wait for her, and her body began to regain control of her throbbing heart and her panting lungs. It took longer than she would have wished and all the time, the only thought she could recall was her shout of "Gerard!"

She did not dare risk getting out of bed. She was shaking too much. Rani remained watchful until finally dawn came and the light was put out, and only then did they both return to a sleep that remained mercifully undisturbed until the sun was well risen.

Chapter 8

A ring on her front doorbell took Aunt Gwendoline's attention away from her index copy of *Antiques Collectors' Weekly* and its list of articles on Victorian Hunter clocks.

"We weren't expecting anyone, were we?" she asked Rani.

She had not been fully concentrating on her search for a reason why her Hunter clock remained so obstinately unregulated in spite of her efforts to introduce it gently into its new surroundings. She was worrying about Gerard. He was the single individual their family had managed to produce down to the most recent generation, and if he did not soon cease his far-flung expeditions and settle down with some sensible young woman, he could very well be the last of the line. He had never been short of female company ever since he climbed into long trousers and there had been some promising prospects among them, but they all eventually proved temporary for which she was ultimately relieved. She tried not to interfere, but it was difficult.

"Ms Penderrick?" the young man asked when she opened the door.

"Miss Penderrick, yes," she corrected him.

"I'm Detective Sergeant Chak from the local police. I'm a friend of your nephew, Gerard." He held up his identification.

"Indeed, you are," she smiled. "He has told me a lot about you. Do come in."

He grinned in return and followed her into the sitting room, noting as he went the polished and dust-free hallway with its tall grandfather clock and the fine antique wood engravings along the walls.

"Would you like a cup of tea?" she asked.

"Thank you, no," he answered, taking the chair she indicated. "This is just a social visit and not an official one. I've called on the off-chance that Gerry might be here. He wasn't in his department, and his research assistant told me he might have gone up to Glasgow. I had quite a chat with her. She's an interesting girl, certainly a looker, big smile, long legs, very friendly. Australian, said her name was Anne Blaise. I gather Gerry brought her back with him from his last trip."

"He hasn't mentioned her to me," she smiled, adding to herself that indeed, he had not, and given the sergeant's enthusiastic description of her, she would have to wonder why.

"Why did you want to see him?" she asked. "I hope you are not going to tell me he has got himself involved in another murder, at least not one in the present day. He tells me he often finds graves in his archaeological digs, although I cannot think they would be of much interest to you, even as cold cases."

Sergeant Chak grinned broadly. The old lady was much as Gerard had described her, slender and elegantly dressed, her clothes new, understated and of good quality and worn in a style which suggested a bygone age, much like his own grandmother wore her sari. He had the impression that, like his grandmother, she too had been taller in her younger days and was now slowly shrinking under her years, although in contrast to his grandmother, she seemed only to carry enough weight to stop her being blown away by the next puff of breeze.

"It's nothing like that," he reassured her. "A telephone call came through to the police station asking if Gerry still worked at the university. The caller identified himself as 'Anderson', no rank or title, and said he was from the Data Intelligence Unit. The station sergeant passed the message on to me because he knows Gerry and I are pals, and he was puzzled that Anderson, whoever he was, did not want Gerry's telephone number when he was offered it."

"Odd," Aunt Gwendoline agreed. "I presume Mr Anderson is not someone bent on mischief."

"I doubt it," Sergeant Chak shrugged. "We practical coppers tend to regard the data intelligence people as a bunch of pale, otherworldly beings who spend their days in closed rooms dimly lit only by the glow of their computer screens. They collect huge amounts of data in the pursuit of criminal activity, and I have to admit they have provided us with the intelligence for some notable police successes. But they are a strange bunch."

"I cannot imagine Gerard being involved in any criminal activity, at least not since 5000 BC which is where he seems to spend most of his days," she answered.

Sergeant Chak laughed again. He was beginning to see why Gerard loved this old lady and her steel sharp mind.

"I can't imagine it either," he agreed. "But given the state of security in the world today, and Gerry's track record of departing for places not on the usual tourists' itinerary, the pale ones were probably just checking to see he was safely back from his jaunt in Vietnam."

"Well, if Mr Anderson should call again, feel free to tell him that Gerard is once more home, much to his great-aunt's delight, and if he wishes to dispute the matter you may give him my telephone number," she ended.

"I will do that," he answered.

He smiled into her steady eyes and hoped that Anderson did call again. He imagined she could still wilt a recalcitrant maharajah and his rebellious rabble at a distance of more than forty paces if she needed to, so he could only wish Anderson the best of luck in his data gathering if he had to deal with her.

"Meanwhile, if he is looking for somebody to find, perhaps you could ask him to see if he can locate a Dr Witheney," she continued.

"Who?"

"Dr Witheney. Has Gerard not mentioned him to you?"

"No, he hasn't," he replied. "But I've only seen him once since he got back. I gather this Dr Witheney is someone who is absent on duty?"

"Apparently so. He called from the airport, left a message with Gerard's secretary and then disappeared. Not something we like to think of happening in this country."

"Certainly not," Sergeant Chak agreed. "I'll get a few more details from Gerry and check with Missing Persons. In the meantime, don't worry too much. I'm sure Anderson's enquiry is nothing more than someone wanting an expert in old graves to help with an investigation into a recently discovered skeleton."

"Let us hope so," she smiled back to him.

For some minutes after the sergeant left, she stood in the hallway and listened to the syncopated beat of the pendulum of her oak-cased grandfather clock as it simulated the sound of a workman's boots and the clopping of a Cleveland Bay on their way to work at Felderby Pit.

"I wonder what it was that really brought the good sergeant to our door?" she asked Rani. "He already knew that Gerard has gone to Glasgow. Was it simply to deliver the message that someone by the name of Anderson was looking for him?"

It was not much of a message, but in her core, it made her feel uncomfortable.

She looked up at the clock. It had been her dad's wedding gift to mother, and she had listened to its voice all her childhood years and drawn strength from the certainty of its beat as it trod the minutes of her life. Her dad had always kept it wound and oiled, but it had stood silent and empty in the parlour at home after he died, and it was only after mother died that she had rescued it and polished it and wound it up and heard its voice ring out once more. She looked into its face then over to a silver frame holding an ancient photograph of a young man. Dashing and handsome, he looked a swell with his moustache, waistcoat and watch chain, the fashion of the era, and as the years went by, it was with pride and joy she saw his features emerge again in his great-grandson, Gerard.

She wandered back to her sitting room.

"Our Gerard is not telling us everything about his trip to Australia, is he? A good looking and friendly research assistant with long legs and a big smile who goes by the name of Anne Blaise, for a start," she summarised to the aspidistra.

"Nothing to do with you, I suppose. I wouldn't be so sure. If our Gerard is collecting good looking research assistants from the antipodes and bringing them home with him without so much as saying a word to us about it, then I cannot see how you would ever think it is none of your business."

The plant feigned indifference.

"It is a mystery, and I don't suppose we will know any more until our Gerard comes to tea next Wednesday," she ended. "Still, you like Sergeant Chak, don't you Rani, so that is something."

The dog happily agreed.

Chapter 9

"I see you have your spies," grinned Gerard. "How did you know I'd been to Glasgow?"

"Your friend, Sergeant Chak, called to see me, and he in turn, was told it by a certain Australian research assistant he happened to meet when he went to your department to enquire your whereabouts. She seemed very well informed."

The tea was Darjeeling, the sandwiches smoked salmon, cream cheese and watercress, and the cakes were a selection of iced and chocolate sponges.

Gerard chuckled. "Anne Blaise, our wombat expert," he confirmed. "I met her in Canberra where she was finishing a master's thesis in zoology at the Research School of Biological Sciences, tracking wombats around Tidbinbilla Nature Reserve. Since wombats live in burrows, I thought her expertise might be useful."

"Sergeant Chak said she was very good looking," Aunt Gwendoline persisted, holding Gerard with a gaze that in his childhood years he had referred to as her 'hairy eyeball'.

"One has to be slim and athletic if one is going to follow wombats down their burrows," he parried. "I was thinking of the two pieces of iron we found in Ban Long. When we put them together, it was difficult to believe they were not two fragments of the same iron blade, and we archaeologists are always concerned about animals digging burrows and churning up the layers of the dirt in which we find things. It is possible that burrowing animals could have disturbed the soil around them so that they only coincidentally ended up alongside charcoal from a fire lit 3000 years ago."

"And do they have wombats in Vietnam?" she asked.

"No," he conceded. "But the principle is the same."

She was clearly not persuaded, and he grinned back to the laughter in her eyes. He knew that old as she was, she could still remember the time when she too was young. "The folly of youth," she had once said to him as he struggled through the aftermath of a particularly intense relationship. "In spite of all evidence to the contrary, you young people still persist in thinking you are the first to discover what every generation has discovered before you. In case you hadn't realised it, that is precisely why you are here." Anne Blaise was unquestionably attractive as well as being a very capable zoologist. He chuckled and settled back in his chair.

"So, I had better tell you about my trip to Glasgow," he began. "I had another e-mail from Chris Fadden. It was a strange message, and I could make very little sense out of it other than he wanted to see me again. I called him and the conversation was even more odd. He talked very fast, muffling his voice to the point of being almost inaudible. I was beginning to wonder whether or not he was having some sort of choking fit.

"'Gerry. Oh god. I can't talk. Security, you know. Can we make arrangements just like last time?'

"'You said in your e-mail you wanted to meet,' I reminded him.

"'That's right, exactly like last time. Get your secretary to call the department here with the time. Don't call me direct. Must go.' He rang off.

"I was utterly perplexed. When we had last met, he had been very excited about his new bug, but I could not imagine what might have upset him in the meantime.

"I arrived around late lunchtime at the café where we had previously met. He joined me almost immediately and bustled me inside. I got the impression he had been hiding somewhere nearby, waiting for me to arrive before showing himself.

"'What's the excitement?' I asked as soon as we had ordered.

"He was even more twitchy than he had been previously.

"'My bug, *Methylococcus faddenii*,' he whispered across the table to me.

"'What about it?'

"'It's showing itself to be everything I hoped it would be and more. I've had to be careful, keeping it hush-hush and top secret and all that. Even so, I think some of the commercial boys may have got wind of it. But I think I've now got enough data to get it patented, set up a company and start offering its services to anyone who wants to pay. It will be worth a fortune. As I promised last time, I'll cut you in on the proceeds, Gerry. In any case, you could claim a small role in my discovery.'

"'Me? How?'

"'It was your guess about a link between reduced pollution around the American plastics factories and the improved survival of Andy Tan's albatrosses in the Southern Ocean. That got me thinking about my data. You deserve some credit for that, say five per cent of the profits? They will

44

be huge, so five per cent will be more than enough to set you up for life.'

"Fortunately, our sandwiches and drinks arrived at that point. I was beginning to feel a little dazed trying to keep up with the pace and direction of his thinking. I stirred my tea until the waitress was out of earshot.

"'Chris,' I began before he could take off again. 'I'm not a microbiologist, but neither are you a businessman.'

"'I think five per cent is fair,' he fired back, suddenly not quite so friendly. 'In view of the fact that I am the one who has done all the work and the only thing you contributed was an off-the-cuff suggestion. I could have offered you only two per cent, but I thought I would be a bit more generous seeing that you are a friend. If you are going to be sniffy about it...'

"'It's not the five per cent, Chris,' I interrupted him. 'In any case, it is Andy Tan who is working on the albatross data, not me.'

"'You haven't told him about my idea, have you?' he demanded.

"'No, of course not,' I replied. 'I don't even know what your idea is. All I said to Andy was to look out for your report, and I gather you sent him a copy. That is all.'

"He calmed down a little and pulled back from across the table, but the direction of the conversation was starting to worry me. He had become very possessive of his discovery and was behaving as if I was trying to steal it from him.

"'Stop and think a minute, will you, Chris?' I continued. 'You have made a remarkable discovery, and it might turn out to be worth some money. But you, like me, are an academic and a scientist. We discover things, add to the sum of human knowledge and open up new horizons for the rest of humanity.

45

We don't make money and generally speaking, we don't have the mercenary skills or the street cunning to do so. But as scientists, we have something that no simple money maker can ever have. We have the certainty that at the moment we make a discovery we are standing in a place where nobody in the whole of the history of humankind has ever stood before. We are standing at the very frontier of human knowledge, and no other human eyes have ever before seen what we are looking at. That is what being a scientist is all about, Chris, that instant of first discovery. It is the payoff we get for all our work, and it is what we work for, and I don't know any of us who would ever swap that feeling for a mere pile of money. So, shut up about your five per cent.'

"I was annoyed with him. Most academics view the world with a certain amount of avarice when it glints the prospect of gold at them, but Chris seemed to have become lost to the idea that *Methylococcus faddenii* was going to make him rich beyond his wildest dreams."

Chapter 10

"He calmed down at my outburst.

"'Tell me about your bug,' I invited him. 'How exactly is it going to make you squillions?'

"He leaned back in his chair and giggled, and I saw the mischievous undergraduate reappear in his eyes.

"'Bioremediation,' he replied.

"'You've lost me already, Chris,' I sighed.

"'Bioremediation,' he repeated. 'It means cleaning up the environment using natural, biological agents such as bugs as opposed to using nasty, synthetic chemicals like detergents. It is a very fashionable thing to be doing these days.'

"'True. We are all being encouraged to be more environmentally friendly,' I agreed.

"'But did you know the role bugs play in the process?' he asked. 'Somewhere in nature, there is a bug that, given the right conditions, will break down almost any pollutant our great industrial lifestyle produces. Did you know that there are bugs in the soil that can digest crude oil? After some of our more spectacular oil tanker disasters, they were spread around and were so effective they were able to clean up the contaminated foreshores without damaging the shellfish and other creatures that live there.'

"'And this is going to make your money for you?' I asked.

"'It most certainly is,' he replied. 'After oil, plastic pollution is a massive problem. Did you know that we, mankind, manufacture in excess of one hundred million tonnes of it every year?'

"'I didn't know, but I will take your word for it,' I shrugged. 'It's very useful stuff.'

"'Unquestionably useful, but did you know that even the most dedicated local authorities only manage to recycle half of the plastic rubbish that gets thrown out by our consumer-oriented society,' he continued. 'The rest gets incinerated, chucked around the countryside, or left to float around the oceans where it chokes Andy Tan's albatrosses. A good quarter of it ends up as rubbish in landfill sites where it will stay for the next four hundred and fifty years or more before it finally rots away. That is twenty-five million tonnes a year, increasing at around five per cent per year, buried in the ground. I would have thought that you as an archaeologist, would have wanted to know about that.'

"'It's useful information,' I agreed. 'What ancient peoples threw away can tell us an awful lot about how they lived, but I would have to regard plastic as a bit recent.'

"He looked at me with exaggerated patience.

"'Local authorities spend millions every year trying to deal with waste plastic,' he expounded. 'Just finding new landfill sites is a major headache for them. Think how they will welcome me when I tell them I can get rid of all the plastic rubbish in their landfill sites and massively reduce their future landfill requirements in a completely environmentally friendly way, using my patented, plastic-devouring Methylococcus fadennii which recycles waste plastic back to its harmless constituents in only a few months. And I wouldn't be greedy. I'll only charge them eighty per cent of what it costs them to get rid of it now.'

"I looked at Chris. He was as fired up and excited as only an academic who thinks he has sighted a pot of gold at the end of a rainbow can be.

"'You think they'd pay you?' I asked.

"'Of course, they would,' he spluttered. 'What alternatives do they have? Keep trying to find more landfill sites and build more waste disposal incinerators against the opposition of increasingly well organised residential and environmental protest groups? Avoiding the legal battles alone would make it worthwhile to them. The problem is not going to go away. Do you know that there is so much plastic buried in some landfill sites that it has even been suggested they be mined for it? Just think how much more rubbish dumping space I could create for them by making it all disappear. They would love me for it.'

"His voice had risen with his excitement. He stopped himself short and again looked hurriedly around the café in something like a panic before relaxing a little.

"'You will keep this quiet, won't you, Gerry?' he stressed. 'Please don't say anything to anybody. I still have some work to do before I can get the whole process patented, and it's such an immensely valuable piece of intellectual property that somebody is bound to try and steal it if word gets out.'

"'You have my promise, Chris,' I repeated. 'Not a word to anyone. It does sound as though you've latched on to something potentially useful. Good luck with it, and if you can clean up the countryside and save Andy Tan's albatrosses in the process then you have my full support.'

"He beamed at me.

"'It is big,' he nodded. '*Methylococcus faddenii* could just clean up the world.'"

Chapter 11

Aunt Gwendoline let her mind skip over the details of what her grand-nephew was saying. It was not a strange idea to her that nature had a way of cleaning up the mess left behind by mankind. Carrion birds lived off the roadkill beside the lanes she travelled on her outings and with the spread of suburbia, foxes now fed their cubs from the contents of domestic rubbish bins rather than the farmers' chicken coups of days gone by. Poppies had grown in the devastated fields of Flanders after the War to end all Wars, and trees and forests inevitably reclaimed the sites of the abandoned towns and villages that millennia later, Gerard and his colleagues would rediscover on their archaeological digs. It simply amused her that the current generation had created words such as 'bioremediation' and 'recycling' to describe what she and her sisters considered common knowledge when they were growing up.

"I suppose it could work," Gerard resumed. "If a bug exists that can live on something as noxious as crude oil, I see no reason why a bug should not exist that can live off waste plastic. I hope Chris has discovered something that will help clean up our world, but at the moment, he is tending to be blinded by thoughts of money, fame and glory to the extent that I worry he is going to make a fool of himself."

"Apart from a transient loss of dignity, it will be a relatively harmless crash to earth for him," she smiled.

"I hope it happens soon," he shrugged. "Chris does seem to be getting a bit paranoid about the whole business. He keeps impressing on me how hush-hush everything must be kept."

"'You're one of the very few people I can trust,' he says. '*Methylococcus faddenii* is literally worth millions and there are a lot of very nasty, industrial people around who would love to steal it, either to kill the idea or else make millions out of it for themselves, all without giving me or you or the university any credit or financial return for the work I've done. Industrial espionage is a very dirty business, so please do not say a word to anyone.'

"I can only do as he asks. The industrial applications of archaeology are extremely limited, so I have never had anybody try and pinch any of my ideas."

"Loose lips sink ships," Aunt Gwendoline quoted. "It was a wartime slogan we had drilled into us to remind us to be careful about careless talk. There's no harm in it."

The tea was finished, the sandwiches eaten and only one non-chocolate sponge cake was left.

"There could be something in what Chris says, though, about the industrial espionage business," Gerard continued as he rose to leave. "I had an e-mail from Andy Tan yesterday. He is back on Heard Island, no doubt very cold and homesick. I know that feeling when you are far from home, so I keep in touch with him."

"And did he mention Dr Fadden?" she asked.

"No, but he told me he had a visitor last week."

"Not Dr Witheney by any chance," she prompted.

"No," he smiled. "According to Andy, Heard Island is a very small island in the Southern Ocean, closer to Antarctica than anywhere else. It is cold, wet, windy and usually covered in mist. It has no airstrip, so the only way to get there is by a stomach-churning, four or five-day sea crossing from Hobart, and because there is no harbour you have to scramble yourself ashore from an inflatable dingy. It has World Heritage listing, so you need special permission to be there and even then, parts of it are restricted in order to protect the albatross and other bird nesting sites where Andy is working. All in all, it is not a place where people drop in for a casual chat."

"And somebody did?" she asked.

"Apparently so. One morning, Andy was startled by a helicopter landing outside his hut on the very south of the island. Out popped a public service type who announced he was from the International Antarctic Scientific Resources Policy Committee and started talking about plastic pollution in the Southern Ocean. He asked if Andy had seen Chris Fadden's report and Andy just happened to have his copy with him, something to read during the long sub-Antarctic nights. He was completely surprised when the visitor took the report from him, said 'thank you' and put it in his briefcase, declaring that he did not have time to read it immediately and that he had to leave before the weather closed in. He then got back into his helicopter and left."

"Literally a flying visit," Aunt Gwendoline commented.

"Exactly," Gerard agreed. "And it started Andy thinking. All anyone needed to do to get hold of a copy of Chris's report would be to write to Chris or the US Environmental Protection

Agency and ask for one. Making the uncomfortable trip to Heard Island and back seemed a bit extreme. When a week later, he got back to the main base on the north of the island, Andy found nobody on any of the research teams had ever heard of the International Antarctic Scientific Resources Policy Committee, and nothing showed up on an internet search. It also transpired that the head ranger had been annoyed by the visitor refusing to be accompanied by an official guide when entering a sensitive area like Hurd Point, and had sent off a report to National Parks headquarters to advise them. He received a reply saying that the visitor had full clearance to go wherever he liked."

"A powerful man," Aunt Gwendoline nodded. "And did Dr Tan's visitor have a name?"

"He introduced himself as Dr Anderson, although if he is one of Chris' industrial spies that probably would not be his real name. Aunt Gwendoline, are you all right?"

Aunt Gwendoline gripped the front door catch as she felt the floor tremble beneath her.

"Anderson?" she repeated.

Rani stood beside her, pointing intently towards the front door, ready to attack or defend as the instant required.

"Do you know him?" asked Gerard.

"Not at all," she replied.

"That's a pity," he shrugged. "I might have been able to put Andy's mind at rest. Anyway, dear aunt, before I go, you mentioned that Sergeant Chak called and wanted to see me about something."

Aunt Gwendoline paused with her hand still on the front door.

"He said something about someone looking for an expert in old graves," she answered dismissively.

"I'll call him and get some details," Gerard smiled. "And don't worry about Dr Witheney. I've given up on him. He hasn't presented himself in the department, and I really cannot remember ever meeting him. Thanks, as always, for the tea. Take care of yourself, and I'll see you again next Wednesday."

He gave her a quick hug and tried not to show his surprise as she hurried him out of the door and closed it quickly behind him.

Chapter 12

Aunt Gwendoline lowered herself gently into her favourite chair and furrowed her brow in concentration.

"Dr Anderson, indeed," she muttered. "First, he telephones Sergeant Chak's police station asking the whereabouts of our Gerard. Next, he goes on an uncomfortable and apparently unnecessary journey to an isolated Antarctic island to collect a copy of a report which he could have obtained simply by asking for it. There is certainly something not right about that."

She had no doubts that the two Andersons were one and the same.

"You don't like Mr Anderson, do you Rani?" she continued. "We haven't yet met him, and it is very bad to have an opinion about someone one has never met, but I cannot help thinking you are right. Should we have told Gerard about him? Perhaps it is better that he finds out from his friend, Sergeant Chak."

She began shuffling the deck of her thoughts, cutting them and then dealing them out in sequence, looking for an answer in the order of their fall. None appeared, so she cut them and shuffled them again, adding in the wild card of the missing Dr Witheney. Still, no picture emerged. She included the trump card of a Cleveland Bay and the missing card of mister doctor Anderson, but still, no pattern took shape. Eventually, the strike of her grandfather clock told her that any further puzzling would achieve nothing more that day.

"One of the problems of old age," she sighed to Rani as they settled into their respective beds. "It carries with it too many memories, and they tend to become jumbled."

Rani contributed a sympathetic wag of her tail stump to the discourse and watched as her mistress closed her eyes.

There was the smell of staleness in the air, of stone dust and damp, of grease and men and sweaty horses and pipe tobacco. It smelt like her father. No matter how much he washed down at the tap in the back yard after finishing his shift, or how much mother boiled and scrubbed the shirts he put on afterwards, he always smelt the same even after his weekly bath. When she sat on his knee and snuggled into him in front of the fire after dinner, she imagined he smelt like it all the way through. She wondered whether all fathers smelt like it, but she did not think so. Not all fathers were below ground miners like her dad.

He was good with the horses. He talked to them and could calm them when they took fright, but it puzzled her that Gerard was leading the Cleveland Bay back to work. It had been injured when the big jed fell in, and her dad had brought it out to Pit Entrance and daylight, even though he knew it would never work again.

From a safe distance, she followed them, the bay and the man, all the way to Pit Entrance where, without knowing why, she whispered "Goodbye" to the horse as it was led off down the drift. The light from its handler's lamp reflected thinly off the metal of the rail tracks that carried the ore wagons, and beckoned her to follow, but fear clawed at her. She should not be there. She swallowed hard on her stubbornly dry mouth but could not tear herself free from the waning daylight behind her.

The man had given no sign he had seen her, but suddenly he looked straight back at her, causing her to jump with fright. And in the heavily shadowed light of his makeshift lamp she saw him as clearly as if it was day. It was Gerard. He should not be going down Felderby Pit. It was too dangerous. He was an archaeologist, not a miner. She desperately wanted to call out to him but it was not a woman's place. Her fear of the darkness and the prohibitions against her being there stopped her throat.

He did not look back at her again. Without breaking his stride, he led the horse on. It was half a mile down the drift to the steeper slope of the incline, and then it would be more than a mile further down before he arrived at Pit Bottom. Fear knotted inside her. She would not be able to reach him once he was there.

Rani watched patiently over the following days as her mistress fiddled with the Hunter clock, until its refusal to become properly regulated was eventually declared more than wilful disobedience and verging on criminal recalcitrance. Hr mistress also refused to engage with the aspidistra until eventually, she could stand the silence no longer.

"There's no point in just sitting there looking smug, Mother," she fumed at it. "You know something, but you are simply not going to tell me, are you? Why is our Gerard going down a mine? And if it is not a mine, then what is it? Is it a cave where he can do some of his archaeology? He tells me caves often contain very good digging sites because they are where primitive peoples used to shelter, although why he should be taking a Cleveland Bay with him is beyond my understanding. Perhaps he is going into a cavern to look at an old gravesite for whoever-he-is Anderson of the police intelligence unit and the whatever-it-was Antarctic research committee."

None of her suggestions drew a response.

"Perhaps it is a wombat burrow he is going into, to try and rescue the slim, athletic and long-legged Miss Anne Blaise with the wide smile from the antipodes," she tried. "That would be a danger he might find it difficult to escape from, although I don't see how taking an injured horse with him would help."

Aunt Gwendoline woke tiredly on Saturday morning and took her first, tentative steps of the day to make her early morning cup of tea. She was only halfway down the stairs when the ever-attentive Rani suddenly dashed forwards between her legs, nearly tripping her so that she had to grab the bannister quickly to prevent herself from falling. She turned to deliver a sharp scold, but Rani had run on ahead and was sitting on the newspaper that had been delivered through the front door only a few minutes earlier. She was looking up at her mistress and wagging her tail stump vigorously.

The reprimand caught in Aunt Gwendoline's throat as her eyes fixed on the banner headline. There had been a terrorist attack on a northbound train travelling from London the previous day. It had been on the West Coast line, the line that ran between London and Glasgow, the line that Gerard took when he travelled north to see his friend Dr Fadden. And the attack had been made not in a mine or a cave, or a cavern or even a wombat burrow. It had been made in a tunnel.

Chapter 13

"I don't know that I can tell you much more than you will have seen on the television," Gerard answered through a mouthful of cucumber sandwich. "You are quite right, I did go to Glasgow last Friday to see Chris Fadden, and coincidentally I was on that train. But I knew nothing about the bomb attempt until the train made an unscheduled stop just south of Birmingham and police swarmed all through it. I was in one of the front carriages, so I was nowhere near where the three bombers tried to blow themselves up, although if they had been successful, I can only imagine I would have known about it. The journey back was a nightmare, what with the antiterrorist people keeping the line closed for their investigations and disrupting all the train schedules for the next few days. My return trip ended up taking around five hours longer than normal and all the trains were packed. No spare seats anywhere, but I suppose that is better than being blown up."

He chatted as if he was describing a mildly amusing episode at an afternoon tea party, and Aunt Gwendoline was relieved to see him so apparently unaffected by his escape. Perhaps all his years of archaeology in wild and lawless parts of the world had given him a view on life that allowed him to dismiss a terrorist attack on an intercity train as a normal part of living. Perhaps he had more stiffness in him than she thought, or perhaps he had inherited something of the family gift, and it was that ever watchful sense that was keeping him safe. Or perhaps she worried about him too much. Even so she could not relax. Whatever the reason, his treating the incident so lightly was incompatible with the sense of threat she felt whenever she recalled her dreams.

"The bombers had their devices in their backpacks, and their plan was to explode them simultaneously as the three of them huddled together somewhere in the middle of the train as it passed through Kilsby tunnel," he continued. "It would have created a major disaster had they succeeded, what with the carnage and the wreckage and the difficulties of rescuing people so far underground. But I cannot say I understand it. Deliberately setting out to kill oneself and innocent others, even if in a cause, makes no sense to me."

"It is a strange mix of thinking that convinces three young men from loving families to blow themselves up in an attempt to damage the society that nurtured them," she agreed.

"I can only assume they would have regarded it as a sort of martyrdom," he concluded.

"Martyrs do not kill themselves," Aunt Gwendoline countered. "Martyrs die at the hands of others after consciously putting their lives at risk in the defence of something or somebody they hold more important than self. It is an act of bravery, and your great-grandfather was named in a dispatch by his commanding officer for such an act in the trenches of the First World War, which fortunately he survived. What your bombers attempted was nothing more than suicide."

She watched her grand-nephew closely. In spite of him telling his story in the manner of a young boy's adventure tale, the experience had shaken him. It was not surprising. Kilsby tunnel was a mile and a half long and dug through quicksand and clay. It was still new when her dad was a boy, and he had told her about it and how twenty-nine navvies had died in its construction. Perhaps his great-grandson sensed it.

"But fortunately, they did not succeed," Gerard continued. "At the appointed moment when their bombs were supposed to go off, there was no bang. All that happened was three puffs of powdery smoke whoofed out of their backpacks. After a few shocked seconds, a couple of the more alert members of the public managed to grab one of the attempted bombers and sit on him while the other two tried to escape by running through the carriages. They didn't get very far before they too were jumped on by train staff and other passengers who held on to them until they could be handed over to the police."

"That is all to the good," Aunt Gwendoline summarised. "Everyone was safe. But tell me, you were on the train to go and see Dr Fadden. What prompted the meeting and was it a success?"

For the first time in the afternoon, Gerard smiled. He knew his much-loved aunt worried about him even though she tried not to show it.

"I don't know that I would call it a success, and I'm not sure I could even say it was useful," he replied. "But, it was interesting."

Aunt Gwendoline waited while her grandfather clock struck the hour and noted with some interest that her new Hunter clock was agreeing with it.

Chapter 14

"Chris had chosen a particularly dark and dubious café for our meeting," Gerard began. "He sent me the address, somewhere down a narrow back street on the edge of old Glasgow. It was small and cramped with a smoking gesture of a fire in the grate, an eating hole that even the students seem to have abandoned. It took me a while to find it, and I was also late because of the incident on the train. It was mid-afternoon by the time I got there. Chris gripped my hand firmly as soon as he saw me.

"'I was beginning to get worried,' he whispered. 'I thought you might have been intercepted or been leaned on and advised not to come.'

"'The train was delayed,' I answered. 'Some sort of security scare and you know how the authorities react to those. Everything and everyone had to be examined and questioned, and nobody could go until they had filled in their security and safety checklists at least three times.'

"I did not know then that there had been a terrorist attempt on the train and my explanation did nothing to ease Chris' state of anxiety. He visibly jumped at the words 'security scare'.

"'You weren't singled out or anything, were you?' he asked quickly.

"I assured him I had not been, but he still did not relax.

"The food was mediocre, but the café allowed us to take our own wine. Chris had taken in two bottles, one of which he had already started. He poured me a glass, and I noticed his hand was shaking.

"'So, how are you getting on with your work on your bug?' I asked him, more in an attempt to ease the tension than extract information from him.

"He grinned immediately.

"'It is a remarkable creature, a real masterpiece of nature,' he beamed. 'It has a ferocious appetite for plastic waste and can metabolise it under almost any set of conditions. It doesn't seem to care what sort of plastic it is, polyethylene, polypropylene, polyvinyl, polyurethane, polystyrene, high density or low density. It turns its nose up at natural polymers like rubber and doesn't much care for neoprene, and it leaves celluloid and cellulose-based plastics to lesser bugs, but apart from that, almost any synthetic polymer we make is breakfast as far as it is concerned. It is most effective under anaerobic conditions, such as underground at the bottom of landfill sites, but it can still degrade most plastics even when in the fresh air, all of which makes it a superb candidate for the bioremediation of any location blighted by plastic waste.'

"'It sounds an attractive little beast,' I commented.

"'It is, and it is not only the council-run rubbish dumps we are talking about,' he ploughed on. 'Since I last saw you, I have been thinking about Andy Tan and his albatrosses and the plastic rubbish floating around our seas. Did you know we dump about twenty-six million tonnes of plastic into the sea every year? There are around three million tonnes of it swirling around the Pacific in a vast area that has become known as the East Pacific Garbage Patch, and there is a similar one in the Atlantic in what used to be called the Sargasso Sea. It is either old food or drinks containers, lost toys, bits of fishing gear, or just unidentifiable bits of plastic pounded to splinters by the waves. No wonder marine life is in trouble.'

"'It is a big problem,' I agreed.

"'But it is more than that,' he continued. 'All that plastic tends to wash up on people's beaches. Every year something like twenty thousand tonnes of it washes up on the shores of this country alone, and it is happening all over the world. There are beaches in Hawaii that are buried under more than twenty centimetres of plastic waste. Just think of the problem this presents to all those expensive seaside holiday resorts that market themselves with glossy brochures showing glamorous couples walking along pristine, golden sands. They face a never-ending battle to keep back the tide of plastic that threatens their cash line. There's a fortune to be made in just keeping them happy. I could seed their beaches with *Methylococcus faddenii*, collect my cheque, and leave knowing that over the next few weeks every scrap of plastic would disappear from their beautiful sands and the expensive resorts would have their glossy brochure conditions returned to them. There is no telling how much they'd pay me for that.'

"By now, my eyes had adjusted to the dim light, and I could see him more clearly. I was shocked by his appearance. He was pale and drawn in an ill, sweaty way, and he looked as if he had not slept for days.

"'Chris, you look awful, and you are behaving as if you are sitting on hat pins. What on earth is the matter with you?' I asked.

"He waited until our food was set in front of us and the waiter had departed before taking a large gulp of wine and leaning across the table to me.

"'It's my bug,' he whispered. 'I don't know what's going on, but I'm being watched and followed wherever I go. The people doing it are difficult to spot, but I'm sure I've been followed here. You've probably been marked out too by now. I'm sorry to have got you involved, but this industrial espionage stuff is all new to me, and I have to admit it is getting on my nerves.'

"'I'm not involved in anything,' I replied. 'I have travelled up to see you, and we are here having a late lunch together, nothing more. Don't you think you might be getting a bit paranoid?'

"He looked around again to check that nobody else was within earshot, then looked straight at me.

"'Don't start disbelieving me,' he pleaded. 'I don't have many friends I can trust with this. I am being followed, and I'm sure my 'phones are also being monitored. Big commercial organisations have incredibly sophisticated setups for these sorts of things, and they are not averse to using them on anyone they see as a threat to their business, and my bug is a big threat to them. Yes, I know I sound paranoid, and maybe I am a little, but I'm facing a paranoid reality. Stay with me on this, Gerry. Please, I need your help.'

"He was in a bad way, but paranoid or not, he was not such an imaginative individual that he would dream up vistas of men in overcoats with collars turned up, and hats pulled down watching him round the clock.

"'Tell me what evidence you have that you are being followed,' I invited.

Chapter 15

"He ate hungrily for a while and continued to plough through the wine at a great rate. He had already opened the second bottle.

"'You don't know the power of big business,' he insisted. 'My *Methylococcus faddenii* is potentially huge. It could clean up all mankind's plastic waste across the whole globe.'

"'Which is what you are aiming to do, isn't it?' I asked.

"'Certainly,' he confirmed. 'But that would be a big problem to all those companies involved in the waste disposal business. Imagine all the plastic waste being tipped into rubbish dumps around the world and which we are adding to every day. Add in all the beaches and plastic polluted wastelands and industrial sites. Then imagine all the money being made by all the rubbish collection and environmental clean-up services across the world that deal with it all. It is a massive industry. Then think of all the people employed in that industry, and the interests of governments like our own who are desperate to keep people off the unemployment lists. Put all that together, and you have a massive, combined government and commercial, vested interest needing to make sure that *Methylococcus faddenii* never sees the light of day. Whoever owns my bug can destroy a global industry, and that is why big business wants to get its hands on it. Why else am I being followed and watched and monitored wherever I go?'

"'That is all speculation,' I countered when he finally drew breath. 'I asked you for evidence.'

"He was breathing hard and sweating, partly because of the hot food and the wine he had galloped down, but I was beginning to suspect he was also running some kind of a fever.

"'I don't have any evidence,' he answered at last. 'I knew these people would be clever, but I never suspected exactly how clever they are, nor the sheer intensity of what they can do, or the inability of their victim to prove any of it. And it's not just big business. It is also the police.'

"'Come on, Chris,' I snorted. 'This is going too far. I think we can take it that the police in this country are, in general, fairly free from commercial corruption.'

"He almost broke down and sobbed. I didn't know what to think except that he was in a bad way. I let him recover and tried a different tack.

"'You say that your bug is worth a fortune and that you are being harassed by commercial organisations,' I continued. 'Your assumption is that they want to kill off your bug so that they can go on making their less than environmentally friendly billions around the world. Am I right so far?'

"He nodded.

"'But are you really sure you've got what you think you have? Is your *faddenii* bug really capable of making such a difference?'

"'Almost certainly,' he replied. 'Apart from my culture experiments, I also have the data from my factory inspections in the United States. The most vigorous growth of *M. faddenii* occurred in the soil samples I collected from around those factories that had the most environmentally clean sites. That is either an amazing coincidence or else my bug is doing the environmental clean-up job for them. Then there is what happened in my laboratory in Adelaide.'

"'What happened in Adelaide?' I asked.

"'One of the technicians in the laboratory grabbed hold of a biohazard rubbish bin one day, and its bottom fell out.'

"'I'm lost Chris. Why is that significant?'

"'Biohazard rubbish is put in special plastic bins with a thick plastic liner so it can be taken away and incinerated. That way, everything nasty is contained and destroyed,' he explained. 'My guess is that some of my bug had been discarded with a paper tissue or a pipette tip or something, and it had then eaten its way through the plastic bin liner and then through the plastic of the bin itself. We had to scrub the whole place down with bleach and alcohol before we could do any more work.'

"'Isn't that a problem?' I asked. 'It might be all right for your bug to clean up landfill sites and beaches, but eating the rubbish bins as well might be seen as going a bit far.'

"He waved away my concern.

"'We applied standard decontamination procedures. That fixed it. We're not talking about anything that is going to give us nasty diseases. It was just a nuisance getting out into the laboratory.'

"He seemed to think it was not a problem, although I was not convinced. I tacked again.

"'Look at you, Chris,' I reached over to him. 'You are not well, and you are being driven to an emotional edge by what is happening. It doesn't matter to me whether what you have told me about *Methylococcus faddenii* is real or not...'

"'It is real,' he insisted. 'I have the data.'

"'All right, Chris, it's real. But is it worth your health and sanity? Maybe your idea is ahead of its time. Its time will come eventually, but not just yet. From what you tell me *M. faddenii* is perfectly happy living in the soil under our feet, so it is not going to go away and nothing is going to be lost. So, if you can find out who it is that is following you and watching you, and you have the data, then why not offer them a deal? Tell them you will sell them all you have on your bug for a couple of million and let them have it. You might not make the umpty squillions you first thought of, but at least you will have a nice little addition to your retirement fund, and you will regain your peace and quiet.'

"He looked down at his plate and then back at me. There was a touch of desperation in his eyes.

"'It's too late for that,' he replied.

"'How do you mean, too late?' I asked.

"He drew on a deep breath to calm himself.

"'I've had a visit from the police,' he replied."

Chapter 16

Aunt Gwendoline felt the same sense of menace that once flowed out of the darkness of Felderby Pit fill the room. It made it stuffy with the unease that had become so much part of her recent days and tightened her breathing. Rani looked up at her with concern in her eyes, but she avoided the dog's gaze and said nothing and concentrated only on what Gerard was saying.

"I couldn't see any connection between Chris' bug and the police, or why his dealings with his presumed industrial tormentors should interest them," he continued. "Chris had done nothing illegal, and I did not go along with his idea that the police were somehow commercially corrupt.

"'I'm being a bit dramatic when I say "police". I'm not sure they were the real thing, although they did a very good impersonation,' he agreed. 'They walked into my laboratory as if they owned the place and flashed some sort of official-looking identification at me, which could just as well have been a sports club membership card for all I know. I'm not exactly familiar with police warrant cards so "pretend police" might be a more accurate description of them.'

"'You think they were some of your industrial spies?' I asked.

"'A few days earlier, someone had been through my office,' he nodded. 'They were very careful about it, making sure they put everything back as they found it and not leaving any mess. But it doesn't matter how tidy spies are, they can never put all your books, pencils and general clutter back exactly how you yourself would leave it, and your own familiarity with your own habits tells you if something has been moved. It would not have been obvious to anyone else, but I knew immediately someone had been in my office. It was the same with my computer. They had been through that as well, bypassing my passwords and everything. I asked the lab staff and the university security people if they had seen or reported any strangers wandering about the place, but nobody admitted to knowing anything, so I left it at that.'

"'You didn't call the police?'

"'No, I didn't,' he confirmed. 'Then a couple of days later someone broke into my home and searched it in exactly the same way. I knew they would be after my notes, so I anticipated them and hid my papers and files where they wouldn't find them, but I spotted their traces as soon as I got home from work. They had searched everywhere and then left, leaving everything as undisturbed as possible.'

"'So, this time, you did report it, and the police came to see you in response to your call about a burglary,' I shrugged. 'There's nothing suspicious about that.'

"'Except that I did not report an attempted burglary to the police or to anyone else, either on that day or on any other, and neither did the university security people unless they are spinning me a story. What was there to report? There was no mess, no vandalism, no broken window, no evidence of a forced entry in either my office or my home. All the doors

74

were locked, and nothing was stolen. There was nothing to show in either place that could not be dismissed as the ravings of a highly stressed university lecturer who should probably be sent on a long spell of gardening leave. I tell you these people are very clever at what they do, so it was a complete surprise to me when two of them arrived unannounced in my laboratory, pretending to be plainclothes policemen, and began questioning me about my work.'

"I could see his point.

"'You said they flashed some sort of identification at you. Did it carry their names?' I asked.

"'I don't remember what was on the constable's card,' he replied. 'But the name on the other one was "Inspector Anderson".'"

Aunt Gwendoline felt her blood pressure surge and then fall precipitously. She fought momentarily to hold on to her consciousness as the fear she had felt in her dream ricocheted back and forth through her. No breath or sound reached into the sitting room to counter the tension that had erupted into it, and Rani pawed at her knee to offer support and reassurance.

"Anderson," she echoed. "Oh, dear."

"Exactly my thoughts," agreed Gerard after a pause. "I felt a bit of a jolt when Chris said that. With someone introducing himself as Inspector Anderson visiting him in his department, I can only think that some at least of what he has described is not entirely the product of his overactive imagination. Some of it has to be real."

Aunt Gwendoline reached down and stroked Rani's head, a gesture that helped settle them both.

"Did you tell Dr Fadden about the other occasions we have come across a mister, doctor and now inspector Anderson?" she asked.

"Absolutely not," Gerard replied. "Chris is too emotionally stretched at the moment and telling him about Anderson's other appearances would more than likely have sent him into a tailspin. As Chris says, Anderson, whoever he might be, is clearly very clever at what he does and has huge resources to call on. All tools of the trade for an industrial spy I suppose, and deeply worrying if that is the sort of dirty tricks his profession gets up to. My concerns only deepened as Chris told me about the questions he asked.

"'He didn't ask me about the burglaries. He didn't mention them at all, which was not surprising since I hadn't reported them,' he told me. 'But he did ask me a lot of questions about *Methylococcus faddenii*. He seemed to know an awful lot about it, far more than he should. He had a lot of precise information about how it behaves, things which I had only just discovered myself and had not yet told anybody about. I can only think he must have found some scrap ends of notes either in my rubbish bins or on my computer when he burgled my home and office. Of course, I knew more than he did, so I was easily able to field his questions, but he should not have known what he did. And ever since then, I have been followed and watched. Everything I do or say is being recorded. They're watching me now, Gerry, all around the clock, everything I do.'

Gerard paused again, his thoughts blocked by his efforts to try and fathom a meaning in them.

"You don't suppose that Anderson, whoever he is, might be someone official?" Aunt Gwendoline suggested.

"I don't see how he can be," Gerard replied. "Chris is a minor academic who has always lived a life that is blameless to the point of being boring. As he says, there is nothing in his work that is illegal or worthy of police notice, so why should the authorities suddenly focus any attention on him? What he has is something which could clean up a lot of the world's mess and is potentially very valuable, so the motive behind Anderson's impersonations can only be commercial. It's the only possible explanation."

Aunt Gwendoline nodded. There was no reason to disagree.

Chapter 17

Gerard lapsed into silence once again. He was more unsettled than he was prepared to acknowledge. "He has left a chocolate biscuit on the plate and he has never done that before in his entire life," Aunt Gwendoline noted quietly to herself.

"So, how did your meeting with Dr Fadden end?" she asked finally.

Gerard took his time replying.

"It ended in what has become the fairly standard format," he sighed. "Chris described some studies he is doing with his bug, most of which meant nothing to me, but telling me the technical details, even if I didn't understand them, seemed to be therapeutic for him. He relaxed as we talked and became once again the boyish academic excited by the prospect of new discoveries.

"'It seems to break down plastics mostly into methane and ethylene glycol,' he told me.

"'That doesn't sound very encouraging,' I argued. 'Methane is an inflammable gas which contributes to global warming, and ethylene glycol is used as an antifreeze and is also inflammable, and generally considered poisonous. If you are looking for a bug that is environmentally friendly then perhaps you ought to try looking again.'

"He brushed aside my argument.

"'The amount of methane is negligible compared with what the world's herds of cows, sheep and goats produce every day simply through the process of digesting their food, and our global chemical industry manufactures several million tonnes of ethylene glycol annually, most of which goes into making plastics of various kinds anyway. My *faddenii* is simply breaking those plastics down into what we manufactured them from in the first place.'

"We finished our meal, and I was pleased to see he didn't call for any more wine. He had drunk one and a half of the two bottles he had brought with him, and after around three hours he finally ran out of conversational steam. As we prepared to leave, I saw the tense, suspicious and deeply unsettled Chris return. He pulled his coat close around him, turned up his collar and perused the few other customers in the café. He checked the street outside through the café windows before deciding it was safe to leave.

"'Thanks for coming, Gerry,' he said, gripping my hand tightly and speaking very closely and quietly. 'Can you come again next week, same time same place? I'm almost at the end of the first bit of my work and it is important I keep you up to date as I get my bug patented.'

"I promised him I would be back and I watched him walk off up the street, staying as close to the walls of the shops and buildings as possible and trying to keep in the shadows. It was hardly a discreet performance, and even an amateur private eye would have had no difficulty following him. I saw him turn down an alleyway then after a few seconds come back out, cross the road and disappear down another narrow lane on the opposite side. I shook my head in despair of him.

"'Don't ever take up spying, Chris, not with your sense of direction,' I whispered after him.

"I scanned the street but saw no sign of anyone following or watching him, and after a few seconds, I headed towards the train station for my tedious journey home."

Aunt Gwendoline waited. "Was that all?" she asked.

Her Hunter clock was persisting in showing the correct time.

"More or less," he shrugged. "As I said, I don't know that my going to see Chris was particularly useful other than to keep in touch. I did ask him if he could remember a Dr Witheney from his Adelaide days, but he could not recall anyone of that name, so she remains a mystery."

"She?" she echoed.

"Yes, Dr Witheney is a she," he grinned. "My secretary returned from her holidays on Monday, so I was able to ask her if she had any more details about our absent visitor. She couldn't recall very much. I gather she was distracted by her own holiday preparations and my imminent return from Vietnam when the call came through. All she remembered was the quickly scribbled note I found when I arrived back in the department, and that the voice on the other end of the telephone was female."

The grandfather clock in the hallway led the chorus to the strike of six.

"I must go," he smiled. "As always, I must get back to the university. I've had some more data about the two pieces of iron we found at Ban Long. The department in Adelaide have had their dating of 1000 BCE confirmed by another laboratory. I have to tell Professor Nguyn."

"See you next week," she smiled and acknowledged his cheery wave as he strode off up the street.

Chapter 18

Aunt Gwendoline closed the latch on her front door and wandered back to her sitting room. She felt the floor judder under her feet.

"What do you make of it, Mother?" she demanded of the aspidistra. "Our Gerard is puzzling about two pieces of rusty iron he found in the jungles of south-east Asia that, no doubt, he will eventually conclude were made in China like so many of the other manufactured goods we purchase these days. He is distracted by a mislaid visitor, another 'she' he has managed to collect and about whom we know nothing, just like the good looking and Australian Miss Anne Blaise who, at some point, I suppose I shall have to have a word with him about. Not only that, but we have a man by the name of Anderson who is popping up in various guises and beginning to be a nuisance."

She looked hard at the potted plant and was surprised to see how well it set off the lines and polish of the table she had recently purchased for it. She had sold the solid, round, Victorian table inlaid with Mother of pearl that had been its previous support and replaced it with a smaller, square, Edwardian piece of much finer lines. The plant was preening itself and spreading its leaves affectedly over the finely worked edge, posing and draping them elegantly across the exquisite inlays of ash and walnut that decorated the top.

"Gathering pretensions again are we, Mother?" she sniffed at it. "Let me remind you that you would not be sitting on your new table if I had not spotted it sitting dusty and ignored in the corner of the saleroom, having just made a modest profit on the old one. And I can assure you the price I paid for it was considerably less than your airs and graces warrant."

It may have been a bargain, but she could see no reason why a mother should claim any of the credit for it. She looked down at Rani, sitting at her feet.

"I am talking to myself again, aren't I?" she smiled. "Why don't you stop me? You know it is a bad habit I am getting into."

Rani looked up at her mistress, less than convinced under her examining stare.

Over the next two days, she enjoyed enormously the extra-long forays among the trees and undergrowth during her daily bounces in the park, even though it did take a lot of tail wagging and insistent pointing to encourage the eventual movement of her mistress homewards for lunch. Back at home, her mistress fiddled endlessly with the Hunter clock while the aspidistra in its decorated pot was studiously ignored other than to be told, "And we know exactly where I get my stubbornness from, don't we, Mother?" Mostly, though, there was very little else for a dog to do other than sit in the afternoon warmth of the sitting room, yawn and settle one's chin on one's paws and wait while her mistress' eyes closed and her head nodded forward over yet another back copy of *Antiques Collectors' Weekly*.

"Muscles of stone and tendons of iron," her dad boasted as he pulled up his shirt sleeves so she could try and poke her child's fingers into the hardness of his arms.

She was proud of her dad. He was a below-ground miner, one who drove tunnels into the stone under the Cleveland Hills and hacked out the iron ore using shot powder, pickaxe and muscle. Sometimes of a night time, she would lie in bed and listen to the voices coming up through the floorboards from the parlour below where her dad and her uncles were chatting and drinking beer around the fire.

"A mine is a living thing," they said. "It moves and breathes, sometimes hot, sometimes cold and often wet. There are rivers down there that no one except the hills know about."

She heard them tell how they cut into the hills' entrails, marking out pillars the size of houses that were then butchered for their ore. She heard how it took two tonnes of pitiless rock to fill an ore wagon and how the wagon was pulled by a Cleveland Bay up the incline to the drift, where a steam cable took it out of Pit Entrance and away to fill the bellies of the blast furnaces of Felderby Iron Works. She heard how the hills complained as they were emptied, of how the rocks stretched and cracked and spat fractured boulders into the paths of the men and horses as they worked. They told her how the tunnels that the men dug writhed and twisted in protest, and how the rail tracks squealed as the floor beneath them buckled and the ore wagons jumped their tracks.

"Everything is always moving," they said. "It never stays still."

She listened in the darkness while they told how the jed, the cavern they left behind under the hills after they had taken

84

out the stone, grew ever bigger with each shift as they hewed at the ore seam and sent its riches flowing out through Pit Entrance. She heard how, as the jed grew, so the chorus of complaint from the hills became ever louder, even though the men offered them timbers to prop them up and appease them while they continued to wrench out the iron bounty from beneath them, and how the timbers in their turn added their protests to those of the hills, groaning and splintering under the ever-increasing weight they had to bear until the rising crescendo drove out even the rats.

"Muscles of stone and tendons of iron," her dad said, and in the darkness of the night, her own lips mirrored his words.

"The jed. It must be as big as Low Felderby by now," the voices told her.

"Bigger," others said.

"We'll have to bring it down," they all agreed. "We'll have to draw the jed or else it will come down of itself."

Aunt Gwendoline let out a small cry and her eyes flicked open as she heard the timbers splitting and the rocks cracking under the weight of the hills. She pushed out at nothing, then her eyes and ears adjusted to the sights and sounds of the afternoon in her sitting room. Rani was sitting up whimpering quietly beside her, and her oak cased clock was just finishing striking five in the hallway. And as her ears adjusted, she realised it was not the straining in the rock seams or the splintering of the pit props that she could hear. It was her telephone ringing. She struggled out of her chair still half in her doze and reached for the receiver.

"Hello. Wych Green four-five-oh-four," she announced.

"Hello, Aunt Gwendoline. It's Gerard. I know it's short notice, but could I pop round to see you? I have something to tell you that I'm sure you would be interested in."

She was awake immediately. He sounded excited but also apprehensive.

"Of course, dear boy," she replied. "If you don't mind sausages for tea, then you are more than welcome to join me. Could you give me some clue as to what it is that is so urgent?"

She shot a scowl in the direction of the aspidistra and braced herself to receive the news that he had managed to get himself engaged to a certain Miss Anne Blaise, friendly and athletic wombat expert with good legs and a nice smile from the antipodes. He hesitated only briefly before answering.

"I've just had a visit from Commander Anderson," he replied.

Chapter 19

"Commander Anderson indeed," Aunt Gwendoline snorted as she replaced the receiver. "I knew there was trouble at Pit. It seems that mister doctor inspector Anderson has just given himself another promotion. Come along, Rani, it is time to beat to quarters and clear the decks for action."

She shook herself into full wakefulness. The sausages went under the griller, the potatoes were peeled and put in a pan to boil, and fresh green beans were topped, tailed and sliced ready for their two-minute blanching. A tin of doggy chunks was mixed with a handful of meaty bites and salads and put down for an excited Rani, and the table was set with water glasses and English mustard. The cruet had just been placed when the doorbell rang.

"A pleasant surprise," she greeted her grand-nephew with the calmness of one whose philosophy of life did not include the need to rush under any circumstances. "Dinner won't be long. The sherry is in its usual place if you would care for one too."

She offered her cheek to be kissed, then disappeared back to the kitchen.

Gerard smiled to see his elderly aunt returned to her more usual, indestructible self and wandered into the sitting room where the Waterford crystal decanter of sherry sat on one end of the Sheraton sideboard. He opened himself to the sense of shelter the room always gave him. It was a harbour he cherished and unconsciously sought whenever he was agitated, and his meeting with Commander Anderson had undoubtedly left him well stirred. He inhaled the scents of brocaded velvet and lavender furniture polish and renewed his acquaintance with the room's contents; the carved rosewood Victorian grandmother chairs, a horn carving of a pair of elephants from Africa, an ivory carving of Shiva on its hardwood stand from India, a pair of rosewood pole screens with their floral embroidered panels, and so much more. It was an eclectic mix, timeless and harmonious, and he had always imagined that Aunt Gwendoline had heard the story of each piece on first meeting it and came to an agreement with it before acquiring it. He savoured the shelter of the room, poured two glasses of sherry and tipped his glass in greeting to the aspidistra. He had no idea why he always did that. It just seemed natural to him to do so.

"I hope you don't mind, but I am going to put dinner directly on the plates," Aunt Gwendoline informed him as he joined her in the kitchen. "There are a couple more sausages if you are hungry, and I have a chocolate walnut cake bought from the bakery this morning for our pudding. I hope that is satisfactory."

"It most certainly is," he smiled back to her.

They were the only words she heard from him for the entire meal. She waited for his preoccupations to disperse and for him to begin chatting about his two pieces of rusty iron from Ban Long or some other inconsequentiality, but he said nothing and distractedly helped himself to the last two sausages. She cut him a piece of the chocolate walnut cake and served it with cream, and he demolished it wordlessly without seeming to taste it. She looked down at Rani who twitched her tail stump in agreement.

"Commander Anderson," she finally prompted, emphasising the rank in order to jolt him out of his silent depths.

He raised his eyes to her for the first time in the best part of an hour.

"Yes, Commander Anderson," he smiled, echoing her inflection and finally putting down his spoon. "I think we can dispense with the idea that our hitherto mysterious Anderson is merely an annoying, industrial gumshoe."

Chapter 20

"So, who is he?" asked Aunt Gwendoline.

"Someone official, although at no point did he say exactly what he was or who he represented," Gerard answered. "But when he came to see me, he was accompanied by Sergeant Chak who introduced him very deferentially."

"That would certainly imply he is someone official," she agreed.

"He was quite sinister," Gerard continued. "I didn't ask him if he was the same Dr Anderson of the fictitious Antarctic Scientific Resources Policy Committee who went to see Andy Tan on Heard Island, or the Inspector Anderson who paid a visit to Chris Fadden in Glasgow, but I got the impression he knew I was aware of his other presentations and it did not bother him. In appearance, he was average height, average build, his clothes were neither cheap nor expensive, he wore no colours that did not merge in with the background, his shoes were neither scruffy nor polished. He did not stand out in any way. He was a perfect study of someone who you could pass in the street and not notice. Even now, I cannot recall exactly what he looks like."

"An undoubted talent for someone engaged in subterfuge," Aunt Gwendoline commented, pouring the Lapsang Souchong. "What did he want?"

"That too is a good question," Gerard answered. "Even after spending three- quarters of an hour under his close scrutiny, I have no idea. At first, his questions were all rather vague and general. He asked about some details of what I remembered from the terrorist attempt on the London to Glasgow train I took last Friday. My answers were as detailed as I could make them but necessarily short on specifics. I explained again that I was in a forward carriage and nowhere near the middle of the train where the bombers tried to blow themselves up, so I did not have anything to add to the statement I had already given to the police. I saw nobody acting suspiciously, did not see the bombers board the train and was not aware that anything serious had happened until we pulled up outside Rugby and armed police began swarming through the compartments. He asked me again what carriage I was in, what seat I was in, what my return arrangements had been, and went on in that manner for about twenty minutes.

"He began to remind me of some of the officials I have met in some of the less democratic countries I've worked in over the years. When digging up prehistoric sites in Asia, one almost expects to come across them. Sooner or later, they turn up at the dig site accompanied by some armed and uniformed minions, and after looking vaguely around the place, they approach and start asking inconsequential questions in a manner that implies they have some authority but leaves their exact status deliberately vague. They are never specific about the reasons for their visit but eventually the subject come up about the need for some sort of permits or government documents, and the reminder is given that these are advised if the work is to continue uninterrupted by officialdom. It's all hokum, of course, because all official clearances are obtained before we even turn the first sod, but after some pantomime discussion one usually ends up giving them a handful of cash, notionally a payment for the required permits, and they go away. I was beginning to wonder whether this was what Anderson was after, except that Sergeant Chak was with him and in this country police officers at Commander level do not usually look for such undeclared cash handouts. Then he sprang his first surprise question on me.

"'When are you seeing Dr Fadden next?' he asked.

"The question was clearly intended to throw me. His voice had not altered in pitch or tone, and he never shifted in his position, but I had not to that point mentioned Chris or said anything about going to meet him, or even that I knew anyone of that name.

"'Probably next week sometime,' I replied. 'Why?'

"He ignored my question.

"'Where did you first meet him?' he continued.

"'I met him in Adelaide a few months ago.'

"'And what is your connection with him?'

"'We are fellow academics, that is all.'

"'Fellow academics with separate interests that hardly provide much common ground for a trip up to Glasgow for lunch?' he persisted.

"'Then you do not understand academics,' I answered. 'Academics talk to each other regardless of their fields of study, simply because they find the world interesting. I am currently working with an organic chemist from Tianjin, a molecular biologist from Heidelberg, a software designer from Auckland, and an anatomist from Hanoi. My research assistant is a wombat expert from Australia, and Chris Fadden is a microbiologist from Glasgow. That is not unusual among academics.'

"He had annoyed me, and he knew it. He paused and looked down at the carpet. He may also have smiled.

"'I've already met your research assistant,' he replied. 'But let's get back to your train journey last Friday.'"

Chapter 21

"'You were on your way to meet Dr Fadden in Glasgow when three young men selected the train you were on as the target for a suicide bomb attack,' Anderson continued.

"'I suppose you can say I was unlucky,' I shrugged. 'I don't normally go out of my way to board trains that are about to be blown up by terrorists.'

"'A coincidence,' he nodded.

"'Exactly,' I replied.

"'And is it another coincidence that you selected a seat in a forward compartment where, if the bombs had gone off, the momentum of the locomotive and first few carriages would probably have carried you clear of the blast and significant injury if not certain death?'

"I had no idea what to make of his insinuation.

"'I happen to prefer travelling at the front of the train,' I answered.

"He smiled again, stood up and wandered over to the window, letting a silence of a good few seconds hang over my interrogation, for that is what it had suddenly become. I looked at Sergeant Chak, who avoided my gaze. He had said nothing and only concentrated on taking notes in the usual policeman-like manner.

"'Dr Fadden is working on a microbe that has the ability to degrade plastic,' Anderson continued. 'I presume you know about it?'

"'Chris' bug, yes, of course, I do. He talks of little else when we meet.'

"'What do you know about it?' he asked.

"For the first time, it sounded like a genuine question.

"'He found it in some soil samples he picked up in the United States when he went there to do a report for their Environmental Protection Agency,' I replied. 'I gather it has an appetite for plastic and Chris has visions of making a lot of money selling it to local councils who want an environmentally friendly way of reducing the amount of plastic waste in their landfill sites. He also believes it could solve the problem of plastic pollution in the world's oceans, clean up beaches around the globe and save various threatened marine life forms in the process. It's a nice idea, and I wish him well with it.'

"'Is that what he told you?' asked Anderson.

"'Yes.'

"'And has he told anyone else about his little find?'

"'Not as far as I know,' I answered. 'He is keeping his work very hush-hush because he is afraid someone else will steal his idea before he can get it patented.'

"'And you believe him?'

"'Yes, of course, I do,' I retorted. 'It's a wonderful vision of benefit to us all if he can make it happen. Why shouldn't I believe him?'

"'Because this beneficent microbe which is going to clean up the world, and which your academic friend just happened to find in a handful of dirt, is resistant to every antibiotic known to mankind,' he replied.

"His statement perplexed me.

"'I was not aware of that,' I answered. 'I'm not an expert in microbiology or the genetics of bugs, but I could imagine that the same gene that allows it to break down plastic might also help it break down other chemicals such as antibiotics.'

"'So, its antibiotic resistance just happened by chance then. Another coincidence?'

"I didn't answer him. It was his conclusion as far as I was concerned. He returned to his chair.

"'You don't think it is possible that this bug did not come about by chance?' he continued. 'You don't consider that it might have been deliberately made, a genetically engineered organism created in a laboratory by someone with the right expertise, someone such as Dr Fadden?'

"'It had never occurred to me,' I replied.

"'Tell me what you know about home-made bombs,' he asked.

"That was the last straw.

"'I don't know anything about them, but I can imagine that there are times when detailed knowledge of them might come in very useful,' I sniffed at him.

"Over his shoulder, I saw Sergeant Chak stop taking notes and look at me with a sudden, stern expression. He shook his head almost imperceptibly at me. The warning was clear.

"'I've never had any occasion to enquire about them,' I continued more calmly. 'Archaeologists don't blow up things these days. The most dangerous implement I have ever used is a shovel.'

"'Well, let me tell you about them,' Anderson resumed unperturbed.

"He settled himself into a more comfortable position.

"'They consist of a combustible material, usually in a finely powdered form such as rice flour which is what our attempted train bombers used. The idea is to make it all ignite and burn in the same instant, so producing that sudden expansion of burnt gases that we call an explosion. Are you with me so far?'

"I nodded. There did not seem much else to do.

"'To help it burn, it is mixed with something that will provide extra oxygen,' he continued. 'Ordinary garden fertiliser will do that, which our train bombers also stirred into the contents of their backpacks, and they included some bottles of hydrogen peroxide just to help the whole business along.'

"'This is all very educational, Commander, but I can't see it as any real use to me,' I sighed. 'As I said, archaeology is a very genteel pastime these days. We do not blow up things.'

"'You're right,' he smiled. 'It was very amateurish. But if our three train bombers had succeeded in exploding their backpacks in the middle of Kilsby tunnel, they would have caused a lot of damage. At the very least the carriage they were in would have been torn apart, taking it off the rails so that all the following carriages would have piled into it. On a crowded train, the carnage would have been enormous, except in the front carriage where you were travelling, of course. And following the explosion, the access to the wounded by the rescue crews would have been extremely difficult and dangerous being so far underground, and that is after the bomb squad had been in to make sure there were no further

97

bombs to go off killing and maiming the rescuers as well. The death toll would have been huge, Kilsby tunnel itself would have needed extensive repairs, and a major line on the national rail network which carries forty per cent of the nation's rail freight and a large portion of its passenger traffic would have been put out of action for several weeks if not months. Substantial damage all the way around, wouldn't you agree?'

"'But it didn't happen, did it,' I countered.

"'No, it didn't. And that is the interesting part.'

"He was still talking quietly, and he paused for dramatic effect. Over his shoulder, I could see Sergeant Chak sending me signals of extreme caution.

"'Having got their explosive cocktail into their backpacks, all our train bombers had to do was fire the detonators in them in order to produce the damage they were after,' Anderson continued. 'But when they did that, nothing happened. There was no explosion, only three puffs of smoke. It turns out that the wires linking the batteries to the detonators had short-circuited.'

"'We were all very lucky then,' I summarised.

"'Possibly, but let us see why that happened,' he replied. 'The short circuit was caused by the plastic insulation around the detonator wires breaking down, allowing them to come in contact with each other.'

"'As I said, we were all very lucky,' I repeated.

"'Maybe,' he smiled. 'That is until you consider the reason why the plastic insulation around the wires broke down. It turns out our bombers' backpacks had become contaminated with the same hush-hush, environmentally friendly, plastic-eating microbe that your friend Dr

Christopher Fadden is working on. It ate through the insulation around the wires. How do you suppose that might have happened? Another coincidence, do you think?'

"I didn't know what to think. It was too much information for me to take in at one hit, and the implication that Chris had anything to do with an attempted terrorist attack on a crowded passenger train was ludicrous. In the background, I noticed that Sergeant Chak had gone visibly pale under his natural colour. I didn't say anything."

Chapter 22

Aunt Gwendoline did not feel she could make any comment either. There was, as her grand-nephew said, too much information to digest in short order. Her sitting room became muted around her, and she felt a pressure in her ears. She adjusted her sitting position to let the blood begin flowing back to her ankles and toes while Rani lifted her head and sniffed the air.

"Can we infer that Commander Anderson is from one of the police antiterrorism units for which there is regrettably an enhanced need these days?" she asked.

"I'm beginning to think so," Gerard answered, grateful his great-aunt had reached the same conclusion as himself. "But if he is some sort of police intelligence, antiterrorism spook then I would have to wonder why he is interviewing me in such a threatening manner."

Aunt Gwendoline could only agree. Commander Anderson had made Gerard angry, which had no doubt been his intention, but his reasons for doing so were worryingly obscure. She recalled the officers in military intelligence she had met during World War Two. Without exception, they were all charming young men, invariably good dancers, and their undiscussed exploits were part of the cut and thrust of war, but it was understood that it was only the enemy who treated their own law-abiding citizens with mistrust and suspicion.

"Did he ask anything else?" she prompted.

Gerard grinned for the first time that evening.

"He did have a couple of parting shots," he replied. "As he got up to leave, he hesitated in a manner that was almost theatrical.

"'By the way,' he said. 'What is your connection with Dr Witheney?'

"I found the question so unexpected I burst out laughing.

"'I have no idea,' I replied.

"'You seem to know very little about some of your associates,' he pressed. 'She called you from the airport saying she was on her way.'

"'So my secretary tells me,' I confirmed. 'But she didn't turn up. I can only assume I must have invited her to visit and that at the last minute, she changed her mind.'

"He paused, pretending to be convinced.

"'It might interest you to know that nobody by the name of Witheney appears on any passenger list for any flight arriving or departing from the local airport for forty-eight hours either side of the time she called you,' he stated.

"'Well, let me know when you find her, and we will both be the wiser,' I replied.

"'Thank you for your time,' he smiled superficially. 'Remain available. We may need your further help with our enquiries. In the meantime, do you own a car?'

"He knew I did, of course.

"'Yes,' I replied. 'It's outside in the car park.'

"'Then you might like to consider that if your friend Dr Fadden has released a genetically engineered microbe into the world, one that can eat plastic and cannot be controlled by any known antibiotic, it could cause a lot of trouble. Twenty per cent of your car is made of plastic. Be careful how you drive home.'

"With that sinister comment, he left. Sergeant Chak gave me the most imperceptible of nods and followed him out, leaving me wondering what sort of insanity Chris has got himself mixed up in."

Aunt Gwendoline listened to her sitting room. It all seemed quiet although Rani was unusually alert. For no obvious reason, the image returned to her of a blindfolded Cleveland Bay and its handler going down into Felderby Pit.

"I can't say I understand it," she summarised.

Gerard stifled a yawn and shook himself as the last of the tension he had been incubating since his meeting with Commander Anderson finally spent itself.

"Me neither, but thanks for listening, Aunt Gwendoline. I don't know what I would do without you." he sighed.

He looked at his elderly aunt and once again felt it wrong of him with his youth and vigour to lean for support on such an old and frail frame.

"You will be careful, won't you?" she cautioned.

He looked at her with puzzled affection.

"I'll do that, but it is Chris Fadden I am worried about," he replied. "I feel I have to at least let him know that Commander Anderson, or whatever rank he wants to give himself, is not a run of the mill industrial spy. I don't know that telling him will be of much help to him, but it might keep him out of more serious trouble. I cannot believe Chris is involved in anything like terrorism. It is not in his nature. At worst, he might have become cynically snared into a criminal plot by others, but any involvement would have to be a very naïve and innocent on his part."

He collected his coat, then leaned forward and kissed his great-aunt's cheek softly in farewell.

"Thanks for the dinner, Aunt Gwendoline, and I'm sorry to leave you with the washing up, as usual," he shrugged apologetically.

"Don't forget to come next Wednesday," she reminded him. "And if Miss Blaise is free then perhaps you might like to bring her with you too. I'm sure she could tell me a lot I don't know about Australia."

He looked at her quizzically, then smiled.

"I'll ask her," he called as he left.

She waved him goodbye and closed her front door.

Chapter 23

Aunt Gwendoline stormed back into her sitting room.

"Why did I issue an invitation for Gerard to bring his young Australian research assistant to tea?" she demanded of the aspidistra. "That was your doing, Mother, and certainly not my idea. You are interfering again."

She looked sternly at the plant, but it ignored her.

"Our Gerard has escaped unharmed from a brush with three incompetent young terrorists and has survived an unsatisfactory interview with the dubious Commander Anderson," she persisted. "That, I should hope, is the end of the matter. What other danger could he be in? And we certainly don't want to be encouraging him into any adventures with long-legged wombat enthusiasts with nice smiles, do we?"

Rani sat upright beside her mistress and added her contribution to the display of annoyance at the plant.

Aunt Gwendoline sighed and set about clearing the dining table, but her thoughts kept dragging her back to her dream that was interrupted by Gerard's telephone call.

"Our dad was chatting with his brothers in the parlour, as they often did before they went on shift," she recalled. "They were talking about drawing a jed."

The vast space left between the worthless rock above and the unprofitable rock below after the iron ore had been removed could only fall in, so the only sensible course for the men who had to work under the threat of it was to collapse it before it did so of its own accord. They had to draw the jed.

"The jed," she repeated, reaching for a tea towel to begin drying the dishes. "I remember that jed. Who could forget it? It was the biggest jed that had ever been dug out at Felderby Pit, or anywhere else as far as anyone knew. It was the full thickness of the ore seam, and it stretched for miles underground. It should never have got so big, but the mine owners were never going to declare it worked to its limit while there was still an ounce of profitable ore to be taken out of it."

The whole village felt the fear of it, and she shivered as the memory came back to her.

"It became unstable, and we all felt the ground straining beneath our feet for more than a week before it fell in. All the hens went off lay, the ducks flew off the ponds, and all the sheep came down off the hillsides, and no end of shepherding would send them back up again. And in the middle of the night, we would be woken by the geese honking and the dogs barking and we would feel the rocks settle a bit more in preparation for giving way. Do you remember it, our Mam?"

A shudder in the floor rattled through her, and two plates slid on the draining board driving some cutlery to clatter into the sink. The half-dried cup in her hand crashed to the floor as she grasped the edge of the draining board to steady herself.

"I'm asking the wrong person," she gasped.

She dropped the tea towel and ran into the hallway to stand in front of her oak cased grandfather clock.

"It's not our mam I should be asking. It's you I should be talking to, isn't it our Dad? What are you trying to tell me? Is it something about the jed?"

The solid beat of the clock's pendulum was her only answer.

"We all felt it when it gave way," she appealed to it. "Layer upon layer of rocks fell down one on top of the other as the hills collapsed into it. The accident siren sounded, and a great hole appeared in the ground just outside Low Felderby, big enough to swallow a farm and half its fields. The whole landscape was undermined, and it changed forever. Is that what is happening, our Dad? Is the landscape changing with our Gerard in the middle of it?"

She waited, but nothing came back to her. She looked down at Rani sitting patiently by her side.

"It has been a long day, and it would appear that we have broken a cup," she sighed. "Stay outside the kitchen until I have swept it up. We don't want you getting bits of sharp china in your paws, do we? I am too tired to be dealing with anything more tonight."

Chapter 24

Aunt Gwendoline was surprised to see how late it was when she woke next morning.

"Goodness me, Rani, you must be wondering where your breakfast is," she declared.

Her sleep had not been the most restful, but in spite of her tiredness she felt surprisingly alert. Tea was briskly brewed, Prince of Wales to start the day followed by Ceylon for breakfast, and afterwards, Rani allowed herself to suffer a brisk brushing in preparation for an expedition to town for the weekly shopping. That done, she sat and watched while her mistress applied a small amount of face powder and lipstick in front of the hallway mirror.

"We don't want to put on too much," she was informed. "Otherwise we might be mistaken for one of those young women who were taken off for delousing before being issued with their Women's Auxiliary Air Force uniforms in 1940. I was not one of them."

Coat, gloves and hat were gathered, and finally satisfied, Aunt Gwendoline fixed her fox-fur stole about her neck and reached for the dog's lead.

"Come along, Rani," she announced, encouraging herself as much as her companion. "'There are mountains to climb and worlds to conquer', as our dad used to say."

She turned to attach the leash, but far from bounding around her feet in excited anticipation, Rani sat very solidly beside the grandfather clock, watching her and not making any attempt to approach.

"Walks?" Aunt Gwendoline prompted, but Rani did not move.

The lead was held out and shaken, but the usual command for calm so that it could be affixed was not needed. Rani remained stuck firmly beside the clock, quivering slightly and intermittently, dipping her head and flicking her tail stump in apology for her disobedience.

Aunt Gwendoline listened to her house. There was nothing amiss that she could sense. She peered into the grandfather clock's face and then went through into her sitting room where the aspidistra also avoided her gaze. She returned to the hallway.

"What's the matter, Rani?" she soothed, bending down and stroking the dog's ears. "We have to do the shopping, otherwise we shall have nothing to eat."

Rani remained rooted to the patch of floor, awkwardly refusing to budge while Aunt Gwendoline sighed in exasperation.

"What is it, Rani? Are you worried about the jed falling in? Well, don't be. It all happened a long time ago and a long way from here. The ground shook, cracks appeared in some of the houses and tiles fell off their roofs, and one house lost its chimney stack. The accident siren sounded at Felderby Pit, all the women gathered at Pit Entrance and smelling salts were passed around, but all the men came out of it alive. No dogs were hurt. It was a horse, a Cleveland Bay, that took the worst of the rockfall. It was very badly injured, and it came out limping and bloody and had to be taken to the farriers to be shot."

The thought pulled her up with a jolt. The horse would, of course, have been shot as it was too badly injured ever to recover. She faced the knowledge as if for the first time.

"I do hope nobody is going to get themselves shot," she gasped.

She returned her attention to Rani, but her reassurances had no effect on the dog. She found herself uncharacteristically at a loss as to what to do next and was so concentrated on her indecision that the ring of her doorbell startled her. Rani was on her feet immediately, rushing past her to the front door and fussing uncontrollably behind it, her tail stump enthusiastically wagging the whole of her body in happy greeting.

Apprehensively, Aunt Gwendoline opened the door.

"Sergeant Chak," she beamed.

Chapter 25

"Good morning, Miss Penderrick," the Sergeant smiled back to her. "I hope I'm not interrupting anything."

Rani greeted him most warmly and had clearly lost all interest in the idea of an outing.

"It can wait," Aunt Gwendoline replied. "If you are looking for Gerard, I'm afraid he is not here."

"I am looking for Gerry although I didn't really expect to find him with you," he confirmed. "I would guess that at this moment he is on the train to Glasgow going to see his friend Dr Fadden."

Aunt Gwendoline looked into the disturbed eyes of the young man.

"Why don't you come in and have a cup of tea," she invited. "Irish Breakfast sounds about right, and black I presume."

"Perfect," he replied with a tense smile.

Sergeant Chak found his own way into the sitting room and once again cast his detective's gaze around the fascinating and well-organised clutter of knick-knacks and collectibles it held. His focus was drawn to a small statue of Shiva he had noted on his previous visit, not more than twenty centimetres tall, extremely finely carved and surprisingly undamaged

110

given its age betrayed by the discolouring of the ivory from which it was made.

"Destroyer of worlds," he muttered.

It fitted his mood.

"So, what is it I can do for you, Sergeant?" asked Aunt Gwendoline as she returned with the tea.

He looked down at the springer spaniel sitting obediently at her mistress' feet, a nice looking dog who looked straight back at him, wagging her tail stump as if pleased to see him.

"Commander Anderson and I had a meeting with Gerry yesterday at the university," he began.

"Yes, he told me about it. I understand the Commander was rather abrasive," Aunt Gwendoline replied.

"He was, but that is maybe just his style," he continued. "My concern is that Gerry might not be taking him seriously. I think Gerry ought to know that Commander Anderson is not someone to be toyed with. He has a brief he is pursuing and can call on a lot of resources to back him up if necessary."

"A powerful man," Aunt Gwendoline nodded. "Gerard and I had already deduced he was not an ordinary policeman."

"That, he is not," Sergeant Chak agreed. "The best guess at our local police station is that the Commander is something to do with antiterrorism, but he might be national intelligence or something even higher. He himself is not saying. All we know is that he arrived at the front desk and demanded to see our chief superintendent. One telephone call to someone very high up and we were all being ordered to provide him with anything and everything he asked for, including the chief superintendent's office, with no questions asked. I was assigned as his run-around, and I have subsequently learned that I was selected for that role because I was known to be

111

Gerry's friend. I would like to make it clear, Miss Penderrick, that I don't like being commandeered or used in that way, but I wasn't given any choice."

He paused and sipped his tea.

"A powerful man indeed," Aunt Gwendoline repeated.

Sergeant Chak put down his cup and took a deep breath. He looked at the old lady sitting in front of him and thought again of his grandmother, and how the fact that he had become a policeman had made her very proud of him. He thought of the wisdom she had so freely shared with him when he was a child, and he knew he was saying more than his training and instincts as a police officer should properly allow, but he was having difficulty working with Commander Anderson.

"Whatever investigation Commander Anderson is pursuing includes the attempted terrorist attack on the London to Glasgow train that Gerry was on," he continued. "Beyond that, I am only being given as much information as the Commander thinks is appropriate. I don't think for one moment that Gerry is a terrorist, but it has been made clear to me that what I think is not important. It is what Commander Anderson thinks that carries the weight, and that is why I feel Gerry ought to be very wary of him. He can generate a lot of heat, furnace heat, in his enquiries if he needs to."

"Are you saying that Commander Anderson suspects Gerard of being a terrorist?" Aunt Gwendoline asked.

"He's keeping the possibility open," Sergeant Chak replied guardedly. "Gerry's frequent excursions to out of the way places that do not have reliable intelligence exchanges with this country have been noted, particularly his visits to those countries where terrorist organisations are known to be able to establish themselves below the radar of any western intelligence organisation. Gerry has visited quite a few of those."

She could only agree. "Too many," was her long-standing opinion.

"Look at it from Commander Anderson's point of view," the sergeant continued. "Three politically motivated young men try to blow up a train in a tunnel on one of the busiest stretches of the rail network. Gerry is travelling on the same train. The bombers are foiled in their plans by a genetically modified bug, a bug that is the special interest of Dr Fadden in Glasgow, the man who Gerry is on his way to meet. It is a set of coincidences that someone like Commander Anderson will not ignore."

"But they are coincidences nonetheless," Aunt Gwendoline replied. "Surely, in order to blow up a train one needs to have a motive. I can understand how three disillusioned young men might acquire a destructive political idea and try to act on it. I saw not just young men but also young women from good families pick up the flag of fascism in the nineteen-thirties, but I cannot see how that would apply to Gerard. He has never been politically active in his entire life."

Sergeant Chak took a sip of tea from his refilled cup and shook his head.

"At the moment it is a confused picture," he agreed. "In our latest briefings, Commander Anderson is painting a picture of three deluded young men who were just foot soldiers. They have been questioned intensively, and it is clear they do not have the brains between them to put together a successful plan to blow up a train in the middle of a tunnel. The fact that they attempted it means there must be someone

113

else behind them who does have the brains and who could devise the whole plan, and convince the three mules to put it into operation."

"I hope he is not suggesting Gerard is that person," interrupted Aunt Gwendoline.

"He is keeping the option open," Sergeant Chak replied.

Aunt Gwendoline said nothing. No sound of creak or strain called to her from any floorboard or furniture piece. Her whole house, including her Hunter clock, seemed to be concentrating on what the sergeant was saying, while Rani sat erect and statue-still at her knee.

Chapter 26

"This is beginning to sound rather far-fetched," Aunt Gwendoline dismissed. "Are you sure Commander Anderson lives on the same planet as the rest of us?"

Sergeant Chak gave a wry smile.

"I'm pretty sure he doesn't, but that doesn't mean he is insane," he shrugged. "The Commander has to be hypercautious about anything that might affect our national security. It is his job. So, his starting point is that a successful attack on an express train in a tunnel requires the bombers to have sophisticated bombs, accurate detonation devices and for them to know how to use them. Our bombers fail on all three counts. The bombs they concocted were crude to the point where they were more likely to fail than not; their detonators were no better; and the potential bombers themselves are three individuals who would struggle to get through primary school. Commander Anderson is reasoning that whoever sent them out on their mission deliberately set them up to fail."

"It seems a very strange terrorist attack, being designed to fail," commented Aunt Gwendoline.

"Perhaps," agreed the sergeant. "But what if it did not fail? In Commander Anderson's thinking, perhaps the bombs were not the real weapon. What if they were merely devices designed to set off three puffs of smoke in the middle of a crowded rail carriage?"

"And what damage would that cause?" she challenged. "Three puffs of smoke aren't going to hurt anyone."

"They are going to cause a lot of panic," he countered. "Remember, this country is permanently on a high level of security alert because of the threat of terrorism, so even an amateurish attempt is going to set off alarm bells all the way up to the Prime Minister's office."

"And how does this involve Gerard?" she asked.

"Commander Anderson is pursuing the idea that the real weapon in the train attack was the microbe being worked on by Dr Fadden. We know it was in the bombers' backpacks because it was the cause of their bombs failing to explode. It ate through the plastic insulation of the detonator wires. The bombs misfired and three puffs of smoke were created, and that smoke sprayed the bug over everything and everybody up and down the carriage before it settled. All those people sprayed, after they had given their statements to the police, went home, spreading the bug further and further as they went. Not only them but the cleaners who cleaned up the mess and anyone else who walked through the carriage afterwards."

Aunt Gwendoline did not move. She could sense nothing in the world around her to indicate that it was about to change. Everything seemed solid and still, just like it was in Low Felderby on the morning before the jed fell in.

"But my grand-nephew was not in the carriage where the train bombers tried to blow up their devices," she countered.

"That is not the point," Sergeant Chak continued grimly. "It seems that every piece of electrical wiring manufactured since the 1940s has been insulated by coating it in plastic, and today, that wiring brings electrical power to every part of every building where we live and work and every domestic and industrial appliance we use. Dr Fadden's bug demonstrated its ability to degrade that insulation when it short-circuited the detonators of the bombers on the London to Glasgow train, and everyone who was in that carriage has now taken it home with them. So, the question becomes, what will it short circuit next? We do not know how fast Dr Fadden's bug can spread on its own, but we do know that every factory, office block, domestic dwelling and hotel, every school, hospital and every lock up garage and place of work that has ever been built is now in danger of catching fire when somebody switches on a computer, bedside lamp, power drill or microwave oven. If it gets really hungry, the bug could attack the national grid itself and bring down the entire electricity generation and distribution network of this country. That makes what happened on the London to Glasgow train a major bioterrorism attack, hence Commander Anderson's interest in it."

Aunt Gwendoline heard the doubts in the sergeant's voice and watched as he leaned back in his chair and forced himself to relax.

"It sounds like a lot of conjecture," she summarised. "Even if true, who would do such a thing? I know nothing about Dr Fadden other than what Gerard has told me, and the image he gives me is quite the opposite of a terrorist."

"Maybe Gerry doesn't really know him," he countered. "The world has moved on since the nineteen-thirties, Miss Penderrick. Anarchists are no longer strange-looking men who throw little round bombs with fizzing fuses. There is a report that Dr Fadden may be carrying a grudge, something to do with an argument he had with the university a few years ago. According to our intelligence services, he has the expertise to make the bug and he works in a university department that has a specialist research interest in antibiotic resistance. He has also had the opportunity to distribute it in the United States where it can do a lot of damage. None of that can be discounted."

"And where else does Commander Anderson's speculation lead him?" she asked.

She was anxious to ascertain where Gerard was envisaged as fitting into the Commander's highly imaginative scenario. It was, after all, Gerard, who in her dream, was leading the Cleveland Bay down into the unstable darkness of Felderby Pit.

Sergeant Chak hauled on a deep sigh.

"We know Dr Fadden's bug eats plastic," he summarised. "When we look around us, Miss Penderrick, plastic has become ubiquitous in our lives. It is in the clothes we wear, in our shoes and handbags, our carpets and furniture fabrics and the chairs we sit on. It is in the tools and appliances we use in our kitchens and workplaces. It is difficult to pick up anything these days that does not have plastic in it. It is everywhere in our world, and our whole way of life depends on it, and in the extreme, Dr Fadden's bug seems to be capable of eating it all. The consequences of it getting loose in our lives could be disastrous, and at the moment, we have no way of stopping it."

Like the rest of her sitting room, Aunt Gwendoline had almost forgotten to keep breathing. She wondered whether a microbe could mine out the stuff on which society was built in the same way that the men of Low Felderby had mined out the iron ore under the Cleveland Hills, causing a rockfall that changed the landscape about them forever. Perhaps it was possible. Rani wagged her tail stump intermittently in hesitant agreement.

"But you still have not told me where my grand-nephew fits into this picture, and why he should be particularly wary of Commander Anderson," she repeated.

"That would be because of Dr Witheney," he replied.

Chapter 27

Aunt Gwendoline sat a little more upright in surprise.

"The mysterious Dr Witheney," she echoed. "I cannot imagine how she might fit in. For all the enquiries Gerard has made about her she might not even exist."

"That is why she is in Commander Anderson's thinking," Sergeant Chak continued. "People in antiterrorism don't like people who don't exist. It is the perfect cover that allows them to move around the world unnoticed. We know Dr Witheney arrived in this country because she made a telephone call to Gerry's office from the airport, but her name does not appear on any of the passenger lists for any flight arriving or leaving around the time of her call. She made her call to Gerry from a public telephone which limits the possibility of it being traced and it was of too short a duration to be tracked if by chance the intelligence services were listening in. She then disappeared. Commander Anderson is considering the possibility that her call to Gerry saying 'I'm on my way' was a coded message for Gerry to board the London to Glasgow train."

"That is utterly preposterous," Aunt Gwendoline protested. "I have known my grand-nephew all his life. You will find nobody more tolerant of other cultures or with fewer motives to do them any harm, including his own. He is a highly regarded academic, and all his expeditions overseas are fully documented in the archaeological descriptions he has published."

"That may be so," fired back the sergeant. "But I'm sure I have no need to remind you, as someone who lived through the nineteen-thirties, of the long queues of respectable academics who lined up to sign their allegiance to the Nazi Party during a time when all sense of rationality and humanity went out of the window in Europe."

He stopped and drew back on a long breath. He had not meant to be quite so sharp with the old lady. It was the stress of having to deal with Commander Anderson and the way he operated. He noted with mild surprise that Rani had not moved against him but had remained sitting and looking at him with her moist brown eyes, and Aunt Gwendoline herself remained impassive with only a reprimand in her expression.

"For what it is worth, Miss Penderrick, I don't believe Gerry is involved in any terrorist activity," he resumed more calmly. "I think I know him too, but against that I have to acknowledge that the intelligence and security services of this country continue to do a magnificent job protecting us from genuine terrorist atrocities. Sometimes you do think they end up with a warped view of the world but they have had some real successes to their credit, and part of the way they do this is by generating a lot of heat in order to get the answers they want."

"Geheime Staats Polizei," Aunt Gwendoline replied quietly.

"I'm sorry?"

"Geheime Staats Polizei, the Secret State Police," she translated. "That's how they started in Germany in the nineteen-thirties, the Geheime Staats Polizei protecting the homeland. Only they found 'Gehieme Staats Polizei' was a bit of a mouthful to shout out when they hammered on some innocent's door in the middle of the night, so they abbreviated it to 'Gestapo'. You are right, Sergeant. It does pay to be careful."

The conversation closed.

"I must be leaving," Sergeant Chak nodded. "Thanks for the tea, Miss Penderrick, and I'm sorry for disturbing you. If you could tell Gerry when you next see him that it would be helpful if he could produce Dr Witheney so we can all see she is only a lost academic and not a terrorist messenger."

"Thank you, Sergeant, I will do that," she answered.

She noticed his glance at her statue of Shiva standing on her display cabinet as he rose to leave.

"Was there anything else you wanted me to tell him?" she asked.

He looked away from the statue and from her and pulled his coat around him as she opened the door for him to leave.

"You could also tell Gerry that his passport has been withdrawn," he replied. "It should be only temporary and all being well, it will be returned to him when we have finished our enquiries. In the meantime, he can't leave the country."

He did not wait for her response but strode off up the road without looking back.

Chapter 28

Aunt Gwendoline closed her front door but could not let go of it. The floor shuddered under her feet and all sounds came to her as if from far away. The straining in the rocks as they resisted the hills sitting heavily over the jed ran through her, and she felt them slip, stretching further towards the point where they must break.

It was a minute before she felt she could release her grip and feel her way along the walls and past whatever pieces of solid furniture that were within reach, and find her way back to her favourite rosewood grandmother chair in her sitting room. Even then the world was not completely still around her, and it was a few minutes longer before Rani felt able to stand down from her anxious watching.

"I lost my temper with Sergeant Chak, didn't I Rani?" Aunt Gwendoline confessed. "That was not a good thing to do. Sergeant Chak is a friend to our Gerard, and he was not comfortable delivering his message."

She remained in her chair until her heart steadied its beat against the tread of her grandfather clock, and she could once more view the world with some equilibrium.

"Why do I keep coming back to the jed, our Dad?" she asked. "It was so long ago, yet my sleep is being repeatedly disturbed by it."

She brought forward her memories of that distant time.

"The jed at Low Felderby became the biggest ever mined. The weight of hills bearing down on it, and the threat to the men who had to work in it, had never been greater. It had to be drawn before it collapsed of its own mind."

She knew from memory the sequence of drawing a jed. First, the ore wagons with the last of their payable rock were pulled out. Then the rail tracks upon which they ran were taken up. Her memories raced to complete the picture. Anything else that had any value was then brought out, and after that, one by one, the timbers holding up the roof were taken down. Good timbers cost money and could be reused in another part of the mine, and the mine owners were not ones to waste money. So, down the timbers came starting at the furthest part of the jed until there was nothing left holding up the hills except the rocks stretched across the emptiness where the ore had once been. The men sweated, ever alert for the giddying roar that announced the unsupported rocks were splitting and that the hills were spilling their entrails into the empty space created by their labour. With luck, the collapse would start at the furthest point where the props were fewest, and they would have time to retreat. With luck, the collapse would stop short of the full jed and let them walk out with nothing more than a covering of dust. Without luck, it might follow them and engulf them wherever they ran, taking not only the space of the jed but also parts of the mine where men still worked. A rockfall, even a deliberate one, was never a controlled beast. No one could foretell it. Only the hills knew.

"You were so proud, our Dad. 'Muscles of stone and tendons of iron' you said. You should have added 'ay and nerves of steel too'."

"And sometimes, very occasionally, the hills teased you," Aunt Gwendoline recalled. "That is what happened at Felderby. The last timbers were taken down and disbelieving men retreated on tiptoe from the vast and unsupported cavern, never taking their eyes off the black underside of the hills, not talking lest the smallest whisper should trigger the stretched rocks into splitting and taking them all in a single strike. The rocks held and the big jed stood open and empty waiting to fall with only the hills deciding when that should happen. I remember you coming home, our Dad, and saying 'they've drawn the big jed an' t'bugger has not come down'. It did not come down that day nor the next and not for almost a week, and when it did fall in it was a wonder that nobody was killed. There was only the one horse that was injured and the whole landscape changed around Low Felderby. A great hole appeared on the surface that swallowed half a farm and in time, the hole filled with water and gave us children a lake to play beside. And then the water percolated down through the rocks and caused flooding in the mine and later still, after all the mining had finished, the council decided the hole would be a good place to bury rubbish so it became a landfill site. So much of the landscape changed and it kept changing, didn't it, our Dad? Fifty years later the council were still putting up road signs saying 'road liable to subsidence'. It was a big jed."

Aunt Gwendoline sat sharply upright in her chair.

"I've got it wrong," she announced. "I've got it back to front."

She hurried out to the hallway and stood in front of her grandfather clock, her unsteadiness forgotten.

"I thought I dreamed our Gerard was taking the Cleveland Bay back to work after it had been injured in the rockfall," she panted. "Yet that could never have happened. The horse could never have gone back to work after being injured like that. So, when I saw our Gerard leading the horse down into Felderby Pit, it was before it was injured, not after. That is the proper order of events, isn't it our Dad? I've had it back to front. Our Gerard is leading the horse into Felderby Pit where the jed is yet to fall."

She held on to the wall for support while an icy wash of fear ran through her and Rani whimpered anxiously at her feet. She choked on a deep breath and looked pleadingly up into the clock's face.

"The jed has not yet fallen," she repeated to it.

The clock struck the half-hour in reply.

Chapter 29

"The bronze drums of the Dong Son are most exquisitely cast, and probably the technical endpoint of a tradition that started off with simple bashing on metal sheets and evolved into a musical tradition that saw finely crafted gongs and bells dominate Asian music even to this day."

Aunt Gwendoline listened to Gerard talking about ancient Indochinese civilisations, bridging the hours and aeons with an ease that indicated a total absence of any knowledge of the jed that was going to fall and change the landscape of his world around him.

"In Europe, our forebears took a different approach," he chatted on. "They took catgut, or the gut of whatever animal they had recently killed, dried it and stretched it across bits of wood and twanged it, so giving us our musical heritage based on strings."

"I would have to say I prefer strings to gongs," she commented. "My limited exposure to Chinese opera and Kabuki music did not leave me looking for more. I am much happier with Strauss and Mozart."

"Yet all your clocks strike with a metal chime," he countered, smiling broadly as he accepted a refreshed cup of tea.

"A mixing of cultures," she conceded. "How we benefit from each other, and I can certainly appreciate the fine tones of a peal of English church bells."

She wondered why, following her surprising and unaccounted for invitation, Gerard had not brought the antipodean Miss Blaise with him for tea. Something must have stopped him although nothing had been said. Not for the first time she looked to see if there was any trace of the family gift in him, that extra sense that would tell him when troubles and dangers were circling. There had been occasions when she believed he had reacted to the world around him just as she did. She had inherited the gift from her mother, so it was not impossible for it to have been transmitted down the family line through her younger sister Lizzie to Gerard's mother and then to Gerard himself. On the other hand, she had just as frequently been exasperated by his blindness to dangers that screamed their approach to him, and at such times, she had felt herself forced to conclude that, loving though she might be, it was against all reason and expectation that such a scatter-brained personality as his mother was capable of passing on anything worthwhile to her son. Ultimately, she blamed her sister Lizzie for it.

"And how is Dr Fadden?" she asked.

Gerard hesitated in his exposition about the Dong Son drums and sat back into his chair. His last visit to Glasgow had left a lot of thoughts churning through his mind and in spite of his worrying them through all his waking hours, he was no closer to saying why they so disturbed him. He leaned back further, took a deep breath and let the room, the artefacts, the afternoon tea, his timeless Aunt and the aspidistra take the strain off the anchors that were holding him unsteady in his mooring.

"Chris is not too bad under the circumstances, although I'm not sure he will be feeling any better after seeing me," he replied. "I felt I had to let Chris know about my visit from Commander Anderson. Even now I can't believe he is serious about linking Chris' discovery of his bug with a terrorist plot on the London to Glasgow train, but he seems to have enough clout to make it unwise to ignore him.

"I called Chris to arrange where to meet, and again he chose another nondescript café down a Glasgow back street. He was tense and anxious on the 'phone and wanting to keep the call short, just as before, but he was pleased to hear from me. I was surprised by his appearance when I saw him. He is beginning to look more than a bit tired and scruffy around the edges and not nearly as neat and tidy as he had always been before.

"'They are still following me,' he announced as soon as we met. 'They are tapping into my 'phone and going through my papers. Nasty commercial spies getting up to all sorts of dirty tricks. I even had a tarted-up female accost me in the street last evening, swinging her perfume suggestively at me and pretending to ask the way.'

"The stress of being a target of what he thought was commercial espionage was clearly telling on him.

"'You think she was one of them?' I asked dubiously.

"'What do you think, Gerry?' he spluttered. 'I'm a nondescript academic two years off retirement who wears a sports jacket that smells of laboratory. I may have a few illusions about myself, but I do know I don't look like a film star or someone who carries around the wallet of a millionaire.'

"I was pleased to see some sign of fight in him after his initial, deflated presentation.

"'So, how are you dealing with them, the spies and the espionage?'

"'I'm not going home,' he replied. 'I'm moving around, staying mostly in cheaper hotels and student digs, trying to keep below their radar. But I am at the department every day if you need to contact me. Just don't say anything identifiable over the telephone.'

"It seemed a bit illogical to hide where you sleep at night but then still turn up for work every day, but I didn't comment on it.

"'I'm sorry to add a further twist to your troubles, but I'm not sure industrial espionage is all that is going on at the moment,' I continued. 'The Inspector Anderson who came to see you and who asked you all those questions about your bug is not an industrial spy. He is someone official. He came to see me last Friday and introduced himself as Commander Anderson. He had with him a very good policeman friend of mine who I know is genuine.'

"Chris looked at me, alarmed.

"'In what way official?' he asked. 'Do you mean police?'

"'In part, yes, although nobody seems to know exactly who he is other than he seems to be connected to antiterrorism. He himself is not telling.'

"'So why is he bothering me?' Chris protested. 'I haven't done anything illegal. All my work is above board, and I'm certainly not a terrorist.'

"'I know you are not a terrorist any more than I am,' I assured him. 'But when Anderson came to see me, he seemed to be trying to put together some screwball scenario whereby you and I are in cahoots with the three young men who tried to blow up the London to Glasgow train last week. Needless to say, I treated his speculations with the contempt they deserved.'

"Chris twitched around to see who else was in the dim interior of the café. He drained his tea and looked around again.

"'Is there any possibility of something stronger?' he asked.

"'I don't think that's a good idea, Chris,' I answered. 'If we are going to deal with this then both of us are going to have to stay in fighting trim.'

"He nodded and slumped back in his chair.

"'One of the things Anderson told me was that your *Methylococcus faddenii* is resistant to antibiotics, not just one but several, as in all of them,' I continued. 'That is what makes him think the bug was somehow man-made.'

"'It probably was,' Chris replied.

"I jumped. I had not expected him to confirm it.

"'Are you telling me that Anderson and his secret service pals are right, that we are dealing with something that a terrorist group might have created?'

"He waved a dismissive hand.

"'Antibiotic resistant bugs are being made all the time. I thought *M. faddenii* might have antibiotic resistance so I checked it out, and there doesn't seem to be much it can't handle.'

"'But why would we want to do that?' I challenged. 'We are having enough trouble in our hospitals with the resistant bugs we've got without us producing more. The ones we've got are already killing people.'

"'It's simply the way we identify bugs when we do research in genetics,' he replied. 'When we have a gene of interest, and we want to splice it into a bug's DNA, all we have to do is shake the bug and the gene together. But not every bug takes up our gene, so we join our gene to another gene for antibiotic resistance.'

"'And?' I asked.

"'Any bug that incorporates our gene then also incorporates the antibiotic resistance gene, and after growing them for a while in a nice, nutritious soup, we hit them with an antibiotic. The ones that survive are the ones we want for our research. The rest get killed. It's standard procedure.'

"'And they all have antibiotic resistance,' I added. 'Is it difficult?'

"'Not in the least. It's an undergraduate exercise.'

"'So, it is something a terrorist could do, splice a gene for antibiotic resistance into a bug?' I asked cautiously.

"'As I said, we do it all the time,' he shrugged.

"This was new information to me, and I began imagining thousands of students in universities all over the world manufacturing antibiotic-resistant microbes by the truckload every day as part of their studies.

"'What happens to all these new antibiotic-resistant bugs that we create?' I asked.

"'They are not a problem,' he dismissed. 'After we have finished with them we drop them into buckets of industrial-strength disinfectant which kills them instantly. The bugs we

132

use do not kill humans anyway, so we are all quite safe. The general public is less likely to catch anything nasty from what we get up to in a microbiology lab than anywhere else on the planet, even if the occasional one does escape.'

"'Do they ever escape?' I pressed him.

"I was thinking about Chris telling me how his bug had chewed its way not only through his plastic culture dishes in his laboratory in Adelaide but also through the plastic waste bins.

"'A couple of years ago foot and mouth disease found its way out through a leaky drain in a supposedly secure government infectious diseases laboratory,' he replied. 'So, I would have to say escape is possible. Bugs are clever little creatures.'

"'Too clever by half,' I commented.

"I looked at Chris and saw the naivety in his smile, and I was suddenly afraid for him. In normal times he is good company and a good teacher, but he is also very trusting. He could be led anywhere, even into the embrace of a terrorist network."

Chapter 30

Aunt Gwendoline could see the turmoil within her grand-nephew as he paused in his recounting, and she wondered whether it was the family gift that was stirring forewarning into his thoughts. She hoped so. She had worried endlessly about him facing bandits, poisonous creatures and vile diseases in foreign places, yet it was here back at home that he was in the middle of events involving terrorists, an attempted train bombing, a more than attractive research assistant, and the withdrawal of his passport by the likes of Commander Anderson. Trouble was brewing up a storm about him, there were tremors all around him and the jed had not yet fallen, and yet he seemed at best only dimly aware of any of it. If he had inherited the gift, then it should be shouting to him as it was to her. She could not help but worry about him.

"I can't help but worry about Chris," he continued. "He only sees his bug as a benefit that would clear hedgerows, beaches and oceans of plastic rubbish, saving wildlife and cleaning up the earth, and incidentally making a lot of money for him. Protecting it has become the focus of his life, and he does not seem to be able to grasp the full picture as Commander Anderson would see it.

"I repeated to Chris what Anderson had told me about the bombs on the London to Glasgow train failing to go off because *Methylococcus faddenii* had chewed its way through the plastic insulation of the detonator wires.

"'In which case, he should be thanking me, not pursuing me like a criminal,' he countered. 'I saved people's lives. Why is he harassing me?'

"'Anderson thinks your *faddenii* bug is man-made, and you seem to agree with him,' I summarised for him. 'The difference is that Anderson believes it is being spread around deliberately by some politically dislocated people who have the intention of causing wholesale havoc. I have no idea what his real thinking is. Nobody does with the possible exception of himself, but we now know he is official and that means he can probably do more or less whatever he pleases and it will all be covered by the words 'national security' and 'Official Secrets Act'. The immunity of government intelligence services to public scrutiny is widely known. There is never any accounting for international arrest warrants issued on innocent people, or for law-abiding citizens being shot by antiterrorist police. All we are ever told is that there was faulty intelligence and it would not be in the interests of national security for the details to be made public. What is worrying for us is that, rationally or not, Anderson has involved us in his thinking.'

"'He could just ask for our help instead of treating us like the enemy,' offered Chris.

"I had no answer to that. I had no more idea than anyone else how Commander Anderson viewed the world except that I could not think it was very benignly.

"'Let's get back to your bug, Chris. Exactly how dangerous is it?' I asked.

"'It's not,' he replied without hesitation. 'It has never hurt anybody. It's simply a harmless little bug which lives in the soil, minding its own business while helping recycle nutrients. It doesn't give us or any other living creature any diseases, not even so much as a sniffle, and it certainly doesn't kill us.'

"'But it is different,' I pressed him gently. 'It eats plastic and as Anderson informed me, about twenty per cent of the cars we drive is plastic. If your *faddenii* starts eating its way through our steering wheels and dashboards as we drive along, not to mention the host of other plastic widgets under the bonnet, it could produce some very nasty road accidents. Could it be that *M. faddenii* has been specially made to cause such mischief?'

"Chris thought for a minute or more, the scientist in him mentally running through all the possibilities. He finally shook his head.

"'We could never tell,' he replied. 'When we splice a gene from a human being into a bug then, as Anderson would have it, we know it has to be man-made because bugs in the wild do not have human genes. They only have bug genes, and the gene for antibiotic resistance is a bug gene. It is one that they created all by themselves in response to our attempts to kill them. It is now so widely spread and so much part of their natural world that we could never tell whether some human had spliced it into *M. faddenii* or whether it was something it inherited from its mummy and daddy or caught from its girlfriend.'

"'Caught from its girlfriend?' I queried.

"'Something bugs do,' he giggled. 'Every now and again, they rub up against each other and exchange genetic information. In higher animals, we call it having sex, in bugs we call it lateral transfer.'

"'But what about the gene to eat plastic?' I persisted. 'That seems mischievous to me. Could someone make one of those and splice it into a bug?'

"Chris was back in his role as the benevolent and slightly paternalistic teacher his students knew so well.

"'We humans are not that clever. We might string together a heap of molecules in a test tube and end up with something that looks like a gene, but if we tried to insert it into a living organism, it would almost certainly kill it. Genes don't work in isolation, and so far, only Mother Nature knows how to create a new gene from scratch and put it into place in a living organism without crashing the rest of life's processes.'

"'You are saying that whatever gene it is that allows your bug to eat plastic is a gene it has come up with all by itself?' I asked.

"'Almost certainly,' he answered. 'Remember, since they first appeared on earth, microbes have lived under every set of conditions imaginable. No matter what the universe has thrown at them, they have adapted to their surroundings and survived. I cannot think that the sudden appearance of industrial quantities of plastic in the mid-twentieth century would present them with much of a challenge. To them, it would simply be a massive, untapped food supply. It only took them thirty years to learn how to turn antibiotics to their advantage.'

"'To their advantage?' I echoed.

"I must have looked perplexed because he grinned at me, clearly enjoying the impact of his statement.

"'We humans began using our first antibiotics to treat infections in the nineteen forties,' he beamed. 'By the nineteen seventies, we not only had antibiotic-resistant bugs, we also had antibiotic dependent bugs, bugs that could use antibiotics as food. The more antibiotic we used to try and kill them the more they grew, and the faster the poor patients who were infected with them died.'

"I stared at him in disbelief.

"'Bugs that use antibiotics as food?' I repeated. 'How do we deal with them?'

"'We keep trying to come up with new antibiotics, although I would have to admit we are starting to run out of ideas on that front.'

"It was my turn to be silent again, trying to digest all this new information. I couldn't share his enthusiasm. In contrast, I felt there was something frankly scary in the whole situation.

"'Your *M. faddenii* has developed its ability to eat plastic all on its own without any of us humans being involved at all,' I summarised.

"'Almost certainly correct,' he agreed.

"'Chris, don't you think this might be a problem? When you look around there is an awful lot of plastic in our world. It might be a useful thing to do to scatter *Methylococcus faddenii* about the place to clean up our oceans, beaches and hedgerows and help local authorities deal with plastic rubbish, but once you have scattered it about, what is to stop it continuing to eat its way through the rest of our existence? Sergeant Chak told me a recent environmental agency survey found an unexpectedly large number of agricultural drains needed replacing across the country. Apparently, a large part of the flood defences protecting our towns and transport systems consist of plastic agricultural drains, and the worry is that if *M. faddenii* starts chewing its way through those we could end up being inundated next winter, with lives lost and houses, roads and farms destroyed beyond anything we have ever seen before. Looking at it through Commander Anderson's eyes, how sure can we be that this bug of yours is not dangerous and has not been engineered by someone with malicious intent? Don't you think Commander Anderson and his people might just have a point?'

"'I hadn't thought about it like that,' he nodded after a pause. 'But I still don't see why he should be so obnoxious about it.'

"Once again, I had no answer to give him, but at least we agreed that for the present, there is nothing we can do about Anderson and whatever title he wants to give himself. All we could do is remain wary and see what happens."

Chapter 31

Aunt Gwendoline could only agree. She had no answers either and neither, apparently, did Rani who had returned to being completely at ease, chin on paws, at her feet while Gerard moved on to other matters.

"I had an e-mail from Professor Nguyn yesterday. The Vietnamese Minister for Culture paid a visit to our diggings at Ban Long and became very excited about what is developing into a major prehistoric cultural site. He has promised us more funding. I only wish our government would get as enthusiastic about archaeology."

Which was all very well except that Aunt Gwendoline still had a Cleveland Bay to worry about, a horse being led to work by Gerard into a place where there was a jed yet to cave in.

"And your research assistant, Miss Blaise?" she asked.

"To be perfectly honest, I have barely seen her," he replied. "I gave her your invitation, of course, but I have been so busy…"

She bid him goodbye with her usual invitation for him to return the following Wednesday and waved him on his way.

It was inevitable that over the next two nights, Rani would sit up frequently from her blanket and sniff at the darkness while her mistress muttered in restless sleep. The days were no more relaxed, in spite of the long-sought article on Victorian Hunter Clocks being found in her vast collection of back copies of the *Antiques Collectors' Weekly*.

"You come from a very distinguished heritage," Aunt Gwendoline was able to inform her still annoyingly disobedient timepiece. "Camerer, Kuss, Tritschler and Co., established in 1788 and patronised by Her Majesty. That would be Queen Victoria, as I'm sure you would know. And you received an honourable mention in the Exhibition of 1862. You really could do better."

She looked up at her uncooperative acquisition and reread the passage about the honourable mention. She had known she was getting a bargain when she bid for it, but an honourable mention in one of the exhibitions following the success of the Great Exhibition of 1851 was a bonus she had not expected.

"With a fine German mechanism such as yours, one would think that you would be better regulated by now," she reprimanded it.

On the other hand, given the honourable mention, a small amount of extended tolerance might perhaps be justified.

"I think I will write to the Victoria and Albert Museum in Kensington to see if they are able to tell me more about you," she mused.

She gave the clock another stern look and was startled to see it was again showing the accurate time, confirmed from the hallway by the striking of her grandfather clock. She put down her magazine.

"I was just about to call you an annoying piece of mechanism not worthy of the attention that went into your manufacture, but I see you have decided to behave yourself again. Just in time, too, I might add," she informed it apprehensively.

She reached out into the world, listening with all her senses, and looked down at Rani. There was a tension in the dog as if she was anticipating a hunt, a readiness to locate and point, to fly and retrieve, but as far as Aunt Gwendoline could tell, there was nothing to pursue. She paced slowly around her chair watching the Hunter clock closely, then walked out to the hallway. It was just before midday, and she held herself defiant before the sentinel of all time in her life and stared straight into its face as its hands moved steadily towards the hour.

"What are you doing, our Dad?" she asked it. "Why are you playing with my new clock? I know you never liked Germans, not since your experiences in the trenches of the First World War, but that was a long time ago and my clock predates that conflict. Not only that, but while both Mr Camerer and Mr Kuss were German in their origins, they were well and truly English by the time they made it, so there really is no need for you to make them so unwelcome."

The hands crept ever more vertically.

"You have led me along the road to Felderby Pit, following our Gerard, who is leading a Cleveland Bay to work, and down at Pit Bottom, there is a drawn jed which has not yet fallen in," she persisted. "I know it is dangerous, our Dad, because I was there when it happened, but you will have to tell me more before I can be of any help to him. What is it I have to do?"

The clock roared out its reply, striking the midday hour with more force than she had ever known it capable. Twelve times it hammered at her until she leaned on the wall for support, and as the echoes of its voice died away in her ears, she heard her telephone ringing behind her.

"Wych Green four-five oh four," she answered it cautiously.

"Hello, Aunt Gwendoline, it's Gerard. Can I come and see you right away?"

He sounded anxious and even a little breathless.

"Of course, my dear boy. I am at home."

"And while I'm getting there, could you switch on the television with the lunchtime news? It is important."

He rang off before she could give a reply.

Chapter 32

Gerard, Aunt Gwendoline and Rani sat without speaking, watching the television in the front room. It was not a room Aunt Gwendoline used very often. It held some of her furniture, a Sheraton corner wall cabinet and a brass handled sea chest *circa* 1840, and also her Landseer and Jacquet wood engravings and a David Cox watercolour of sheep being driven across Morecombe Bay, but it was closest to the road so did not provide the quietness she preferred. It was consequently a good room in which to place the television.

Gerard seemed unduly agitated by the news being reported. Pictures were flickering across the screen of aerial water bombers and ground-based fire crews fighting a fire burning over a large area in southern Germany. The running commentary identified the location as the largest landfill site in Europe.

"It's massive," Gerard commented. "Apparently it started late yesterday evening. It seems that a spark from a bulldozer blade ignited something combustible in the rubbish. The explosion that followed was completely unexpected. Two workmen were killed instantly and a score of others injured, three of them seriously. The resulting fire then spread across the dump very quickly and has gone progressively more out of control ever since. It soon reached the buildings and environs of a neighbouring recycling site and secondary explosions then started to go off, seemingly at random across the whole area with more workmen and fire-fighters being injured in the blasts. At that point all personnel were evacuated until the cause of the explosions could be identified."

Aunt Gwendoline considered the images rolling across the screen then looked at her grand-nephew.

"I am always happy to see you," she declared. "But I am puzzled to know why a fire at a rubbish dump in Bavaria should lead to me receiving an excited telephone call from you in the middle of the day. It isn't one of your archaeological dig sites by any chance, is it?"

"Commander Anderson," he replied shortly.

Aunt Gwendoline looked down at Rani, who seemed equally bemused.

"And why has Commander Anderson suddenly developed an interest in fires at domestic rubbish dumps in Germany?" she asked.

Whatever the reason, she could not believe it would be good news.

"I have just been talking to Sergeant Chak, so I only know what he has told me," he replied. "It seems that the ferocity of the blaze in Bavaria and the speed with which it spread surprised the local fire authorities who were called in to deal with it. They quickly suspected arson, which drew in the local police. By the time the police got there, the whole dump was exploding and too dangerous for anyone to approach, so they cordoned off a huge area and declared a state of emergency. That triggered the next step. The Bavarian authorities notified the German federal government who sent the news all the way up to the Chancellor's office, and that in turn activated the German national security services. At present the official story is that what is going on outside Munich is probably only a serious rubbish dump fire. It could be that arson is involved, but a terrorist attack cannot be discounted."

Aunt Gwendoline raised her eyebrows.

"A terrorist attack?" she queried. "If the intention is to bring down the government, then blowing up people's rubbish is a strange way of doing it."

Gerard smiled, reflecting his great-aunt's bemusement.

"We have to remember the increased state of security that has gripped the Western world since the terrorist attack on the World Trade Centre in New York," he answered. "After that event, any and every unofficial explosion is assumed to be a terrorist attack, and it did not take long for the German security services to decide that a conflagration on the scale outside Munich could not be an accident. It is massive. From what Sergeant Chak tells me, the blaze has drained the firefighting resources of Bavaria and much of the rest of southern Germany. Additional units have been drafted into action from northern Germany and the German government has asked for units in Austria, Switzerland and the Czech Republic to be available to help if necessary. Services in France, Belgium and Poland have also been put on standby."

Aunt Gwendoline looked again at the images on the television screen. Eyewitnesses were comparing the blaze to the firestorms created out of the cities of Germany by allied bombing during World War Two, and two experts began discussing the public health implications of the smoke billowing out from a rubbish tip fire. The running commentary was advising that a dense cloud of thick, acrid smoke was covering large areas of Bavaria and beginning to spread westwards across central and southern Europe. Citizens of Munich and surrounding towns were being advised to stay indoors and prepare for a general evacuation.

"I suppose if there is the possibility of it being terrorism, then that would explain Commander Anderson's interest in it," she summarised. "But I still don't understand why you should be so immediately concerned about it."

"Chris Fadden," he replied.

She looked down at Rani again and saw that the dog was even more agitated.

"I'm not sure Sergeant Chak should have told me all he did, but he is worried," Gerard continued. "Somehow, and Sergeant Chak doesn't know-how, our American cousins became aware of the existence of *Methylococcus faddenii* around the same time that Chris Fadden presented his report to their Environmental Protection Agency. They sent their investigation teams to the factories Chris had visited and found the bug in the soil around all of them, just as he had. Once their scientists had decided that the bug was man-made, it was only a short leap for them to suspect it had been deliberately manufactured and spread about as a threat to their plastics industry, and since the United States plastics industry is huge, that translated into a bioterrorism threat to their national economy. Their national security people then asked 'is Dr Fadden a terrorist agent who is deliberately spreading *M. faddenii* around their plastics factories under the guise of being a harmless academic?'"

He paused, still not convinced by the logic of what he was saying.

"It does sound rather a long extrapolation," Aunt Gwendoline agreed.

"Maybe, but it does explain where Commander Anderson fits in and why he is bothering Chris," he shrugged. "Understandably, the United States does not take kindly to the thought of a terrorist attack being launched against it by a citizen of their supposed friend and ally on the other side of the Atlantic Ocean, so it brought pressure to bear on Her Majesty's government to sort it out. Our government's response was to launch Commander Anderson at the problem with orders to get the people responsible for making Chris Fadden's bug and stop them. Meanwhile, in the United States, they are pumping thousands of gallons of industrial-strength disinfectant into the ground around their plastics factory sites to counter the spread of the infection."

Aunt Gwendoline looked at him.

"Which still does not provide me with a reason why you should be so interested in the fire in Bavaria," she stated.

Gerard shook his head.

"I don't know," he admitted. "It is just a feeling I have. All garbage dumps have large quantities of everyday combustible rubbish in them, and they are forever catching fire. I've seen them burning in India, Thailand and all over the Far East. But this fire is different, and I cannot help but be uneasy about it. I can't help but wonder whether *Methylococcus faddenii* is involved."

She focussed hard on her grand-nephew. The image formed in front of her of a trusting Cleveland Bay standing by his side. She felt the landscape around her straining to hold its shape.

"What are you going to do?" she asked.

Gerard looked down at the floor and pursed his lips.

"I have to warn Chris," he replied. "I cannot believe he is anything other than an innocent party in whatever it is that Anderson is chasing. Whether his bug was deliberately created by some terrorist organisation or simply came into existence as part of Mother Nature's experimenting, his only crime was to find it in a handful of soil. I'm going up to Glasgow."

Aunt Gwendoline switched off the television. In the tickings of her clocks, she heard the treading of a horse on its way to work at Felderby Pit, and in her dream she had seen it wounded and bloody and being led limping to the farrier.

"You will be careful, won't you?" she cautioned as he prepared to leave. "And you will call me the moment you get back."

"I'll do that, Aunt Gwendoline," he replied, giving her a brief hug. "And don't worry. I just want to make sure Chis is safe."

Chapter 33

Peace of mind was out of the question after Gerard left. Aunt Gwendoline brought into her mind the masculine touch of his face against hers as he departed, but no sooner had she done so than the smoothness of his cheek was replaced by the bristle of her father's chin as it was when she kissed him on the morning he left for work on the day of the rockfall, the day the big jed fell in. She leaned back against the corded velvet of her favourite chair and let her right-hand dangle where Rani could nuzzle it. She closed her eyes. She was feeling her years.

"We knew the jed would be hanging over our dad and the other men as they worked, didn't we, Mother?" she recounted to the aspidistra listening in the corner. "The whole village knew it, but no one spoke of it in case the words made the rocks break. We kissed him goodbye as we always did and stayed firmly inside while he left for work. It was one of the few times you listened to me, wasn't it, Mother? I could see further than you, and as I left for school, you grabbed me by the arms and wouldn't let me go. You looked into my face and yet could not speak the words, but your eyes told me. 'It's all right, our Mam,' I answered. 'Our dad is going to be all right. He'll be coming home'."

Her memories gathered momentum.

"He did come home, as all the men did," she continued. "He was shocked and white-faced and covered in dust. He was shaking all over and only just able to stand. He told us later that all any of them could do was to hold hard to anything that seemed solid and keep praying that the dice the hills had thrown would stop their rolling before they reached the particular patch of roof below which their own lives and limbs awaited the judgement of chance. 'It set off a rush of air,' he said. 'A fog of dust and damp as solid as a wall and as fast as a train, it knocked us all off our feet. It blew out all the lamps and nobody could see'. He had gone back to help with the injured and had found the wounded horse, and afterwards you held on to him and walked him home, but he was all right. He came back to us in one piece."

She rose stiffly from her chair and wandered out to the hallway and stared into the face of her oak cased clock.

"Our Gerard will come home to us from whatever awaits him in Glasgow. Is that what you are telling me, our Dad?" she asked. "You came home and he will too. He will be shaken up, and the Cleveland Bay he leads will be injured, but at least he will come home."

The night seemed to confirm it.

A chorus of complaint was coming out of the rocks. The hills were warping and bending, and the timbers that held them up were crying out in pain, yet the men stopped their ears to the sounds and worked on. Times were hard, and on a good shift, they might break twenty tonnes of the pitiless ore, and that would make up for those other shifts when the rock would not part so willingly with its treasure. The tunnels

twisted and fired a shrapnel of boulders at them, and snorting
horses hauled the fruits of their labour to the weigh station
and on up the incline where mercifully a steam-driven cable
replaced living tissue to drag the uncaring stone up the drift
and out to the Works. The steel of the rail tracks rucked and
buckled and a juddering in the earth hailed another fracture
in the weakening crust that stretched over their heads,
holding back the hills from the hole they had created.

"The jed," they cursed. "They've drawn the big jed,"

"Aye, an' t'bugger has not come down."

They nodded to each other and pretended not to care.
Work was pay and pay was food and shelter. They could not
stop.

"It can't hold much longer."

A ferocious jolting knocked them all off their feet, and she
heard a horse scream.

Aunt Gwendoline woke, calling out into the darkness. Her
heart was pounding, the timbers were cracking, and she was
pushing at her pillows in an effort to break through a wall of
rock.

"Just a minute, Rani," she gasped. "Just give me a few
moments."

She slumped back on her much-punished pillows and
dropped her hand so it could be comforted by the dog. She
made herself breathe in a more regular rhythm until her world
settled back into place and she could hear once again the tread
of her grandfather clock as its hands moved across the minutes
of her denied sleep. Eventually, she felt confident enough to
push back the bedclothes and swing her feet into her slippers,
and let her trembling limbs and a firm grip on the bannister

carry her downstairs, first to the kitchen to make a pot of tea and then to the comfort of her favourite chair.

"I heard a horse scream," she recalled. "The jed fell in, and the horse was caught in the rockfall. I heard its cry."

It was the single memory that drowned out all others. How long she sat with it she did not know until she took a sip of her tea and recoiled at the taste of it long past cold. She was stiff and shivering.

"It is still very early," she sighed. "I can do no more for the moment."

Next morning Rani looked on puzzled as her mistress tinkered with the Hunter clock, set it to the correct time, checked it after a short while and then began fiddling with it all over again. There seemed to be neither distraction in the task nor relaxation in the avoiding of it. The regular morning bounce in the park was delayed until the key and oil can were finally thrown down in exasperation, and yet another pot of tea was made and sampled briefly before the half-empty cup was left along with a regiment of its fellows in the sink to be washed up later. A notepad was found which waited interminably under a poised pencil for coherent thought to begin a letter to the Victoria and Albert Museum.

"Come along, Rani," Aunt Gwendoline finally announced. "What we need is some fresh air. We really do have more profitable things we can be doing."

She took her coat from the hallway rack, adjusted her hat and lipstick in the hallway mirror and nodded acceptance of the result to her tired and drawn reflection. She snapped on Rani's leash, but once again the dog appeared unenthusiastic about an outing.

"Rani, come along," she instructed. "We are going out, and I really do not have the energy to argue about it. We have comestibles to purchase for next Wednesday when our Gerard comes to tea, possibly bringing the antipodean Miss Blaise with him, and I am sure there are other things we need as well."

Rani gave two twitches of her tail stump but declined to stand.

"What is the matter?" Aunt Gwendoline asked again and tugged at the leash.

She was about to haul the dog towards the door when the doorbell rang. Much to her surprise, Rani remained anchored to the floor and did not rush forward to call the visitor friend or stranger as she always did. More surprisingly, she ignored the bell when it rang a second time.

"A visitor," Aunt Gwendoline stated, bending down to be more on the level with the dog. "One whom we need to see and not necessarily one bearing good news. It's not Sergeant Chak again, is it?"

She was feeling tired and a little dizzy, but that was no reason to be unsociable. She pulled herself erect and stepped forward to open the door.

"Good morning, Sergeant," she smiled. "Won't you come in?"

Chapter 34

Sergeant Chak smiled stiffly. The old lady looked fragile, which did not help his task.

"I'm afraid Gerard is not here," she informed him.

"We know that," he answered. "He left for Glasgow almost as soon as he left you yesterday. It is Dr Witheney we are looking for."

She glanced over at her Hunter clock and noted it was showing the correct time. Rani whimpered briefly beside her.

"Dr Witheney isn't here either, nor has she ever been," she replied.

"We know that too," the sergeant smiled tightly again. "We didn't expect to find her here, but I have to ask you whether Gerard, when he was here yesterday, mentioned anything that might tell us where she might be."

She was surprised by his statement and annoyed by the implication that her home was being watched. It did not please her, whatever reasons Commander Anderson might use to justify it.

"Are you sure you wouldn't like some tea?" she invited.

Sergeant Chak reigned in his frustration. He knew he was on a nonsense errand. His instruction was to come and question this frail old lady about the phantom Dr Witheney, and he knew it was only a device to get him out of the office while Commander Anderson and his team discussed matters they were not prepared to share with him. He also remembered that his last visit had ended on somewhat tense terms.

"Tea would be nice," he replied.

She left him to prepare it, and he tried to settle his thoughts. His attachment to Commander Anderson's team was leaving him increasingly conflicted. He had tried to talk to his own chief about it, but all he was told was, "You are a vital part of the liaison between the investigating team and the local police," from which he deduced his chief knew no more than he did, had no choice in the matter and so could do nothing about it.

"Are you allowed to tell me what has happened to excite your interest in Dr Witheney?" Aunt Gwendoline enquired as she returned with the tea.

"She's a running thread which connects all the known events relating to Dr Fadden's bug," he answered. "Dr Witheney calls Gerry, and he gets on a train where, under the cover of it being a suicide bomb attack, three young males set off puffs of smoke which scatter a dangerous bug over everything and everybody within range. She then disappears. We believe she left this country and we need to know where she went next."

"You think Gerard might know?" asked Aunt Gwendoline. "He tells me he cannot recall ever meeting Dr Witheney."

"He is the one person we know who has had contact with her and we need to find her," he stated.

He found he could not meet the old lady's gaze. He was deeply aware that the script he was working to contained a lot of speculation.

"You would be aware of the major fire that is burning a few miles west of Munich and that the German government has declared it a state of emergency," he continued more calmly. "You may also guess that there are internationally agreed protocols that require the governments of Europe and the United States to notify each other if they declare a state of emergency and suspect terrorism is involved. In accordance with those protocols, Germany notified her allies that the fire in Bavaria was a potential terrorist attack and everybody began trawling their data sources for intelligence leads. It was the US authorities that were the first to come up with an answer. Being already sensitised by what they are treating as a bioterrorism attack on their plastics industry, they quickly declared the incident in Bavaria to be a similar bioterrorism attack with Dr Fadden's bug being the likely weapon. I'm not a biochemist, but most rubbish dumps these days have more waste plastic in them than anything else, and Dr Fadden did tell Gerry his bug breaks it all down to produce large quantities of methane and other inflammable chemicals. Apparently, that is what blew up in Munich."

"So, it is Dr Fadden's expertise with his microbe that is needed to help control the fire in Munich, not Dr Witheney's," Aunt Gwendoline suggested hopefully.

Sergeant Chak shook his head.

"Not quite," he replied. "The thinking of the security people is that either on her way to contact Gerry or on her way out of this country, Dr Witheney stopped off in Munich and made a similar 'phone call to another person as yet unknown.

That person then began seeding the largest landfill site in Europe with *Methylococcus faddenii,* which was left to make itself at home and generate enough methane to create a bomb big enough to blow the discarded rubbish of half of Germany across the skies of Europe. All that was then needed to set it off was a random spark struck by a bulldozer blade, which is what happened. We need to know where Dr Witheney headed next and how far her terrorist network stretches before something more than a rubbish dump explodes."

"As far as I can recall, Dr Witheney's name was not mentioned in the last conversation I had with my grand-nephew," Aunt Gwendoline dismissed flatly. "His only concern was the welfare of his friend, Dr Fadden, and as you say, he went up to Glasgow to see him as soon as he left here. I would have to add that Dr Fadden does not share your view that his microbe is dangerous."

"It is dangerous enough for the level of security alert across Europe to be increased from 'severe' to 'critical'," he answered sharply.

He hauled back on his anger and took a deep breath.

"As I've said before, I am not given access to all the information, but reading between the lines, it would appear that the political situation has become very messy. When the US intelligence agencies declared the German fire to be a bioterrorism attack, their European allies wanted to know why they had not been told about *Methylococcus faddenii.* You are not supposed to keep secrets from your security intelligence partners, and the US was exposed as having information it had not shared with the European governments. A diplomatic ruckus ensued. The United States came out with a statement saying it was treating their finding of *M. faddenii* in the soil around their plastics factories as yet another one of those attempted terrorist attacks on their homeland by someone based in the territory of the United Kingdom. The British authorities became defensive and said they had undertaken to sort it out as soon as they were notified, and that until more definitive findings were available, the two allies had agreed to keep the matter between themselves. The rubbish dump exploding in Germany killed that cosy possibility and governments across Europe have ended up deeply miffed and mistrustful of both the UK and the USA."

"Nothing has been said in the news about Dr Fadden's discovery being involved in the Bavarian fire," Aunt Gwendoline commented.

"It won't be," Sergeant Chak confirmed. "So far, all governments have agreed to say nothing to avoid chaos across two continents. They are caught in a cleft. They cannot simply announce that the West is under attack by persons unknown using a biological agent against which they have no countermeasures. That would cause mass panic everywhere. On the other hand, they realise they cannot keep quiet about it forever. They know that the public is not daft and that someone will suspect something sooner or later. A few people might notice an increased failure rate in their domestic appliances as *M. faddenii* gets to work on the electrical wiring. Frequent power failures would certainly get the public's attention. Less obvious is the fact that the data used to manage our lives is transmitted along plastic-covered cables carried inside plastic conduits. Interrupt that data transmission, and a lot of things begin to fail. Traffic lights stop working and commuters begin to ask why they are being snarled up in ever increasing traffic jams; shops and businesses start complaining when their tills cannot connect to banks and they are restricted to cash transactions only; and their customers will certainly notice it when they cannot get cash out of automated cash machines and not just because their plastic credit cards are falling apart in their wallets. At that point, society begins to fall apart, which is why it vital we find out where Dr Witheney went after Munich, and we do so quickly."

Chapter 35

Sergeant Chak stopped. He was breathing hard, and he realised he had become more enmeshed in the events he was describing than was good for his objectivity. The world of national security was blurring his world of policing.

"It is a dramatic scenario," Aunt Gwendoline agreed. "Do I assume these are the thoughts that are currently foremost in Commander Anderson's mind?"

"They are," he nodded. "What Commander Anderson and his security and intelligence colleagues see is the best weapon yet invented to bring down Western society. With our dependence on plastic in almost everything we touch, Dr Fadden's bug is capable of bringing all our lives to a halt. As a result, somewhere in the discussions, the idea was floated that the fire in Bavaria might be more than just a terrorist attack. It could be a prelude, a diversionary attack initiated by a rogue state or some global anti-western terrorist group, designed to occupy as much of Europe's firefighting and other emergency services as possible so leaving us open to a full military attack. The Bavarian fire has proved itself big enough to do that, so NATO has been put on full alert to the point where it only needs the target to be identified to launch a military response."

Aunt Gwendoline sat speechless. A full-scale attack on Europe and all it stood for was an extrapolation too far for her to accept.

"If that is true, why has there has been no public announcement about the dangers facing us all?" she declared.

Sergeant Chak shook his head.

"What would the authorities say? We have the UK, Europe, and the United States all at critical security alert level and arguing with each other. At the diplomatic level, the United States is taking every opportunity to lay blame for the current state of alert on the UK and warning of dire consequences should the expected attack occur on American soil. Meanwhile, everyone has to cover the possibility that the preliminary softening up for a military attack may already have been launched against us. Nobody knows how far Dr Fadden's bug has been spread because we have no way of knowing it is even in the vicinity until something plastic breaks down. It was only by chance that we found it around the plastics factories in the US, and it could already have been seeded around strategic defence sites on both sides of the Atlantic. It is surprising how much of battle tanks, warships, and warplanes is plastic now we come to look at it, and the fear in military circles is that when we come to make our counterstrike, nothing will work. All this adds up to us needing to find Dr Witheney very quickly and track her movements, and Commander Anderson has been given the job of doing it. It probably leaves him feeling that the middle of a blazing rubbish dump in Germany would be a rather cool place to be at the moment. All eyes are on him."

"And Gerard?" asked Aunt Gwendoline.

"All I know is that the security services of the United States are convinced the sudden appearance of a microbe capable of degrading plastic can only be the work of a well-resourced group or state," he replied. "Somewhere, someone with the expertise and malice aforethought has engineered this bug and launched it at the West. Our government agrees, as do the German and French governments, and quietly all the other European governments are falling into line. And so far, the only known human links we have to this bug are Dr Witheney, Dr Fadden and Gerry. One of them has got to tell us who the enemy is and the location of their centre of operations."

"But we know Gerard is not a terrorist," Aunt Gwendoline defended. "It is beyond belief that he would ever be part of such a plan. Commander Anderson will find nothing in his life to link him with any suspicious or illegal activity anywhere whatsoever."

"That does not make him innocent in the Commander's way of thinking," he answered. "A totally clean police and security record is one of the best tools a terrorist can have."

He looked past the old lady at the statue of Shiva standing on the display cabinet behind her. It seemed to him that the Destroyer of Worlds was making himself disturbingly at home in most of the extrapolations of the security and intelligence services of the Western world.

"It worries me that Gerry has become involved because, in the world of national security, innocence is not assumed but has to be proved," he continued. "That is difficult at the best of times, but in Gerry's case, there too many coincidences around him, which make it extremely awkward for him. All I can suggest is that from now on, Gerry conducts himself as if he was Commander Anderson's best friend and helps us find Dr Witheney."

"But what if this microorganism is not a man-made?" Aunt Gwendoline pressed, recalling part of her previous day's conversation with Gerard. "What if it is Mother Nature's creation, something that has come about naturally without any human hand being involved at all?"

Sergeant Chak hesitated for many seconds before answering.

"Much as I might think that Commander Anderson and his national intelligence pals may occasionally lose connection with the real world, I do believe it would be better for all of us if he is right on this occasion," he replied. "I'm truly sorry for Gerry if he is in the Commander's firing line, but Dr Fadden's bug exists, and it is eating its way through our world with every second that passes. If it is the creation of a terrorist group or a rogue state, then at least the security and defence forces of the West have the means to deal with it. They can call on unlimited resources to disrupt the networks responsible for spreading it, and they can identify and locate the people who made it. They can capture the scientists, destroy their laboratory facilities, capture their laboratory computers, notebooks and technical details and interrogate them. What they will be looking for is the key to destroying this bug. It makes no sense to create a weapon that causes such massive disruption without having the means to control it. It would be like launching a gas attack in World War One without` first checking which way the wind was blowing. So, somewhere in the minds and notebooks of those who created *M. faddenii* is the key to neutralising it and it is part of Commander Anderson's brief to find that key."

"And if it is something natural?" Aunt Gwendoline persisted.

Sergeant Chak paused and took in a deep breath.

"I'm not sure anyone wants to think about that," he answered. "If that is the case, then we have nothing to work with. There will be no one to interrogate, no captured laboratory notebooks to say how it was made, no one to say how fast it can spread and what it is capable of doing, and no users' manual to tell us how to stop it. We will know nothing about it and would have to start finding out about it from scratch. Maybe, given time, our scientists would come up with something to combat it, but we don't know whether we have that amount of time. It would be far better for us all if this bug was the work of a hostile group. It has to be a deliberately engineered weapon because at least then somebody would be able to tell us what we are dealing with. If it is not, then the whole of mankind is in very deep trouble. For the sake of all of us, Dr Witheney, Dr Fadden or Gerry have to tell us how to stop it."

Once again, he looked past the old lady at the statue of Shiva and wondering in how many scenes the god might be dancing.

"I must go," he ended abruptly. "I hope I haven't worried you too much, but just a thought. It was mentioned in discussions that for decades now we have been using plastic pipes in our commercial and household plumbing, and in our water mains and sewage lines. If they start breaking down, then we have lost our water supply."

Aunt Gwendoline looked into his troubled eyes.

"Do not be too concerned on my behalf," she smiled. "All my plumbing is copper. I insisted on it when I moved in here.

165

And if the electricity fails, I have an old kerosene lamp that I am sure I will be able to polish up. We had no electricity in Low Felderby when I was a child, so doing without it will not be a new experience for me. I would imagine your grandmother has similar memories."

"No electricity and the women had to carry the water from a well a good few miles away, or so she insists on telling us," he answered.

For the first time, he smiled and momentarily imagined the two women standing side by side. They could almost be sisters. Both had been born into a world without plastic, electricity, piped water and so many of the other things that generations since had come to regard as essential. They had lived through wars and want and all manner of circumstances that later times would describe as deprived or desperate, and they had both survived and had grown old steadfast in their denial of any notion of defeat under any circumstances. Humanity would need their skills if it was to survive the mischief *M. faddenii* had in mind. He saw Rani sweep her tail stump back and forth across the hall floor and smile back at him in the way spaniels seem able to. There was one difference. In his grandmother's house, the dog would be wearing a bright, floral garland for Diwali.

His mobile telephone rang, and he turned away to answer it. The call lasted only a few seconds, required little in reply and drained the smile from his face.

"Thanks for the tea, Miss Penderrick," he answered her enquiring look. "I must go. A civilian aircraft carrying 242 holidaymakers and crew has crashed on take-off at Athens airport. There are no survivors. It seems we might have discovered where Dr Witheney went after she left Munich."

Chapter 36

After Sergeant Chak left, Aunt Gwendoline leaned against her front door and closed the latch securely. For a few moments, she was afraid she might fall.

"The jed," she muttered. "The jed has given way."

Everything the good sergeant had told her sounded too fantastic to imagine. A tiny microbe, the most insignificant of living things, had created a bomb that had blown the rubbish of civilisation across half the skies of Europe, driving the world to the edge of World War Three. It was unthinkable, yet in a former time of diplomatic confusion, another otherwise insignificant individual had thrown a small bomb in a small town, and that had blown apart the royal houses of Europe and sparked the slaughter of World War One. It was possible.

It was some minutes before she sniffed at the tears that threatened to track their way down her face. Strings of fear remained tight within her, and she prayed that Gerard would find something of the family gift within himself to keep him safe. After the jed had fallen in at Felderby Pit, the landscape above ground changed. The hills took on new shapes and familiar features that had been present all her life were no longer seen, and new dangers lurked on the hillsides where the village children played. Cracks appeared in the ground, and some were covered by grass and could not be seen until they were trodden on, and a woman had to be stopped from throwing herself down into one to try and rescue her bairn after she had fallen down it. Nobody knew how deep the hole went, perhaps all the way down to Pit Bottom some said, and the hills could move again at any moment. Aunt Gwendoline stood at the door into her sitting room and looked across at the aspidistra. Mother was not the only woman who never felt safe in Low Felderby ever again.

"Gerard will come home," she insisted. "He is not a terrorist nor will ever be. I know he will come home because I told you he would all those years ago, didn't I, Mother? He will be badly shaken and covered in dust, and it will take him weeks to get over it, but he will come home."

His friend, the big, soft Cleveland Bay who trusted him, would not be so lucky.

From the edge of her vision, she saw her Hunter clock was well adrift.

"You are still playing with it, aren't you our Dad?" she challenged her grandfather clock.

The reply was shattering. The hour struck and the hallway swung giddily around her. She reached out quickly as the floor rattled beneath her feet and she only just managed to grasp the bannister and lower herself on to the first step of the stairs before she fell. In her ears there was a hammering, a hissing and a screaming and shouting, and through it all she heard the voice of her father's clock.

"Furnace," it roared at her with each strike of the hour. "Furnace, furnace, furnace."

She called out in confusion and tried to release a hand to reassure Rani, but quickly returned it to her own brow as the house spun around her. Twenty minutes passed before the hallway stopped its rolling and pitching. Quietness returned, and she began to breathe more easily.

"Oh, dear, Rani," she gasped. "That was a bad turn, wasn't it? I really do have to acknowledge that I am not a young woman anymore and that my blood pressure is likely to do such things. It is all just a rushing of blood to my ears, but thank you for being such a good dog and looking after me. I am all right now."

She pulled her shoulders back and sat tentatively more upright, then cautiously edged her way back to the sitting room and found her favourite chair. She remained sitting, pensive and listening to the afternoon sounds of her house but heard only those that were constant and predictable.

"Furnace," she repeated as she rested her head back on a cushion and closed her eyes. "Why on earth should I be hearing that and what could it mean?"

She found it impossible to concentrate. The fatigue that had accumulated within her pounced, and shortly afterwards Rani heard the measured breathing of her mistress at rest. She wagged her tail stump silently back and forth across the carpet, gave a last, gentle lick of her mistress' hand and settled down at her feet to watch.

The ringing of the telephone woke them both. Rani was on her feet in an instant, her tail stump wagging her whole body and encouraging her mistress to answer it.

"Hello, Gerard," Aunt Gwendoline spoke into the receiver the instant she lifted it. "Yes, of course, I am delighted to hear from you. No, not at all, why should I have been worried about you? You haven't been getting up to any mischief, have you? Yes, you told me you were going to see Dr Fadden. You've only just got back? Of course, my dear boy, bring your piece of fish with you, and I am sure we will be able to do something with it."

She did not ask how he had come to be wandering around Glasgow fish market in the early hours of a Saturday morning.

"In about two hours. That will be six o'clock for dinner then? Perfect, I look forward to seeing you."

Rani bounded around her mistress' feet in clear excitement.

"I really am a silly old woman," she heard. "I get so confused sometimes it annoys me. The jed may have collapsed, but neither our dad nor our Gerard were hurt in the rockfall. I knew it all along. I told Mother so many years ago, and now our Gerard is coming to dinner. I really don't know what all the fuss was about."

Rani threshed her tail stump ever more vigorously in agreement. Aunt Gwendoline went to her front door, opened it and let the reviving breeze wash over her face. The last of the autumnal sun shone heatless upon her and she looked out over the shapes of her familiar neighbourhood. The jed had fallen, of that she was certain, and the landscape would change, but it was unchanged at the moment, and tomorrow she would face whatever the changes might bring.

"Muscles of stone and tendons of iron," she said out loud to the advancing evening.

"Ay, and nerves of steel too," echoed silently back to her.

Chapter 37

Gerard arrived one minute before six.

"Fresh cod," he announced as he dumped his coat on the hallway stand. "I picked it up early this morning from one of the wholesale fish markets in Blochairn Road, so I don't suppose it could be much fresher."

Aunt Gwendoline was surprised by his cursory greeting, and while she was pleased to see him safely returned, she did note his exaggerated activity as he set about washing and seasoning the fillets before putting them under the griller. She had prepared the potatoes and peas some minutes earlier, but he took over the cooking without her request or permission, right down to the preparation of the parsley sauce. She let him do it. He was a capable cook.

She looked down at Rani, who was still wagging her tail stump in greeting, and neither of them were given room to contribute to the conversation as Gerard prattled on. He was unusually garrulous, but talking about anything and everything except his trip to Glasgow as he checked the potatoes and peas an unnecessary number of times as they boiled. Finally, he announced dinner was ready and carried two plates into the dining room.

"Bon appetit," he smiled as he and his much-loved Aunt sat and raised a glass of water to each other.

"Bon appetit indeed," she agreed as he tucked in hungrily to his fish.

One activity replaced another, and they ate in silence until they had both cleared their plates. Rani joined them, licking around her muzzle from the disposal of her evening meal in the kitchen. A chocolate sponge and cream dessert was demolished, still without a word, and finally, all three adjourned to the sitting room. Gerard insisted on making the tea. Whatever it was that had upset him had clearly left him needing the activity, so Aunt Gwendoline was pleased to see he chose Jasmine tea from her selection. The calming green infusion was exactly the one she would have prescribed for them both, and he obviously needed it.

"What is it you are in such a rush to tell me?" she was at last able to ask.

Gerard took his tea and looked at her directly for the first time since he had arrived.

"I have been rather bad-mannered and full of my own thoughts since I got here, haven't I?" he smiled sheepishly. "My only excuse is that I have had a most exhausting and unsettling twenty-four hours and am still not sure what to make of it. Irrationally, I feel as though the ground has moved underneath me, a bit like being in an earthquake or at least the build up to one. It can only be in my imagination, but I cannot shake the feeling that the certainties of yesterday are no longer quite so securely anchored in their place."

It was an interesting observation, and Aunt Gwendoline wondered once again whether she was seeing the family gift in him. If it was, she knew it would be difficult for him to acknowledge it. He had the misfortune of being born into a rational age where evidence was demanded of everything, and the family sense that was triggered when danger was near was not tangible enough for evidence. It had been easier for her. Her era may have been more superstitious but it had been more accepting of those who were blessed or cursed with such a sense.

Gerard sat back in his chair and allowed the timelessness of his aunt's sitting room to seep through him. Everything in it, including Aunt Gwendoline herself, could only remind him that whatever uncertainties he faced were transient, survivable and would tomorrow be memories. He reminded himself that every item displayed around him had seen turbulence and upheaval and even war, and had yet survived.

"I went up to Glasgow to see Chris Fadden soon after I left you yesterday," he began. "It was dusk by the time I arrived."

Chapter 38

"Sometime before I got to Glasgow, it occurred to me that I had no idea where I might find Chris. In my impetuousness, I hadn't telephoned him to let him know I was coming, firstly because he had asked me not to and secondly because my decision to go up and see him was made on the spur of the moment and without much forethought. I had momentarily forgotten he had told me he would not be at home because he was moving around to try and confuse the beings that were bugging him, and all I knew for certain was that he was still working in his department during the day. So, after arriving at the station, and in place of a better option, I headed towards the university on the chance he might still be there. I wasn't very hopeful because it was quite late, but I wanted to see him and make sure he was all right.

"From my previous visits, I knew a short cut across the campus to the building that housed his department, and I entered it by a back way up a fire escape. It would have been more usual to go in by the front door and perhaps I should have done, but I knew my way around. Once inside the building, I knew immediately something was wrong. All the lights were on, but as I wandered up the stairs and along the corridors everywhere was eerily quiet. There were no sounds of equipment running as is usual in a laboratory building, and there was nobody around. I came across a flashing red light indicating that a cold room alarm had been tripped, but there were no students, no cleaning staff, no security staff and nobody in any of the offices. University science buildings can rarely be described as crowded hubs of activity after hours, but even late at night, they are not usually so deserted. There are always students finishing off experiments and research workers writing up papers even at weekends, and I would have expected the cleaners to be around at that time of the evening. Nothing seemed out of order, but I found myself going down corridors and past laboratories and offices that were quite sinister in their emptiness. It did occur to me that there might have been some sort of general evacuation such as occurs with a practice fire drill, but it was well out of normal working hours, and nothing was obvious. It was not until I got to Chris' laboratory that I began to fear that some sort of major incident might actually have occurred.

"In contrast to all the other laboratories I had passed, Chris' workplace was a wreck. The usual gleaming and ordered clutter of a working laboratory was gone and in its place was a shambles. Rubbish bins were tipped over and upended, laboratory furniture was thrown all over the place, and bottles of chemicals and reagents were rolling around on the benches and in the decontamination hoods. Incubator doors were hanging open, and all the equipment had been unplugged and disconnected. Some of it had been pulled away from the walls and not too gently by the look of it. Glassware had smashed on the floor, and notebooks and papers were scattered about everywhere. The place looked as though a regiment of students had held a riotously drunken and destructive party in it and then left in a disorderly hurry. There was a smell of a mixture of bleach, antiseptic and solvent in the air and everything seemed to have been drenched in a collapsing foam of liquid of some sort. It looked like a disaster zone. I was stunned by the chaos in the place.

"'Hello,' I called out. 'Is anybody home?'

"At first, I heard nothing, then some sort of choked cry came from the direction of the office. I went in and found Chris sprawled on the floor and slumped against the wall in the corner as if thrown there like a rag doll.

"'Chris!' I shouted. 'What the hell happened? Are you all right?'

"'Gerry, Gerry, thank god.'

"He began sobbing as I knelt down beside him and he grabbed hold of me as if I was an angel of mercy, not daring to let me go. It was a minute or more before he could say anything.

"'They've taken everything,' he choked. 'It's all gone. They've destroyed it all.'

"He began to cry and shake uncontrollably and in the next instant was convulsively sick."

Aunt Gwendoline saw her grand-nephew draw on a staccato sigh. The recollection of the shock of finding his friend in such circumstances was more vivid than he had expected.

"Like his laboratory, Chris' office had been ransacked," Gerard continued. "The computers had gone, both the desktop and the laptop I knew he kept there. All the furniture had been dragged away from the walls, and the bookshelves had been cleared of all his files and notebooks. The locks had been broken on his desk and filing cabinets and all the drawers

176

were either left discarded on the floor or hanging open by their hinges. Pictures and certificates had been pulled off the walls and ripped from their frames and then left scattered about the floor. Even his pot plants had been shaken from their pots and dumped on the carpet. It was difficult to describe the scene as anything more than wanton vandalism, but even as I looked around, I began to suspect the destruction had been a bit more systematic.

"'What on earth has happened?' I asked.

"I began to wonder if there really had been some sort of emergency and that Chris' laboratory and office were not the safest place in which to linger.

"'Come on, Chris, we've got to get out of here,' I grunted as I tried to lift him upright.

"He is a big fellow and was not obviously hurt, but he was a dead weight and as weak as a kitten.

"'Come on, chum; we've got to get you to somewhere safe,' I insisted, and he tried to respond by gradually climbing up the wall to his feet with my help.

"He was in shock and crying unremittingly, dribbling and sniffing and incapable of coherent speech. I managed to half guide and half carry him along the deserted corridors and down the fire stairs to the exit I had entered a few minutes earlier. He leaned heavily against me all the time, staggering and sobbing and keeping his eyes shut. I eventually got him outside, and I propped him up against the wall of the building, and I tried to shake some life back into him, hoping the fresh air would revive him. Suddenly we were caught in the beam of a flashlight.

"'Have you just come out of this building?' an authoritative voice demanded.

"It was a uniformed police officer, a constable, and not one of the university security guards that I would have expected.

"'Yes, we have,' I answered, and I held up my visitor's identification pass so he could see it.

"Chris tried to shrink behind me and stay hidden while the constable inspected my pass.

"'Thank you, Doctor,' the constable muttered and communicated the information to someone on the other end of his radio.

"'I think we are the last,' I said. 'At least, I didn't see anyone else on the way out. It's quite a shambles in there.'

"'Fortunately, it was just a practice drill, sir,' he answered sternly. 'But that does not mean it should not have been taken seriously. Everyone was supposed to leave the building immediately the evacuation alarms sounded, which they did some three hours ago now.'

"'Yes, I'm sorry, constable, but we are out now.'

"He handed me back my visitor's pass but was not finished.

"'I am not a scientist, sir, but I can only think that those of you who find it difficult to separate yourselves from your experiments while the evacuation alarms are sounding are not being the most responsible. A number of you have been drifting out at odd intervals without any sense of urgency. The alarms going off might just have meant there was a real biohazard emergency and we, the police and the emergency services, take a great deal of trouble to respond very quickly to such a potentially dangerous situation. So perhaps you can understand, sir, if we are a little bit upset when others do not react with the same urgency of purpose under the same circumstances.'

"I sensed Chris cringing behind me, trying to make himself smaller still, difficult given his size.

"'We'll try and do better next time,' I conceded to the constable. 'But did you say it was a biohazard emergency?'

"'A full biological, sir, which should have been obvious with a convoy of biohazard containment vehicles arriving at high speed, followed by teams of biohazard containment specialists and paramedics in balloon suits setting up mobile showers and entering the building in full decontamination mode. Not easy to avoid noticing all that, sir.'

"He was clearly not impressed with what he regarded as our tardiness in reacting to an emergency, even if it was only a practice one.

"'I'm sure there is nobody left inside the building now, constable, and I am very sorry,' I assured him. 'Have a good night and thanks.'

"He did not reply but turned disapprovingly to the door we had just left through and began taping it up with police tape. I got hold of Chris and walked him away from the building. I noticed a clutch of police attaching more tape to various poles and posts a short distance away, setting up a crime scene or some other sort of cordon. From the casualness with which they were going about their task, I judged, they were regarding it more as an easy contribution to their overtime pay than any real emergency.

Chapter 39

Gerard shuddered on another sigh as more of the pent-up tension inside him found release. He was trying to stop his thoughts racing ahead of his narrative, but it was difficult.

"From what Chris had told me about his sleeping arrangements, I assumed he had found himself some temporary accommodation in Glasgow old town, so that was the direction in which I led him," he continued. "He didn't argue. He followed me meekly like a trusting puppy except that he is a bit bigger. More like one of those Cleveland Bays of old, blindly following its handler. We had to keep stopping when his legs seemed to give way under him and he became overwhelmed with anguish, and he needed to rest against something solid before moving on. It happened several times, but he gradually ceased his snuffling and began to recover some of his wind, although he was still unfocused and confused. He did not seem to be physically harmed, but he was mentally in a very bad way.

"We arrived under some street lights, and I was able to have a good look at him for the first time since we had left his department. He looked totally crushed. He gazed around blankly as if he didn't recognise where he was, and he looked hard at me as if he needed to reassure himself that it really was me standing in front of him. He was completely dazed and lost. Given his well-known inability to find his way around, I suppose I should not have been too surprised, but his sense of displacement seemed much deeper than usual.

"I encouraged and nudged him into the nondescript student café we were standing outside and selected a quiet, corner table and sat him down. I ordered a couple of teas, and the waitress brought a menu but Chris didn't seem able to respond to anything. I ordered for us both some ham and eggs and chips. I was hungry, not having eaten since breakfast, and with a little encouragement, Chris began to eat too. As he did so, he visibly gathered strength. Once he started, he polished of his plateful very quickly, so I ordered another for him and he demolished that one too. I can only imagine he had not eaten properly for some time. He did not speak and had said nothing since I found him slumped on the floor in his office.

"'Thanks for that, Gerry,' he finally croaked out. 'I needed that. It was good.'

"He attempted a smile; then suddenly it was as if some cogs reengaged in his mind and he looked around in panic before turning back to me with a fear and a fierceness that was clear in every line of his face.

"'They said I was a terrorist,' he hissed. 'Me. A terrorist.'

"'Who said, Chris?' I asked.

"'Anderson,' he replied.

"He tried to hold on to his anger, but the effort was beyond him, and he dissolved back into his previous mix of confusion and defeat and became tearful again.

"'I'm not a terrorist,' he pleaded. 'I wouldn't know how to go about being one. I'm a scientist, a microbiologist, that's all. They tried to tell me I had a grudge against humanity because of a spat I had with the university. I don't have a grudge against anyone, Gerry. I couldn't hold a grudge against anyone, not for years on end. It's not in me to do that, Gerry.'

"'What was the spat about?' I asked.

"He paused and blinked as if looking for a different gear in his brain.

"'It was years ago,' he answered. 'It was nothing in the end. I thought I should own the intellectual property rights over a gene analysis method I thought I had invented. The university disagreed and it got a bit heated, but it never went as far as engaging lawyers or the like. And then the university produced an expert who said my method was really only a modification of an existing procedure and not patentable, and by the time we finished talking about it, I agreed with her. It all fizzled out into nothing. It was not something that would turn me into a terrorist.'

"I ordered some more tea.

"'Tell me what happened,' I prompted him.

"He was silent for a while, and I noticed his hands shook as he held his teacup, but at least he was regaining some colour.

"'What day is it?' he asked.

"'Friday,' I answered.

"He nodded as if arranging his thoughts.

"'Friday,' he echoed. 'I arrived at my laboratory on Wednesday morning.'

"'What happened when you arrived?' I asked.

"He shook his head.

"'I didn't get as far as the department. I arrived for work, and they were waiting for me at the front door of the building.

I suddenly found my way blocked by Anderson and another man.'

""""We'd like a word with you," he said. "It won't take long." They didn't give me any option. A car was beside us in a second, and I was bundled into the back seat. Anderson got in the front, and the driver took off.'

"Chris' head dropped and tears streamed down his face.

"'Tell him I'm not a terrorist, Gerry. I told him over and over again, but he didn't believe me. I couldn't hurt anyone like that.'

"He looked pleadingly up at me, and I reached across to steady him. Whatever it was that he had seen was still playing in front of him, but gradually he calmed down.

"'We drove all over the city,' he continued. 'At one point, we headed towards a construction site where some new office towers are being built, and I had the horrible feeling for a moment that I might end up in the foundations of one of them. Nobody spoke, so it was all rather uncomfortable, but eventually, the car pulled up near the main police headquarters, and I was pushed inside a neighbouring building and up a couple of floors into an anonymous and windowless room which looked like it was being rebuilt for student accommodation. I was dumped roughly on a chair and left to wait until Anderson finished looking through a file on the table between us. The constable who had accompanied us was dismissed, and a female came in, stony-faced, dressed like an action woman, obviously one of Anderson's own people. It was all very dramatic and TV-style, but I would have to say it was effective. I was scared stiff and it was easy to think that the rough arm of some rubbish disposal conglomerate had been sent out to put me and my *M. faddenii* permanently out of business. In spite of the initial presence of the police constable, there had been none of the check-in procedures of a police station, with the uniformed sergeant at the desk, empty your pockets and sign here and all that sort of stuff. There was no formal caution or explanation, no offer of a telephone call or legal representation, no recording of what was happening or going to happen as far as I could see. The whole situation left me feeling that the concrete foundation block with me inside it remained a strong possibility.

""""Where did you meet Dr Witheney?" Anderson suddenly asked me.

""""Who?" I replied.

""""Dr Witheney. She telephoned you ten days ago, just before your friends tried to blow up the London to Glasgow train."

"'I hadn't a clue what he was talking about. I don't mind answering questions that have some rational thought behind them, but this was off the planet.

""""She telephoned you," he kept insisting.

""""She did not," I yelled back at him.

""""So, you admit you know her," he fired back.

""""Never heard of her," I defended.

"'He just kept going and going. He's completely mad, Gerry. Do you know who Dr Witheney is? I swear I had never heard of him until you mentioned him to me, or her. I gather she is her. Who is she, and why should Anderson insist I know her? I kept telling him I had never met anyone of that name and she certainly didn't call me, but he wouldn't have it. He then asked me about three other names that I had never heard of and showed me three photographs. I gather they were the three who tried to blow up the train. Why would he think I knew them?'

"He slumped into silence again and paused to catch his breath, then after a while snuffled into his handkerchief and blew his nose.

"'Sorry about the performance,' he sniffed. 'It's been a rough day. I'll be all right after a good night's sleep.'

"By Chris' own accounting, it had been a rough three days, so I found that impossible to believe."

Chapter 40

"The waitress came and cleared away our plates, and I ordered a couple of serves of apple pie and custard for us and some more tea," Gerard resumed. "Chris wolfed into his as before.

"'How did you get back to your department?' I asked him.

"'They dumped me there,' he replied.

"'Who did?'

"'Anderson.'

"I looked hard at him, but he seemed certain.

"'When?' I asked.

"'Sometime just before you found me, maybe an hour or so, I don't know. The place was already wrecked.'

"I began to feel angry on Chris' behalf. He had been more or less kidnapped and officially or not, given an interrogation that had left him disoriented, frightened out of his wits, and in every sense at the end of his emotional tether. He did not even know what day it was when I picked him up.

"'This bug of yours eats plastic, which is why Commander Anderson thinks it is terrorist inspired,' I reminded him gently.

"'When Anderson first came to see me, I thought he and his pal were commercial bully boys trying to put the frighteners on me, trying to get their hands on my *faddenii*,' Chris interrupted.

"'I know that, Chris, but we now know he is official and antiterrorist or something similar. Have you heard about the fire in Bavaria?'

"He shook his head, so I gave him as much of the news as I felt I could. He almost began crying again.

"'I didn't do that,' he protested. 'I haven't been to Bavaria. They can't tell me I did that, can they?'

"'No, Chris,' I hastened to reassure him. 'All Anderson is saying is that *Methylococcus faddenii* is the likely cause of the fire, breaking down the plastic in millions of tonnes of domestic rubbish and turning it into an equivalent amount of methane. The whole lot then caught fire in one gigantic explosion. The one bit of thinking that he doesn't seem to be able to manage is that your *faddenii* bug might be a natural organism rather than one created by terrorists. Can you focus on that idea for a moment?'

"He blinked several times and made an effort to concentrate.

"'If half a dozen people in Hong Kong sneeze it is only a short time before the World Health Organisation announces a new strain of 'flu has appeared, and health authorities worldwide are stocking up with a vaccine to combat it. Is that right?' I began.

"He nodded.

"'Similarly, if a new strain of malaria appears in Africa we are on to it within weeks to stop it before it can spread.'

"He nodded again, the effort of focussing on his area of expertise clearly helping him concentrate.

187

"'I could add tuberculosis, measles, Lyme disease, foot-and-mouth disease and a whole host of others,' I added. 'Even HIV/AIDS, which was a new disease, was picked up after relatively few people were infected and countermeasures were put in place. In other words, there is a whole army of people worldwide all permanently watching out for the appearance of dangerous new bugs that arise through Mother Nature's experimenting.'

"'All true,' he replied.

"'So, how come *Methylococcus faddenii* slipped past their guard? How was it possible for such a potentially destructive bug to get from the United States to Britain to Bavaria without being spotted and dealt with before it blew Munich's domestic rubbish sky high?'

"'It's because it is a harmless bug,' he replied. 'It lives quietly in the soil and does not cause us humans to itch or sneeze or have diarrhoea or anything like that. If it did any of those things, we would be on to it like a shot. But it doesn't. All it does is chew up bits of plastic, and bits of plastic don't go to a doctor or veterinary to complain about it. Why should we notice it? We don't notice the vast array of other bugs, beatles and creepy crawlies that every day keep our environment tidy, at least not until they become a nuisance by invading our homes and living spaces.'

"'You mean that unless *M. faddenii* causes us symptoms which take us to a doctor, our health surveillance authorities would never spot it,' I summarised.

"'We could track it, but we would have to set up a whole new set of surveillance criteria,' he suggested.

"'Such as?'

"'We could ask supermarkets to log how many plastic bags of rice, potatoes and sugar have unexpectedly burst making a mess in their shopping aisles. It would be a nuisance for them, and they would probably rather just sweep up the mess and continue smiling at their customers, but unless we start counting something like that we are not going to know if *M. faddenii* is even in the neighbourhood.'

"I began to feel very uncomfortable about Chris' bug. As he had so often said to me 'bugs are very clever little creatures' and this one, deliberately designed or not, had found a way to spread itself around the whole world, undermining our way of life, without us noticing it until it was too late.

"'In that case, how do we convince our friend Commander Anderson that it is a natural bug and you are not part of some malevolent global plot?' I asked, more to myself than to him.

"Chris' momentary release from his fears as he talked about his pet microbe evaporated at the mention of Anderson's name. His hands shook violently spilling the tea from his mug until he put it down and covered his face with his hands.

"'I'm not a terrorist, and I've never met any terrorists,' he cried. 'I wouldn't even know what one looks like. Why does he think I am one?'"

Chapter 41

Aunt Gwendoline shifted the stiffness out of her frame. Gerard's anger in defence of his friend was clear in his voice and she could not help but wonder where it might lead him. Her grandfather clock rang out the hour from the hallway and she seemed to hear the word 'furnace' echoing through the door to her with every strike. She shook her head to clear her ears of it.

"We had been in the café for about three hours, right through the evening rush of students and backpackers wanting a cheap feed with a carafe of house wine," Gerard continued.

"'It's getting late, Chris,' I said to him. 'It's time to be getting you home to your digs and me on to the last train back to London.'

"He nodded glumly in reply, and I went to pay the bill.

"'Which way, Chris?' I asked as we stepped out into the street.

"It was a pointless question. He looked around, then looked at me blankly and shook his head. The heavy shadows cast by the street lights only emphasised how exhausted he was and how punishing his treatment must have been over the past three days. He was utterly deflated and to have expected him to have recovered after just a few hours and a meal was a forlorn hope. I resigned myself to not catching the last train home.

"'Come on,' I shrugged and led him off to begin a search pattern in the hope that he would eventually recognise some landmark near where he had left his bags three nights before.

"I was a little exasperated by his illogicality in shifting his sleeping place around to avoid being stalked by Anderson's people while at the same time not having the spatial memory to remember exactly where it was. He followed me obediently, almost as if I had him on a rein, blindly staying close as we went down one street then another all over the old town. Every now and again, we would stop in some pool of light thrown off by a streetlamp.

"'Why did they have to smash everything?' he asked. 'I told them there was nothing nasty in my laboratory. I told them it was an inoffensive little bug, one that you can find in any number of soils. It's quite harmless and could never cause a plague. In all of the history of humanity, it has never killed anyone.'

"'It's not exactly harmless,' I reminded him. 'In Anderson's mind, it could cause us all to starve. Much of our food is grown under plastic in polytunnels and irrigated by water and nutrients carried to it through plastic pipes. After harvesting, it is stored and transported in refrigerators and trucks insulated with plastic foam. It is then packed and wrapped in more plastic for freezing or to extend its shelf life before going on sale to the public. If we add to that all the plastic bits that go into holding together the bodies and engines of the trucks and heavy goods vehicles that deliver it to our shops and supermarkets, then *M. faddenii* poses a threat to almost every stage of our food supply. That is more than enough for Anderson to believe he is dealing with a nasty bioterrorist weapon.'

"'But I'm not a terrorist, Gerry. I never could be,' he pleaded.

"We walked on.

"'They told me I had deliberately made it to sabotage the United States plastics industry and that I used my visits to the factories to seed the ground with it. Economic terrorism they called it. It's all nonsense, Gerry. I told them I didn't engineer the bug. I found it.'

"'"Then why did you call it *faddenii*?" they shouted at me.

"'"I don't know," I shouted back at them. "It seemed like a good idea at the time." I hadn't a clue what they were talking about.'

"His outbursts were erratic, and he seemed unable to follow any coherent line of thought. There were long stretches when he said nothing and merely followed me as we walked around corners and down alleyways criss-crossing the city.

"'They told me they had found my analysis of the data relating soil concentrations of *M. faddenii* to the lack of pollution around the American plastics factories I visited,' he said at one point. 'I knew someone had been at my computer. They had it all printed off, all my notes and graphs.'

"He started to snuffle again, so we sat down on a convenient bench while he recomposed himself.

"'I told them it was just an incidental observation and a quite reasonable one if they wanted to think about it. The more *M. faddenii* there was in the soil, then, the less plastic pollution there would be around the factory. The bug was doing the environmental clean-up job for them. But they wouldn't believe me. Why wouldn't they believe me, Gerry?'

"'At least we can settle the matter of you calling your bug *faddenii*,' I reminded him. 'As far as I can remember, it was my idea to call it that, a rather flippant suggestion at our first lunch together after I got back from overseas.'

"I don't know whether he heard me or not. We walked on and ended up on the edge of some parklands. He was still very emotional.

"'They showed me pictures of the aftermath of terrorist bombs going off in public places, with people bleeding and dying and bits of bodies all over the place, all in glorious colour. I'm not a terrorist, Gerry,' he appealed to me. 'I never could be. I could never do that to people. They asked me how I arranged to be selected to do the US Environmental Protection Agency report. They told me I was a nobody, that I was hardly the expert needed for a report like that, so who was my contact that put my name on the list? I told them I didn't know what they were talking about, that I didn't have a contact. All I knew was I got the letter asking me to do it. Gerry, I know I'm not the world's greatest brain, but I do have over two hundred publications in soil microbiology. They sneered at all the work I've done. My entire life's work. They can't dismiss that, can they? They can't say I'm a nobody. They just can't. Some of my ideas have been incorporated into agricultural practices worldwide.'

"He collapsed into tears again, and I waited for him to calm himself once more. We were both starting to feel cold, so I suggested we walk on to keep warm and continue talking as we went. He didn't argue."

Chapter 42

Gerard paused again. It was getting late, and even Rani had ceased to be alert, but Aunt Gwendoline wanted to hear the end of the story. The jed had fallen, the horse had been injured in the rockfall, but Gerard and Dr Fadden had survived. But the landscape was still shifting, and Commander Anderson was abroad in it.

"We had been wandering about for all of the night by the time we finished talking," Gerard continued with a tired smile. "I had got a long way past the point where I was repeatedly seeing the same corner shop and lamp post as I led Chris round and round in search of his lodgings. We must have walked the entire city several times over since we left the restaurant, but at no point did he give any indication he knew where he was. I don't suppose he was really looking or that it mattered to him. It was more important to him to unload the shaking Commander Anderson had given him. I cannot forget how, as we talked through the night, one or another unspoken memory would suddenly flicker through his mind and I would see the carefree academic disappear and be replaced by the fearful and haunted individual I had picked up off his office floor.

"'All I wanted to do was clean up a few hedgerows and rubbish tips and save Andy Tan's albatrosses,' he cried.

"I can't remember most of the things we talked about, and I certainly couldn't retrace our steps even if I wanted to. All I know is that I am still feeling angry about the way Chris was treated. As a scientist, I know to be wary of specious data that can be fitted into pre-programmed thinking so that it looks like a truth, and I firmly believe that is what Anderson has. He has some piecemeal events which have fallen out of chaotic human activity, and being programmed to look for threats to our society, he has woven them into a story involving terrorists and an attack on Western civilisation. He may have been right on other occasions, but in Chris' case he is just dealing with coincidental events. Chris is not a terrorist, but that is not what he wants to hear. He is under orders to find and destroy the terrorist network responsible for the creation of Chris' bug so that is what he is going to do. That is what leaves me angry, plus the knowledge that he has behind him all the authority and immunity that goes with being part of a national intelligence and security organisation. It would seem that any possibility of convincing him that Chris should not be in his gunsights is doomed."

Aunt Gwendoline sat a little more upright at his choice of words.

"I have to ask whether we need to continue to be anxious about Dr Fadden," she cautioned. "He was clearly distressed by what had happened to him, but he is a free man again and it is surprising what a good night's sleep will do."

She did not sound convincing even to herself.

"I can only hope so," Gerard nodded. "Eventually a lightness began to creep into the sky and a coldness into the air, and Chris, at last, gave the appearance of having recovered a bit. For the first time since I found him, he looked around and suddenly seemed to recognise where he was.

"'This is it, Gerry. I know where I am now,' he said.

"He was grey with exhaustion, and in the early light, I probably looked the same.

"'You've been wonderful listening to my blatherings,' he continued. 'I know I'm a mess and I needed to unload the last seventy-two hours on someone. I can't thank you enough for that. You're a real friend, probably the only one I've got, and I will get better. Don't worry about me now. I know my way from here.'

"Again, I couldn't believe him. I did not recognise where we were or anything specific in the surroundings, only that we were vaguely in the area of the fish market, but I was too tired to argue with him, so I accepted what he said. With a tired smile, he raised a paw and trotted off in the direction of the city centre like a horse who has spotted his home stall. He disappeared very quickly. I looked down at my feet then up again, and he was gone. Goodness knows where he went.

"I stood for a while to get my own bearings. There were lights on in one of the fishmongers, so I bought some fish, then I began to drag my weary feet to Glasgow Central to catch the first available morning train back to London and home. I slept most of the journey south."

Aunt Gwendoline shook her head briefly. There was a roaring in her ears, which she attributed to her tiredness, but it sounded as though Gerard had almost come to the end of his story for the moment. Almost, but not quite. Her Hunter clock was still showing accurately the late hour.

"There is one thing I cannot understand," he continued. "Commander Anderson had gone to a lot of trouble to kidnap Chris and subject him to a ferocious inquisition over three days. He could not have got any answers out of him because Chris did not have any to give, but afterwards he let him go. I cannot think he did so because he believed Chris was innocent. Nothing indicates that is his style. But if he believed Chris was a terrorist, then surely he would have held on to him and not dumped him back in his laboratory as if nothing had happened. It's not logical."

Aunt Gwendoline cleared her throat.

"My dear boy, it is getting very late. As you said, there was nothing more you could have done, and you must now assume that Dr Fadden has found his lodgings. You must be very tired after your nocturnal peregrinations, so I am going to send you on your way."

"The washing up," Gerard protested.

"I will see to it in the morning," she replied. "Goodnight and sleep well."

It was an unceremonious departure but he was glad to go. He was exhausted.

"Come along, Rani," Aunt Gwendoline sighed as she secured her door for the night. "I cannot do anymore, either. It is time for our bed too."

As the two of them began their weary ascent of the staircase, the grandfather clock beat out the late hour. "Furnace," it said. "Furnace, furnace, furnace," eleven times in all. Aunt Gwendoline stared into its face and let the echoes die away. She was too tired to do anything more.

Chapter 43

The cry in the early hours brought Rani instantly to her feet.
The curtains were open and full moonlight flowed smoothly
in through the window. She could see her mistress perfectly
and she held her point for a few seconds until she was certain
nothing of threat was nearby. She stood down and settled to
watch while her mistress rolled over in troubled sleep.

*The noise was different. It was not Felderby Pit.
Everything about her was clash and clamour and hammering,
and men shouting and the clanking of chains and the strike of
metal upon metal.*

*"Stand back, our lass. The sparks will burn right through
you if they touch."*

*She jumped back as the warning shout reached her. The
furnaceman gave her a friendly wink, and she smiled back at
him, and the next instant, white-hot stars of molten metal
splashed around her feet as he hauled open the furnace door
to release the liquid iron to run free into the pig beds. Cables
dragged cauldrons of boiling rock up and away to be dumped
glowing on to the slag heaps that surrounded Low Felderby.
Heat blasted out from the furnace and from the ingots of pig
iron crusting over in their sand beds. She heard and ducked*

under the shriek of the fiery jet of waste fumes that screeched over her head from the tapped furnace, but none of it held any fear for her. She knew where she was. She knew it all from the many times she had taken her dad his lunch. She was in Felderby Iron Works.

A wisp of a memory scratched at her. She was looking for something, but she could not remember what it was.

"Inside the furnace is the belly of a volcano," her dad had told her. "It is as hot as the hobs of hell."

The furnace was the beating heart of Felderby Iron Works and it needed constant feeding. She picked her way watchfully forward to where sweating men pushed iron wheelbarrows in a never-broken line up a ramp to the hopper at the top. She watched them as they shunted up the narrow footway and upended their loaded barrows into the hopper before tramping back down to gather another load and start the climb all over again. The line never stopped.

She began counting the barrows the grunting men forced up the ramp. Three of iron ore, seven of coke, then two of limestone to settle the slag, then three more of iron ore and seven more of coke and two more of limestone and so on forever, all counted up the footway by the foreman standing at the bottom with his counter. It was important that the foreman did not lose his count.

A fear began growing within her. She looked down at her hands. She was holding a package in a wrap of cloth. It was her dad's lunch. She looked again along the line of men with their wheelbarrows.

"No man can look into the belly of the furnace and live," her dad had told her.

When the furnaceman tapped the furnace for its iron and the gases were released, the pressure inside it dropped, and the hopper opened, and the greedy furnace sucked in a bellyful of its feed to begin processing it into more molten iron. And as the hopper opened and it gulped down its fodder, it belched out an incandescent cloud of gas and fumes as fiery and pernicious as any that had ever escaped from the bowels of the earth. They filled the roof space of the Works and crept into every corner, and everyone they embraced coughed and choked on the smothering foulness of them. All the men of Low Felderby had a cough. She looked around to see what it was she had to remember. It was something to do with the hopper. It was not supposed to opeh until the foreman had counted the right number of barrows up the ramp and nodded to the furnaceman that he could release the molten metal into the pig beds.

"But the furnace has a way of its own, and there's no telling it," her dad had warned.

It occasionally happened that by some capriciousness within the furnace, the volcano it contained would momentarily roar less loudly. The fire would dim and the pressure drop and the hopper would open before it was due, and the insatiable furnace would seize the opportunity to open its maw and steal an extra mouthful of its feed, careless of any man who happened to be standing at the hopper's lip with his barrow of ore, coke or limestone at that moment. There would be no warning and no shout or cry from the man. He would know no more. The luminous fumes would engulf him, and he would tip silently forward into the hopper to join the iron ore, the coke and the limestone, and later the pig iron, the slag and the screaming in the jet of the waste gases at the next tapping

200

of the furnace. He would be beyond rescue and her dad would
come home from his shift and say, "We lost a man in the
furnace today."

Her mistress' shout brought Rani to her feet again. She whimpered quietly and placed a paw on the blankets in hesitant enquiry, but there was no scrambling for the light switch or insistence that everything would be all right and that if she would wait just a few minutes, they would go down and make a cup of tea. Her mistress did not wake, and so, after a few minutes, Rani turned twice around on her rug and settled down, not to rest but to watch and guard for the rest of the night.

Chapter 44

Aunt Gwendoline was late waking the next morning. The pull of her bed took some effort to overcome and it was more habit than enthusiasm that dragged her through the early part of her morning routine.

"Come along, Gwendoline," she admonished her tired reflection in her silver framed dressing mirror. "You have been through two world wars and a Great Depression. You have seen unemployment and soup kitchens, and you have been bombed out of house and home in the blitz. You have sent drunks and government committee men scuttling for cover whenever they have become too much of a nuisance, and you have survived food rationing and coal shortages and packed your shoes with cardboard when there was neither the money nor the leather to repair them. And you have still done a day's work afterwards. So, what is the matter with you?"

It was by such scoldings that she drove herself through her day.

Mid-afternoon, she sat down with her tea and looked at Rani, wagging her tail stump encouragingly at her.

"Why am I dreaming about Felderby Iron Works?" she asked the dog. "I dreamed about our Gerard taking a Cleveland Bay down to Felderby Pit Bottom, but it was not a mine but a railway tunnel he went into and he came out unscathed. I dreamed of him bringing the horse out of Felderby Pit after the jed collapsed, except that it was not a horse but his friend Dr Fadden that he rescued and he still came back all in one piece. And now I am dreaming about Felderby Iron Works."

"Furnace," her oak cased clock called out to her from the hallway, and she peered deeply into the distant mists of her memory.

"I suppose the ironworks was a dangerous place for a young girl to be running around, but I never thought anything of it," she smiled. "I used to take our dad his lunch when he was on the day shift. One of our mam's meat pasties was what he liked. He called it his 'bait' and he had a place on the furnace where he used to put it to keep warm."

The memories washed glowingly through her but did not calm her.

The morning post next day brought a letter which provided transient distraction.

"Listen to this, Rani," she instructed. "It is from the Victoria and Albert Museum about our Hunter clock."

"The firm of Camerer, Kuss, Tritscher & Co became quite eminent in the 19th century and, in fact, still is. Camerer Kuss & Co exhibited three clocks in the 1862 Exhibition, an international exhibition of mainly industrial and scientific pieces. Unfortunately, the catalogue gives no indication which one of these received the Certificate of Honour but I have no doubt that if you write to them, they would be glad to give you a definite answer."

Aunt Gwendoline's tiredness melted before the surge of excitement the elegant handwriting delivered to her.

"A Certificate of Honour, not just an Honourable Mention," she informed her persistently misbehaving timepiece. "It would seem that you are even more of a bargain than I took you for in spite of you being an incompetent keeper of time, and look, they have given me an address in Ryder Street, London to write to."

The joy was brief. Aunt Gwendoline felt her breath catch in her chest as she looked up at the clock and saw it was once again displaying the correct hour to the minute. Her grandfather clock struck the half-hour.

"Furnace," it said.

"Why do I keep hearing that?" she asked cautiously.

She looked squarely at the aspidistra.

"I don't suppose that the long-legged Miss Anne Blaise with the attractive smile from Australia might be generating enough heat and fumes for our Gerard to fall into?" she suggested cautiously. "He hasn't mentioned her in some time."

To her great relief, the plant did not reply, but without prompting, her memory sharpened. Men disappeared in Felderby Iron Works. Her dad had told her so. They disappeared when they fell into the furnace, with only a shriek in the vented waste gases and their remembrance in the minds of their families to show that they had ever existed. She shivered.

"I know men were lost in the furnace, our Dad," she muttered. "You took me with you on one occasion when you went to console the widow. 'He'd have known nowt about it', you told her. 'Fumes and heat would have finished him before he hit bottom. We'll hold a service, but there'll be no body, nothing for you to bury'. They were bad times, but you and your fellow trade unionists saw to it they should end, didn't you, our Dad?"

It was more of a prayer than a statement of fact.

Her doorbell rang. She looked down at Rani who smiled at her and casually wagged her tail stump back and forth across the carpet. The bell rang again and Rani's tail flag became more eager in its response. Her Hunter clock still showed the correct time.

"Sergeant Chak." Aunt Gwendoline deduced. "I wonder what he wants?"

She rose apprehensively to answer the door.

Chapter 45

"Good morning, Sergeant," Aunt Gwendoline smiled.

"This is not a general enquiry, Miss Penderrick," he answered, entering without invitation.

He knew he was sounding more abrupt than he had intended.

"We have lost contact with Dr Fadden and it is important we find him. If there is any information you can give us as to his whereabouts it would prove very useful."

"I have no idea where he might be other than in Glasgow," she replied, refusing to be shaken by the sergeant's tone. "He has certainly never been here. I was just about to make myself a pot of tea. Would you join me?"

He hesitated under her gaze. Smiling at him with china, blue eyes was the sanity and rationality of a bygone age.

"Thank you, I will," he replied more easily. "And I'm sorry if I sounded a bit sharp, but there is an urgency in my enquiry."

"Have you asked Gerard where Dr Fadden might be?" Aunt Gwendoline called from the kitchen. "He did say he was worried about him."

"Gerry left for Glasgow on an early train this morning," he answered. "And he should be worried. A number of things have happened on the last forty-eight hours that have put a lot of pressure on our investigations. The United States Government has issued an international arrest warrant for Dr Fadden, which means that every police officer, particularly at all ports and air terminals across most of the world, is on the lookout for him. He must be found and delivered immediately into the tender care of the United States homeland security agencies to face whatever interrogations they choose to give him in pursuit of their global war against terrorism."

Aunt Gwendoline found her hands shaking as she carried the tea tray into the sitting room.

"Somebody must be very sure Dr Fadden is a terrorist, although from what Gerard has told me, I would consider it extremely doubtful," she commented.

"Our American cousins are not prepared to take the chance that he is not part of an international terrorist network organised by the rogue state that is behind the creation of such an effective biological weapon as his plastic-devouring bug."

"A state organised terrorist network?" she echoed. "Do you think there is such a group?"

He hesitated before answering.

"I've ceased to know what to think," he replied. "Just as I get to the point of believing that the scenarios created by Commander Anderson and his pals are more farce than fact, something happens to keep open the possibility that they might be real after all. I cannot imagine Gerry as a terrorist either, but that was easier to maintain when the only link between him and the bug was three socially dislocated young men on a London to Glasgow train. But since then, Dr Fadden's bug has also caused a rubbish dump in Germany to blow up and a plane to crash in Athens, and there are a couple of other possible incidents that are slowly coming to light."

Aunt Gwendoline felt the heat of Felderby Ironworks wash over her.

"The aeroplane crash in Athens," she repeated. "By all reports, there was a terrible loss of life. All those people returning from their holidays. But there has been nothing on the news to suggest it was a terrorist attack."

"And there won't be," he confirmed. "As always, I don't have all the information, but I gather the air crash investigators have found that the airliner came down because a plastic connector in the fuel line to one of the engines failed. It cracked under the increased fuel pressure at take-off and allowed fuel to spray out on to a hot engine. The resulting explosion blew the wing off the plane, and the pilot and crew had no time to prevent the crash."

"And the cause of the plastic connector failing?" she asked apprehensively.

"*Methylococcus faddenii* was found on those plastic aircraft parts that survived the fire."

Aunt Gwendoline put down her teacup. She was feeling very hot and clammy and there was a clamour in her ears. It was not easy to hear what the sergeant was saying.

"Our problem is that we have lost Dr Fadden," he continued. "Commander Anderson has had his people following him ever since the United States first identified him as a cog in a terrorist network intending economic damage to their plastics industry. They have had him under close surveillance around the clock, never letting him out of their sight in spite of him moving where he slept each night. They have logged what he ate for breakfast, dinner and tea and they always knew where he was and who he was talking to. They recorded every meeting and conversation he had, right up to the one he had with Gerry last Friday night. But suddenly, after he and Gerry separated on Saturday morning, they lost him. All the hours so far spent reviewing CCTV tapes of Glasgow's streets and localities since then have shown no sign of him. There have been no mobile phone contacts to him or by him, no bank or credit card transactions, nothing. He has disappeared."

"People don't disappear in a well-ordered society like ours," she argued.

"Commander Anderson would agree with you," Sergeant Chak nodded. "His agents do not lose the targets they are tracking. They are too well trained for that. So, his conclusion is that Dr Fadden must have had specialist counter-espionage training in order to be able to slip away from them as completely as he has and that his former amateurish attempts to hide himself by shifting his lodgings every night were simply play-acting to lull them into a sense of complacency. Losing Dr Fadden at exactly the same moment as the United States decided to issue an international arrest warrant for him has not helped the Commander's reputation or that of the UK as a reliable intelligence ally, and nobody likes being made to look a fool. So now the pressure is on to find him. If Gerry is able to tell us where he might be, then I can only suggest he does so."

Chapter 46

Aunt Gwendoline reined in her thoughts. There was a tightness in her chest, and she was having to force herself to keep breathing. The memory of the luminous cloud of toxic gases belching out from the furnace as it fed from the hopper forced its way forward in her mind and she felt the acrid fumes in her throat. Where was Gerard? 'We lost a man in the furnace today,' echoed in her ears. She cleared her throat.

"The air crash in Athens," she queried. "Does the United States think Dr Fadden is responsible for that? Presumably, there will be an announcement restricting air travel until it is confirmed safe again."

"There will not be any public announcement," Sergeant Chak answered.

He drew in a deep breath and held it while his gaze drifted back to the old lady.

"Miss Penderrick, what I am about to tell you is probably classified, and you should not be hearing it from me," he continued. "The report from the air crash investigators has been withheld and placed under a restricted access notice for the time being. The public will only be told that the investigation is ongoing and that the results will be released at a later date. Fortunately, the public expects these things to take time."

"But what about all the holidaymakers who will be flying out for their winter sun, not to mention those travelling on business?" she protested.

"The thinking is that we have been lucky," he stated.

"Lucky?" she challenged. "I would have regarded the loss of so many lives in an air crash as a tragedy."

"For all those who lost their lives and for their families, it is, of course, a tragedy," he agreed. "But for those responsible for the defence of our Western way of life, it is a stroke of luck."

"How?" she asked.

"Military history tells us that success in modern warfare depends on air superiority and that without it, you cannot hope to win. Knock out an enemy's air force, and you have a clear road to victory. The air crash in Athens has told us that *Methylococcus faddenii* can bring down an aeroplane. In that instance, it was a civilian airliner, but the military minds in NATO high command are now aware that we are looking at a weapon that can disable the West's entire air defences. Intelligence thinking is that Athens was not supposed to happen. What was supposed to happen was that someone, most likely Dr Witheney, would make a series of 'phone calls to her various contacts all over Europe just like she did to Gerry. They would trigger the spreading of Dr Fadden's bug in various strategic locations around the West until all of NATO's planes were infected. Once it became clear that *M. faddenii* had done its job and all NATO's planes were either grounded or dropping out of the sky, a full military attack would follow. But some of the bugs managed to escape and

Athens happened, and because of it the West has been given forewarning of an imminent attack. We were lucky."

"What, then, is going to happen?" she persisted.

"There will be no public announcement," he repeated. "Security requires that our enemy, whoever it is, does not know we are aware of his plan and is left with the impression that we are regarding the crash of a civilian airliner in Athens as an accident. Civilian air services will consequently continue as normal unless someone in government can engineer a strike by airline pilots or ground staff to shut the airlines down, and they are working on that. Meanwhile, around the world every carrier-based and land-based aircraft of the United States Air Force and Navy, the Royal Air Force and all other NATO air forces are being grounded for emergency technical checks and disinfection. It is then being returned to the air fully armed and primed with the pilots briefed to respond instantly to an expected attack."

Noise blanketed Aunt Gwendoline's sitting room until finally her ears cleared, and she was able to take a deep breath and hear her surroundings again.

"An academic microbiologist discovers a new microbe in a handful of soil and we end up on the verge of another world war," she summarised.

"Put like that, it does sound barely believable," Sergeant Chak agreed. "But whether the scenario is real or not, those responsible for protecting us believe they cannot take the chance it is not true."

"And who is this enemy that is about to launch an attack on us?" she asked.

"That is the problem," the sergeant shrugged. "We don't know. There are known rogue states that refuse to be bound by the norms of international agreements. There are also other states that have a long-standing grudge against the West. And then there are a couple of others who would just as likely not miss the opportunity to have a go at us anyway. It could be any one of them. Remember, this bug has so far been able to spread itself around Europe without us noticing it, and it is capable of doing damage wherever it goes. It can shut down everything our wired-up plastic world depends on, which is almost everything you might care to think about. Can you imagine hospitals functioning without plastic? No syringes, no blood transfusion packs, no dialysis units, no tubing for the delivery of oxygen, drugs and fluids into a patient's vein, no catheters or drainage tubes, no plastic sheeting for the beds, not to mention no incubators for premature babies. Operating theatres and intensive care units would be unable to work. In short, everything we would need to treat the injured and wounded in the event of a war would be rendered inoperable. This bug leaves us wide open to attack and incapable of responding even to the threat of one, even before the neutralisation of our armed forces. We need to find Dr Witheney and find out who she is working for, and Dr Fadden is our best route to doing that. So, anything Gerry can do to help…"

"My grand-nephew cannot be of any help at all," she interjected angrily. "He is not part of any hostile conspiracy and would never be responsible for such damage as you describe."

"If he does not help us, then I'm afraid Gerry becomes the default suspect who will be the first in line to blame for all the damage Dr Fadden and his bug are likely to do around the globe," countered the sergeant.

"Default suspect? What do you mean?"

She felt the heat of the furnace engulf her once more and the sergeant's voice came through to her as if from the other side of a wall.

"*Methylococcus faddenii* is discovered around all the plastics factories in the USA visited by Dr Fadden under the guise of him doing an environmental review of the US plastics industry. Two weeks later, Dr Witheney makes a telephone call to Gerry who then goes to see Dr Fadden. Commander Anderson believes that after that, Dr Witheney went to Munich and then to Athens, making similar telephone calls as she went. Four weeks later, after the bug has had time to incubate and make itself at home, there is an apparently failed bombing attempt on a mainline train that begins the spread of *M. faddenii* across the UK. Gerry is on that train. A few days after that, Germany blows up and begins the spread of the infection across Europe. Athens follows. Dr Fadden is questioned. He then meets with Gerry, loses his trackers and disappears, presumably down the same previously prepared escape route used by Dr Witheney. Dr Witheney is gone and so is Dr Fadden, so that leaves Commander Anderson with Gerry as the last remaining identifiable link in the hostile network responsible for the spread of this malicious bug across the West. He becomes the default suspect."

Aunt Gwendoline said nothing. There was nothing she could say into the thunder in her ears. All she could do was wait for the world to stop shaking and the heat and fumes of the furnace to dissipate so that she might breathe again.

Sergeant Chak stretched upright in his chair. He knew he had said too much, but the pressure of the situation and the frustration of working with Commander Anderson had boiled over within him.

"For what it's worth, Miss Penderrick, I don't believe Gerry would ever knowingly become involved in the sort of espionage and military endgame that is occupying the attention of our Western governments at the moment," he ended. "But the idea of an imminent attack by a hostile state, an attack that is possibly already underway, is already entrenched in their minds and is one that nobody dares take the risk is not real. All the pressure is pushing in one direction and if it is true, then we are as prepared as we can be. If it is not true, then all we can hope is that someone, somewhere will find a circuit-breaker, something which will interrupt the line of thinking and present us with a less-lethal option before somebody starts pressing buttons. It might be wise for Gerry to know that as he goes about his business between here and Glasgow."

"A circuit-breaker?" she queried.

Sergeant Chak nodded.

"In the meantime, I must remind you that everything I have told you must not be repeated to anyone. If Commander Anderson and all the people behind him are correct, the security of our country, if not the entire West, might be at stake."

Chapter 47

Aunt Gwendoline leaned back against the cushions of her carved rosewood chair in the quietness that followed the sergeant's departure, and waited for breath and normality to return to her. Tiredness clawed at her and she closed her eyes. Immediately, images from her dreams flashed and flickered on the screen of her closed eyelids, pictures of Gerard leading a Cleveland Bay to work down Felderby Pit and bringing it back to Pit Entrance again, injured and bloody after the rockfall that followed the drawing of the big jed. The horse would never work again. Quite possibly, neither would Dr Fadden after Gerard's rescue of him from the wreck of his laboratory. Big, gentle and innocent, his university would probably decide he should spend his remaining time with them on gardening leave. It was a gentler fate than that which awaited the horse. It was taken to the farriers and shot. She opened her eyes quickly to the daylight and pushed the thought away.

"Where are you, Gerard?" she asked. "I have not heard from you."

The question voiced itself. He had not told her he would be returning to Glasgow quite so soon and she tried to console herself with the knowledge that it had been less than two days since he had brought his piece of fish for their late meal together. He had been overseas on his archaeological digs for much longer than that without her fearing so much for him, but the question persisted.

"Come along, Rani," she commanded. "Let us get ourselves some lunch before we fall asleep. Falling asleep before lunch is a very bad habit to get into. It is what old people do, and I am not ready for that yet. Our Gerard is worried about his friend Dr Fadden, and Commander Anderson is worried about terrorists and seems determined to find our Gerard and Dr Fadden amongst them. I cannot make any sense of it. Our Gerard is not a terrorist. And after lunch, we will go for a bounce in the park. That should blow away the cobwebs and clear our heads a bit."

The autumn breeze had enough energy to oblige her. "Bracing" was how she would have described the bluster into which she and Rani set off for their postprandial exercise, but it blew no clear paths to answer the question swirling stridently within her.

"Gerard, where are you?"

Back at home, Rani watched her mistress settle down to an afternoon in which concentration on yet another article in the *Antiques Collectors' Weekly* about Victorian Hunter clocks was never going to be possible. The muffled tread of the grandfather clock paced out the unvarying minutes, the aspidistra withdrew into its decorated pot, the Hunter clock kept to a time all of its own and the afternoon sunbeam through the sitting room window began its silent traverse across the dustless furniture. Aunt Gwendoline's head nodded forward and her eyes closed.

Felderby Iron Works was all around her. She felt the waves of heat and the shrieks of gas jets buffet her as she ran past the sounds of shovelled coke and rattling chains, hissing pig iron and spitting slag, the bedlam of industry.

"Look out for those sparks, lass," a man shouted to her over the din.

She skipped around a splatter of white-hot metal that splashed across her path and breathed in the air laden with the smells of liquid metal and smoking machine oil, of sulphurous gases and molten rock. Everything was familiar to her. There was nothing to startle her or cause her fear.

She glanced down at the cloth-wrapped package in her hand. She had to find her dad and give him his lunch. She looked up to where the men sweated and swore as they fought their loaded wheelbarrows along the narrow ramp up to the hopper at the top of the furnace. She watched the foreman at the bottom check off each barrow and give the man a nod before he started his ascent, and she saw each man at the top upend his barrow into the hopper before tramping back down again. It was a continuous, unbroken line with nothing to stop it.

She looked down the line for her dad and saw the men watching the tension in the cable supporting the counterweight that kept the hopper closed. It was only an occasional glance as they climbed, but it told them all they needed to know. The hopper was getting full. One barrow too many, or a sudden drop of pressure in the furnace, and the hopper would open and the furnace would belch and suck in a bellyful of its feed. Each man estimated his chances as he took his first step up the walkway. It made no difference if he was the biggest rogue in the works or innocent of all crime and a loving head of his family, if he was at the hopper's lip when the furnace opened, he would know no more. The fumes would hit him, and he would tip silently forward with his barrow into the hopper. There would be nothing anyone could do to save him and nothing to retrieve. She looked along the line of men but could not see her dad.

Panic rose in her. Absent-mindedly she turned over the lunch parcel she held in her hands. It felt wrong. She looked down at it. It did not feel like one of her mam's pasties. Puzzled, she turned it over again. A dark liquid stain was seeping through the cloth. She lifted it to her nose and tasted it. It was chocolate. Confusion gripped her. Her dad never ate chocolate. It was Gerard who was the chocoholic of the family. She was in Felderby Iron Works and was carrying a piece of chocolate cake.

Aunt Gwendoline exploded out of her dream.

"Gerard," she called out. "Where are you?"

She had heard less silence from him when he was tramping around the wilds of Indochina.

"Furnace," her grandfather clock's voice echoed from the hallway.

Rani stilled her whimpering and let the sounds of the house take over. The remains of the afternoon dragged their way to evening and a distracted supper that was only picked at. Sleep refused to visit when bedtime finally arrived, and it was only the eventual appearance of the first light of dawn that finally allowed them both a couple of hours retreat into solid slumber before rising to greet the new day.

Chapter 48

It was a struggle to begin the morning, and it was only her determination to shake herself into more wakefulness than she felt that pushed Aunt Gwendoline into maintaining some regularity in her habits.

"A circuit-breaker," she summarised for Rani as she inhaled the steam from her breakfast brew. "That is what Sergeant Chak said we need, although I'm not sure I would know what one looks like. Commander Anderson is looking for terrorists with his single line of thought going around and round that cannot be stopped. Felderby Iron Works had its single line of men feeding the furnace in an endless loop that nothing was allowed to stop, except that it did stop when a man fell into the hopper."

The images in her dreams clung to her like seaweed to a rock on a surging seashore.

"Dr Witheney, Dr Fadden and Gerard," she sighed. "Dr Witheney is nowhere to be found, Dr Fadden has disappeared, and we have not heard from our Gerard since he came to supper. There is silence from all three, yet everything around me is noisy. I can make no sense of it. We must find a circuit-breaker either to break the silence or to break the noise, and how I am going to do that when the police and the intelligence services of this country and no doubt a few others have been unable to manage it, is something else I do not know. I am a person of very few means and very little influence but we must make sure nothing happens to our Gerard, particularly if it involves him disappearing into a furnace with nothing left to show of him. I could not deal with that. I am getting too old. Where are you Gerard? Wherever you are, you should not be in Felderby Iron Works."

She glanced at her Hunter clock and saw it was showing a satisfying discrepancy from the correct hour. Whatever was going to happen had not yet occurred. There was still time.

"Come along, Rani," she rallied. "It is Wednesday, so we must go and buy some chocolate cake for when our Gerard comes to tea this afternoon. I know we haven't heard from him, but that does not mean we won't, and when he arrives, he will expect some chocolate cake."

Rani wagged her tail stump and reflected back the hope in the words and also the doubt that hid behind them. They both knew Gerard would not be coming to afternoon tea on this particular Wednesday, and Rani watched her mistress' hands unconsciously grip more tightly around the imagined lunch pack she carried with her out of her dream.

The breeze boasted of the gale it forecast and ripped at the few discoloured leaves that still hung on to the trees that had given them life. Aunt Gwendoline bent her head to it as it whipped at the flower in her hat and tried to tear away her coat, and with a grimness fitted to meet the hour, she and Rani buffeted their way homewards with their shopping.

"I have been over it so many times, and neither mother nor our dad are being particularly communicative on the matter," she informed the dog.

There was turmoil like the wind inside her and it thrashed at her and denied her all sense except that of danger.

"Where are you, Gerard?" she asked insistently.

They walked back through the park until they came to a sheltered bench just inside the high stone wall that surrounded much of it, a quiet corner where spent leaves piled up as gratefully as she did out of the swirling blast.

"Off you go, Rani. Go and have a snuffle," she instructed as she sank on to the welcoming seat.

She gazed out over the park.

"Dr Fadden is a harmless academic if our Gerard's instincts are not misled," she muttered. "He has found a microbe in a handful of soil and sees only the good it can do, cleaning the hedgerows, beaches and the oceans of the world of plastic rubbish and saving the lives of sea birds and turtles. Against him is Commander Anderson and his antiterrorist intelligence friends who see only the bad that the same creature can do, the floods and the fires it could cause, the aeroplanes it could make crash and everyone being brought to the brink of another world war."

She shook herself to relieve the stiffness in her limbs.

"Furnace. Why do I keep hearing that?" she asked the wind. "And why have I not heard from Gerard?"

Men were lost in the furnace, and she could only hope that her grand-nephew had inherited sufficient of the family gift to warn him of all the trouble a furnace could cause.

Later that night, Rani watched over her mistress as she tossed and turned in disturbed slumber, and it was a few minutes after midnight that she was called to jump to her feet with a quiet 'woof' and reach up with her forepaws to pound on the counterpane. There was no scrambling for the bedside

222

lamp, no call of reassurance, so she pawed frantically at the bedclothes and let out another 'woof' followed by a louder bark and then another yet louder. There was only her mistress sitting bolt upright in bed with her eyes wide open, staring fixedly into the darkness until finally, the bedside light went on. Her mistress turned to look at her in the glow of it.

"I heard a shot," she said. "The Cleveland Bay. There was a cry followed by a loud noise, a concussion of some sort. And then there was silence. Please, our Dad. Please let it not be our Gerard."

Downstairs in the hallway, they heard the grandfather clock strike the quarter-hour after midnight.

Chapter 49

Aunt Gwendoline pushed aside the bedclothes in trepidation as she cautiously approached the next day. She had never felt more like a shrinking leaf that having withered and been left coloured by the reds and golds of age, was just hanging on to its twig. The morning light did not dampen the aftershocks from the night. She had heard a concussion and a cry, as clearly as if it had been shouted beside her, but try as she might, she could not replay the full scene in her mind.

"There was panic and desperation, and then silence," she recalled.

Her hands trembled on the bannister as she descended the stairs and she fought desperately to deny they shook with fear. There had been no word from Gerard and she could only think it was bad news.

She was half way down the stairs before she noticed that Rani had gone ahead of her and was looking up at her expectantly from the vantage point of the morning newspaper, newly arrived on the doormat. She approached it cautiously and pushed Rani aside, and immediately relaxed when she saw the headline. It was nothing, only some problem involving a financial crisis in the city. She picked it up and folded it to put it aside for later reading, but a secondary heading at the bottom of the front page caught her eye and set her heart pounding. A senior academic had jumped to his death from a seventh-floor balcony of a hotel in Princes Street, Glasgow just after midnight last night. A police spokesman said the man had been under stress and they were not treating the death as suspicious. His name was being withheld until his family were informed.

Her tired thoughts boiled and froze in her mind as she reread the meagre few sentences about the anonymous victim. Her frame momentarily refused to support her and she sank on to one of the hall chairs. Was an official knock at that moment making its way to her door? Would she find herself facing two sombre police officers asking, "Do you have a grand-nephew Gerard who may have been in Glasgow recently?" It was not supposed to happen. She was supposed to stop Gerard falling into the furnace, to stop him from tipping forward over the edge of the balcony and into oblivion.

"A circuit-breaker," she cried out, tearfully into the emptiness of the hallway. "That is what Sergeant Chak said I needed to find to stop our Gerard coming to harm. Why, our Mam and our Dad, could not one of you have helped me? Why would you not tell me where I could find one?"

Both her oak cased clock and the aspidistra remained dumb to her appeal.

The doubts and the tears followed her all morning. She tried making tea, but it was left to go cold after only a single sip. She vacillated between confidence that it was not Gerard who had fallen in Glasgow and the chilling fear that it might have been. She sat back in her favourite chair and despaired at not having the energy to engage in any constructive activity, and suddenly, a fragment of image snapped at her.

"I had a dream," she informed Rani. "I had forgotten about it, but it was after I heard the shot and before dawn, although I cannot remember being asleep."

Rani's brown eyes looked up at her full of attention while she bored into her memory to hook the forgotten dream and recreate it.

"I was in Felderby Iron Works, and the men were tramping up the ramp with their loaded barrows to feed the furnace. They were all watching the cable to the counterpoise weight holding the hopper closed. It was vibrating hard, signalling that the furnace was agitating for its next feed. I had our dad's lunch parcel in my hand, and then I saw Gerard. I remember thinking he should not be there. He is an archaeologist, not a foundry man, but I saw him grim-faced and pushing determinedly forward, sweating with the heat of the works and the weight of his barrow as he climbed the ramp to the hopper's lip. I called out to him, but he could not hear me. I held out the lunch parcel to him. 'Take it,' I shouted. 'It's a circuit-breaker. Take it. Break the line,' but the noise and his concentration on his task rendered him deaf to my cry.

"There was only one man ahead of him on the ramp, and again, I shouted out a warning to him, but I was too late. The hopper opened and the furnace fed, vomiting out the noxious, smothering cloud that billowed up into the roof space of the works. I heard Gerard shout and watched as he threw aside his barrow and run forward into the engulfing cloud to reach the man ahead of him. It was futile. Surely, he would know that. The man ahead would be dead. He would have fallen into the hopper, knowing nothing more and lost forever.

"'Gerard,' I called out again.

"I reached blindly into the smog to try and find him and pull him away. I was the circuit-breaker. I felt the foulness burn my throat and the heat blister my hands, and then I saw his jacket, and there were two hands, a woman's hands, pulling at it and hauling him free, back into clean air and life. The circuit-breaker, a pair of woman's hands."

Rani peered up at her mistress, responding to her distress.

Aunt Gwendoline looked down at her hands. Try as she might, she could not recall whether she had been successful. She had woken too soon. She felt a sob kick in her chest.

"I am an old woman, our Dad," she cried silently. "I do not have the strength I once had."

There was only her to look after Gerard and keep him safe, and she looked down again at her clenched fists, opened them and turned them over and examined her hands closely. They were the only hands she had, but there was something about them that was not right.

"What is important is that they reached out into the cloud to grab him and pull him back to safety," she declared.

It was not enough. She could not make her recollection run smoothly to the end she desired. She examined her hands yet again. Had she succeeded or failed? Determined questioning of both her oak cased grandfather clock and the potted aspidistra did not answer the question, and her Hunter clock became uncooperative beyond all reason. The hands were wrong. Had she saved him? She did not know, and she fought to hold her eyes shut against her doubts.

It was Rani who eventually spread a semblance of calm over the household. Sometime mid-afternoon, she left her mistress' side and went to sit on the doormat inside the front door. Once there, she remained fixed and focussed, refusing to be budged and holding her point for more than two hours, looking not so much at the door as through it, drawing her mistress' attention to something that only she as yet could see.

"What is it, Rani?" Aunt Gwendoline asked in tired exasperation.

When it came, the knock on the door startled her beyond mere fright. Her heart thumped resoundingly in her chest and a cough exploded in her throat and kept her choking and gasping for breath so that she had to hold on to the coat stand for support. The knocking came again, more determined, but her shaking hands could only hang on to the door catch. Fear froze them and stopped them from turning the lock. The knock hammered a third time, and through her receding cough she managed to call out, "Just a minute." Puzzled, she noticed Rani was no longer in her point but enthusiastically examining the back of the door and wagging her tail stump in greeting for a friend. A deep breath and a final clear of her throat and she managed cautiously to open the door a fraction and peer through the gap.

Standing on her doorstep were not two police officers looking sombre and tense as if on an official call to deliver bad news. Instead, there was a young woman looking apprehensively at her.

"Oh, hello. Are you Aunt Gwendoline?" she asked hesitantly.

Aunt Gwendoline opened the door further. The antipodean accent registered with her immediately, as did the broad but anxious smile that twitched nervously as it flickered across the fresh and open face. The overcoat the young woman wore did nothing to hide her slim and athletic figure, and her long and shapely legs were set off magnificently by a skirt that was more than a little fashionably short.

Aunt Gwendoline blinked in startled response. She had forgotten all about Gerard's wombat chasing assistant.

"Miss Blaise," she smiled at her. "How nice of you to call. Do come in."

Chapter 50

Aunt Gwendoline decided a light Ceylon tea with a small selection of biscuits was enough of a welcome for the unquestionably attractive young woman who sat nervously across from her. With Gerard inexplicably out of touch and microbes and Commander Anderson on the prowl, the existence of Miss Anne Blaise and the distraction her legs caused the male half of the population had completely slipped her mind. She could see why. They were certainly an outstanding asset. No wonder they constituted most of Sergeant Chak's description of her.

"I hope you don't mind me calling round like this. Gerry mentioned you had invited me round for tea sometime. Is that OK?"

She was looking for reassurance, and the awkwardness in her smile only added to her attractiveness.

"Of course, Miss Blaise. It is so nice to meet you. My grand-nephew has mentioned you on a couple of occasions," Aunt Gwendoline smiled in return.

"Oh, Anne, please. It's just that I was looking for Gerry and nobody seems to know where he is. I haven't seen him for nearly a week, and nobody in the department seems to have heard from him either. I gather it's not unusual for him to go walkabout for a few days at a time, but usually somebody knows where he is. At the moment, not even his secretary has any idea where he might be."

Aunt Gwendoline resisted the urge to pull her own mid-calf skirt down further over her knees. It was annoying that Rani was looking up at their visitor so smilingly.

"As far as I know, he went to Glasgow to see his friend Dr Fadden at the university there," she replied. "I have heard nothing to suggest he is not perfectly safe and well."

She had difficulty saying the words. Although they were in themselves true, she knew there was more than uncertainty in the silence they represented.

"Where did you first meet my grand-nephew?" she enquired.

"In Canberra," Anne beamed.

The memory obviously pleased her.

"He was visiting the university, and I was out at Tidbinbilla Nature Reserve trying to find some wombats I had been tracking for the past two years. I got back to the hut I was camping in, and he was there, going on about how he had found some bits of iron in Vietnam and wanting to know whether they could have been buried by burrowing animals. It seemed quite important to him, so I let him rabbit on for a bit, and he seemed genuinely interested in my opinion, which was rather flattering for a mere Masters student. I mean, someone of his standing wanting to know what I thought. He unpacked his gear and spent the next three days helping me find my wombats; then we drove back to Canberra. The next thing I knew I was on a plane to Hanoi. All very sudden and exciting really."

"You joined him in Vietnam," Aunt Gwendoline summarised.

The story was too self-deprecating and dismissive for there not to be more to it. She looked down at Rani, who clearly had no trouble with it, believing every word of it and looking animatedly at its narrator while wagging her tail stump back and forth across the carpet in a doggy equivalent of applause. Even the aspidistra seemed to be enjoying the performance.

"It was quite an adventure," Anne gushed. "I had never been on an archaeological dig before. Gerry took me to the place where he had found his two pieces of iron. He's a wonderful teacher. He showed them to me, and they really do look like two pieces of the same knife blade, but they really puzzled him. He said that if the knife had been part of a collection of grave goods, then there should have been other items there as well, all part of the burial ritual, as well as a skeleton, of course. But there was none of that. There was no evidence of fighting or battle where it was found, so it had not been lost in conflict. So that left it having been accidentally lost or thrown out, which would have been extraordinary since its rarity alone would have made it an extremely valuable item to whoever owned it in 1000 BC. It would not have been something that would be lost easily. It was a real puzzle for him. So, he wanted me to rat around and see if I could find any evidence of some animal burying a knife from a later age as part of its burrowing. It didn't look like it, but I must admit I found the whole idea fascinating that when wombats and rabbits and the like dig their burrows they are churning through thousands of years of human history and mixing it all up. I had never thought of it quite like that before."

She paused for breath. She was gabbling, and she knew it, and Aunt Gwendoline noted the flush in her visitor's face and concluded that it was probably more than could be accounted for by a newly acquired enthusiasm for archaeology. She also noted that Rani continued to sit transfixed by the story, and to add to the confusion her Hunter clock had decided it was going to show exactly the correct time again.

Chapter 51

"He is a wonderful teacher," Anne resumed more calmly. "It's part of what everybody loves about him, including me. He makes it all come so alive. But it is more than that. It's as if he can actually feel the events that occurred all those ages ago. He seems to be able to sense what happened, and when he suddenly says 'dig here' and they do, they find the most extraordinary things. That's how they found the two pieces of iron. He seemed to know they were there even before they were unearthed."

She looked up and directly into Aunt Gwendoline's eyes and hesitated, uncertain whether or not she should continue.

"One night at Ban Long, I couldn't sleep," she resumed. "So, I got up, and I saw him walking over to the dig site in the moonlight. I followed him, and he went directly to where the pieces of knife blade had been found, and I saw him stand there for a few minutes before starting to move slowly over the ground while looking closely at it. After a while, I realised he wasn't just randomly scouting over it but was doing a sort of dance, a dance where it looked like he was holding a knife and moving around with it. Occasionally he would stop and go back a few steps before moving on again, seeming to build some sort of story centred around the knife. It was quite a performance, especially being in the moonlight and all that. It wasn't scary, but I did start to get concerned. I worried that he might have got himself into some sort of trance, sleepwalking or the like, and I wondered whether or not I should wake him up, act as a sort of circuit-breaker to snap him out of it."

"Circuit-breaker?" interrupted Aunt Gwendoline. "What do you mean?"

The words had caught her completely by surprise, and she spoke more sharply than she intended. She sat more upright in her chair.

Anne retreated momentarily.

"Nothing, really," she answered. "I was just concerned, that's all. But then I saw he wasn't really asleep, so I left him to finish his little dance or whatever it was he was doing, and that was that except at the end of it he saw me. I thought he'd chuck a wobbly, but he didn't. He just smiled and took my hand and we sat on a couple of upturned buckets while he pointed out to me the patch of dirt where the knife fragments had been found, and he told me what he thought might have happened to put them there. He told me the story of a small family community living in the jungle and how they had been hit by a disease, probably contracted through contact with some other tribe. It was killing all their people, and all the women's knowledge of medical herbs and the best skills of the medicine man had failed to stop it. So finally, the head man, the bloke in charge, decided a sacrifice was necessary to satisfy whatever gods they believed in so that the disease would go away. It was the only thing they knew. Their problem was that they were too early to have flocks of animals or anything like that, and too humane to sacrifice one of their own. The care they took over their burials showed how important human life was to them. So, they sacrificed the most valuable thing they had in their possession, the iron knife. It was the only one they had, most likely the first one they had ever seen and as far as they knew the only one in the universe. Maybe the disease came to them through the person they traded with to get it. We'll never know. But they held a ceremony in a clearing in their village, went through their ritual dances, and at the end, they broke the knife with a stone and left the two pieces on the ground never to be touched again until Gerry found them three thousand years later. He just hoped it had worked for them and that they had survived."

It was only a hypothetical reconstruction, but Aunt Gwendoline saw that her visitor had become so wrapped up in the story that she almost willed it to be true. She returned the hopeful gaze and saw the smile twitch involuntarily in the young woman's face.

"You're very fond of him, aren't you?" she suggested gently.

Anne's features flickered then folded, and she covered her face with her hands as tears appeared in her eyes.

"Yes," she nodded, answering in a whisper in case the sound of admitting it destroyed any last hope she had of it not being true. "Which is ridiculous because he doesn't even know I exist," she continued more firmly. "He's gone walkabout and nobody knows where he is, and I'm worried about him, which is garbage. It shouldn't really matter to me, but I've thought about that night so much and really it was just imagination on my part. It's just that at the time, I really felt he was not just describing some academic hypothesis to account for the two bits of iron he had found. I believed he could really feel those events from all those years ago as if he had some sixth sense that could tell him about them just by him walking across the ground. And if he can sense that, then maybe he can also sense how wonderful he sounds and how he can make the people around him feel. He made it all so real. I wouldn't worry about it, though. It was just imagination on my part, and as far as I can tell, he hasn't told anyone else about his theory."

Aunt Gwendoline let the silence lengthen and the time in her sitting room be taken over by the steady treads of her ticking clocks. She thought of the landscape changing around Low Felderby after the collapse of the big jed, and she thought of Gerard in the tropical moonlight, re-enacting a prehistoric ritual of a priest breaking the most treasured possession of a tribe to appease whatever gods that were causing the landscape to change around them, looking for a circuit-breaker to interrupt the progress of what was killing them. "We lost a man in the furnace today." She had heard a cry in the night and it sounded like Gerard, but it was not Gerard who had fallen into the hopper. The fumes would have rendered him senseless before he could do so. He was not lost. For the first time in many days she felt a surge of hope.

Anne Blaise blowing her nose and wiping her tears cut across her thinking. The poor girl was deeply smitten.

"I'm sorry," Anne snuffled. "You must think me very silly."

"Not at all," Aunt Gwendoline replied. "You are a very sweet girl, and I do appreciate your concern for my grand-nephew, and the fact that you came here this afternoon to tell me about them. I can only thank you for it. I confess I am worried about him too, disappearing as he has without a word. But I can reassure you that he is certainly aware of you and

237

he values your opinion highly, otherwise he would not have invited you to tea."

She saw Rani stiffen into a point fixed immovably on their visitor.

"Thanks," Anne answered, giving a final sniff and smiling again. "We can all dream, I suppose. And it won't have done my resumé any harm getting an acknowledgement on one of his research papers, even if it was a bit of a circus trying to get here."

"Circus?" echoed Aunt Gwendoline.

She had lost a connection somewhere.

"I mean when I first arrived," explained Anne. "I got to the airport with no real idea of how to get to the university, so I called Gerry's number from a payphone and got his secretary. I didn't have much change, so I had to keep the call short. I said, 'it's Anne Blaise here. I'm on my way, but how do I get to your department?' It was a bit of a crackly line, so I had to repeat myself. I said, 'it's Anne here, that's Anne with an "e"'…"

Aunt Gwendoline's eyes widened and she almost jumped into a point alongside Rani.

"You said what?"

Her question was too strident for it to be ladylike.

"I said, 'It's Anne here, how do I get…'."

"No. About your name."

"Oh, that! I get all sorts of spelling with my name so I always say 'Anne with and 'e''. It saves confusion later on."

"Anne with an 'e'," Aunt Gwendoline repeated.

She became aware she was gaping and she had not done that since it was knocked out of her by Miss Pryke at Low Felderby Village Primary School.

"That's what the secretary said," Anne repeated. "Then she told me Gerry was not expected back until the next day. At that point, my coins ran out, so I wasn't able to continue the call."

Aunt Gwendoline's dream recreated itself in front of her. She had reached out to Gerard when he ran forward up the ramp and into the toxic fumes as the hopper opened. She saw hands grab him to haul him back, a woman's hands, and she suddenly realised why her hands had seemed wrong. They were not her hands that had grabbed Gerard's jacket. They were a young woman's hands. She looked across at Anne Blaise's hands folded calmly in her lap. Anne with an 'e'. The circuit-breaker.

"Miss Blaise," she smiled, still churning her conclusion in her mind. "You are the most charming and delightful young woman I have met in a long time, and extremely attractive into the bargain. I wouldn't worry about Gerard. He has quite a lot on his mind besides archaeology at the present time, and I'm sure you will find someone who will appreciate your charms to the full in due course. In the meantime, would you excuse me while I go and make a telephone call?"

She hurried out to the hallway and dialled the number printed on a police business card.

"Sergeant Chak?" she requested, and waited while he was found. "Sergeant Chak? It's Gwendoline Penderrick here. Do you think you could come over to see me straight away? I think I have found Dr Witheney. Dr Anne with an 'e'."

Chapter 52

Aunt Gwendoline slept very well that night and had no trouble out-bouncing Rani on their expedition the next morning. She had still not heard from Gerard, but it did not bother her. Nothing was going to happen to him, of that she was sure. He had been pulled safely back from the lip of the furnace hopper, and she had seen the hands that had reached out to grab him. She had reached out too, but it was not her hands that had held him back. It did not matter. The hands that did were younger and stronger and more suited to the task, and it was interesting that it was the fluttering of infatuation that had directed them to where they were needed and had given them the extra strength to complete their work.

As they rode the bus into town, Aunt Gwendoline thought more on Anne Blaise. Perhaps she had been a little too harsh in her initial judgement of the girl, but then she had not met her. Having done so, she could certainly see she had many fine points. Maybe she had been right when she had said that Gerard had felt the events he had re-enacted and described to her in the tropical moonlight of Ban Long. Perhaps she did briefly see in him the family gift telling him of trouble and turmoil, albeit some three thousand years ago. Whatever the possibilities, Gerard had certainly caused a shudder in her landscape. It was, in reality only a small shudder, and she would no doubt recover from it. "Character building" was how her mother used to describe such transient upheavals. "And there's no use saying you don't want your character built because it is going to get built whether you like it or not."

What was important was that her Hunter clock had finally decided to settle down. True, when fiddling with it to find out why it had come to its senses, she had discovered a small inscription handwritten in ink on the inside of its walnut case, giving the date of 1864. That meant it could not have been the timepiece that received the Honourable Mention in the Exhibition of 1862, but at least it was now keeping proper time and she still felt she had secured a bargain.

It was Sunday morning before her telephone rang again.

"Hello? Aunt Gwendoline? It's Gerard. I'm sorry I've not been in touch."

"That's all right, dear boy. I had been wondering what you were up to, but now I have heard from you everything is fine again."

It was not all fine again. He was sounding very tired and speaking as if he was having difficulty concentrating.

"Where are you? It sounds a bit noisy in the background."

"I'm in Glasgow," he replied. "I'll tell you all about it when I get home. I won't be home just yet though, not for a few days. There is something I have to do. I don't know how long it will take, probably till the end of the week, but I'll give you a call as soon as I get back. I just don't want you to worry about me in the meantime."

"I have no idea why I should worry about you, but thank you for letting me know. Do look after yourself. I'll see you on your return."

With that, he rang off. She had promised not to worry about him, and that would not be difficult. She knew he was safe and she would hear all about his adventures in due course.

"All we can do is wait," she informed Rani.

It was more than a week before he called again.

"Hello, Aunt Gwendoline."

He was sounding stronger.

"I'm back from the wilds of Scotland and am looking forward to seeing you. Can we have tea tomorrow afternoon?"

"Of course, my dear boy. I shall be here."

As she wandered out to her kitchen, Aunt Gwendoline had a noticeable lightness in her tread. She sent a wide smile towards her oak cased grandfather clock and a condescending nod to the aspidistra as she decided that a nice, fresh pot of Darjeeling tea was the order of the day.

"There you are, Rani," she announced as she leaned back in her favourite carved rosewood chair and passed half a biscuit to her ever-watchful companion. "We will be seeing our Gerard tomorrow. I must get some chocolate cake for him. Black Forest cake would not be too much, don't you think? It is a bit extravagant, but as our mam used to say 'one never regrets an extravagance' and now is not the time for regrets, don't you agree?"

Rani wagged her tail stump and watched as her mistress smiled at the Hunter clock on the sideboard. She saw her smile at the aspidistra, too, although mother and daughter really had nothing to say to each other. Apart from that, she was happy just to sit at her mistress' feet and agree with whatever she said on the off chance the other half of the biscuit should fall her way.

Chapter 53

Aunt Gwendoline brewed Min China tea to go alongside the Black Forrest cake. Outwardly, Gerard appeared to be in good health, but the instant he arrived, she saw the watchfulness in his eyes. It reminded her of the men who came out of Felderby Pit after the big jed had fallen in. They carried about them the haunted look of shock and dust for weeks afterwards, and were wary of wherever they were.

"It must have been obvious to you when I left you on that Saturday night just over two weeks ago that I was worried about Chris Fadden," he began. "It is difficult to remember all the details now, but when I left Chris in Glasgow at around dawn on that last Saturday morning, he was barely able to hold himself together. I had no real idea then what a rough handling by Commander Anderson and his crew could do. All I knew was that it had left Chris at his wits end and so confused that I could not be sure he would be able to function in his own best interests."

Aunt Gwendoline checked around her house. All was still, including Rani, who rested watchfully beside her.

"I could not get it out of my mind that Chris was in some sort of danger," Gerard continued. "I was right as it turned out, and in very great danger. But at that time, all I had was the unease, the disquiet, the uncomfortable feeling that something was closing in on him. Anderson's people had given him a good shaking in their futile pursuit of imagined terrorists. They had smashed up his laboratory, stripped his office and wrecked his home, and given him such a grilling over the period of three days that he had ended up a complete mental wreck. Anderson, more or less, admitted to me that it had been done deliberately, all in the interests of national security, of course. But Chris was not a terrorist and never had been, and it was all a mistake by our security and intelligence services. I am still angry about it, as angry as Anderson and his people are unapologetic. But that was all for the future to reveal, so I decided to return to Glasgow and see if I could find Chris and help him get himself back together again.

"I had no idea how I was going to find him and did not know that Anderson's people had lost track of him. I knew he had not been to his home for at least a couple of weeks and I was sure he would not go back to his laboratory at the university. There would be no point since it had been wrecked. When he left me, he was heading vaguely in the direction of the city centre, presumably to some temporary digs he had found, but I didn't know where they were, and I'm not sure he did either. We had walked round and around in circles all night long trying to find them so I reckoned my chances of locating them were just about zero. I just hoped that when I arrived at Glasgow Central some instinct would guide me. All I knew was that I had to try.

"It might sound strange, Aunt Gwendoline, but as I walked down the platform at Euston for the fast train to Glasgow, something began nagging at me. I didn't know what it was except that I had the feeling that something was wrong, out of place, like someone was watching me or that there was a question that needed to be asked, but I couldn't think what it was. It was so strong a feeling that I nearly didn't get on the train. I hesitated almost until the last second but eventually, I did board and find my seat.

"The carriage was surprisingly empty. Apart from two men and a woman in business suits at the far end of the compartment there were no other passengers in it as far as I could see. For a weekday mid-morning train, that was unusual, but I assumed the overspill from the other carriages would fill up the remaining seats at the last minute as it usually does. It did not, and as the train left the station, I settled back to an unexpectedly roomy journey and bent my thought towards how I was going to find Chris.

"Soon out of London, there is a tunnel, and I was so wrapped in my thoughts I didn't notice there were no lights on in the carriage as we went into it. It simply went momentarily black for a few seconds, and when we arrived back into daylight again, I was surprised to find Commander Anderson had materialised in the seat opposite me. He must have been hiding somewhere nearby and moved very quickly and quietly in that brief period of darkness. He didn't say anything and just fixed me with a stare.

"I wasn't in the mood to play games with him."

"'Good morning, Commander,' I greeted him. 'Still chasing phantoms in the dark?'

"He smiled grimly at me.

"'Someone has got to do it,' he replied. 'Otherwise, none of us would be able to sleep soundly in our beds at night. Do you have a mobile phone?'

"I was so surprised by the question that I put my hand in my pocket and pulled it out to show him.

"'Thank you,' he said and took it from me before I could react.

"Immediately one of the suited ones from the other end of the carriage grabbed it and rushed away. The move was so practiced it was disturbing, and I suddenly realised why the carriage was so empty. He had arranged it so.

"It was frightening. I had not bought my ticket nor even decided which train to catch until I arrived at Euston that morning, but even so, he had been able to track which train I had booked on and which seat I had selected, and he then had enough time and authority to ensure we had the carriage all to ourselves. The business suits were his people, and one of them began doing clever things with my mobile phone and a laptop computer a few seats away. I began to realise that I had been caught in an ambush.

"'So where is Dr Fadden?' Anderson asked.

"'I don't know,' I replied.

"'You're going to have to do better than that,' he pressed. 'You are on your way to Glasgow to meet him, and you don't know where he is? That doesn't sound very logical for a scientist.'

"'I thought I might call him when I arrived at Glasgow Central,' I answered.

"'I wouldn't bother. His phone is switched off and has been since your meeting with him last Friday night, but then you would know that. So, where is he?'

"He was determined on confrontation.

"'Look, Commander,' I smiled back to him. 'I don't mind you chasing terrorists all over the globe if you want to. Indeed, like most members of the public, I am grateful for the job you do as long as you don't involve me in it. I am not a terrorist, and Chris Fadden is certainly not one. He is a harmless and somewhat naïve academic who happens to have discovered a bug in a handful of dirt.'

"'A bug that eats plastic,' he interrupted.

"'So what?' I countered. 'Why shouldn't nature come up with a bug that eats the plastic rubbish we strew everywhere, and why shouldn't Chris Fadden be its accidental discoverer?'

"'Nice try,' he commented.

"He did not move. He obviously specialised in being able to annoy people and no doubt it is a useful skill to have in his line of work. I was the one who was breathing hard."

Chapter 54

Aunt Gwendoline said nothing but saw her grand-nephew draw on a deep breath to steady himself.

"'You gave Chris a real going over,' I snapped at him," he resumed. "'He was shattered when I found him slumped in his laboratory. He couldn't even think to eat. True, there was not a bruise on him, but that does not excuse the mental beating you gave him.'

"'We asked him a few questions,' Anderson deflected.

"'Over two and a bit days,' I challenged. 'And at the end of it, you let him go. If you were so sure he was a terrorist, why did you let him go? That doesn't seem very logical either for a so-called intelligence spook like you, and I don't get the impression you would ever admit you made a mistake. He would have told you nothing.'

"'Now, how do you know that?' he queried. 'How do you know he told us nothing? It takes a lot of training to reveal nothing under questioning by my officers. Perhaps you would like to tell me where he got that training.'

"'You're insane,' I fired back. 'He revealed nothing to you because he has nothing to reveal. He's an academic who has spent his life looking for bugs in soil. He is a fountain of knowledge about those, but he wouldn't have the first clue about anything in your line of work. He told you nothing because his world is a million miles away from yours and that is all there is to it.'

"We had stopped at our first station, and there was a crush of travellers waiting on the platform. I saw many of them eye the empty seats around us and make a rush for our carriage doors as the train pulled to a halt, but when it moved on again, none of them had joined us. I don't know how Commander Anderson had managed it on a crowded service, but manage it he did.

"We were quiet for a while as the train accelerated away from its stop. One of Anderson's associates came up and put my mobile phone on the table between us.

"'Keep it with you at all times,' he ordered, pushing it towards me.

"'I will,' I answered. 'And if Chris Fadden calls, I will let you know.'

"'There will be no need,' he dismissed. 'We will be listening in to every call made to you and by you. And don't think of switching it off because we will know that immediately too.'

"I did not pick it up.

"'You have answers to everything,' he continued after a pause.

"He was determinedly menacing.

"'I ask you a question, and in every case you come up with a perfectly reasonable and rational answer.'"

"'What's wrong with that?' I asked.

"I wasn't sure whether he was accusing me of something or not.

"'It is not how innocent people behave,' he replied. 'Ask an innocent man enough questions, and he soon begins to contradict himself or at least admit he doesn't know. You don't do either of those things. You always have an answer, an innocent and plausible answer, as if it had been all thought out and rehearsed beforehand.'

"'Maybe you haven't met enough academic scientists,' I retorted. 'Scientific debate can get pretty ferocious even by your standards. One learns intellectual agility when defending one's pet theory against a lecture hall of two hundred or so of one's more sceptical colleagues.'

"'As I said, you have an answer to everything,' he smiled.

"It was a neat trap and I had fallen straight into it.

"'So, who is Dr Witheney?' he asked. 'And where is she?'

"'I don't know,' I replied.

"'And where is Dr Fadden?'

"'I've told you I don't know. I'm hoping to find him. I thought you had people following him round the clock, so how is it that you don't know where he is?'

"'We will find Dr Fadden,' he answered. 'We were worried he might have skipped the country, spirited away down the same escape route used by your Dr Witheney, but your presence on this train tells us he has not done that and that he is still in Glasgow, so we will find him.'

"'It is my wish to find him too,' I confirmed. 'I am extremely worried about him.'

"'I'm sure you are,' he agreed.

"Another train stop came and went without any additional passengers joining our carriage. Neither Anderson nor I said anything until we were moving again. Sometime later, the female business suit brought a laptop to the Commander and

250

showed him the screen. She withdrew on a nod from him, and he turned back to me.

"'You will have heard the news about the fire in Bavaria and know it was caused by your bug eating its way through the plastic rubbish and producing large quantities of methane,' he resumed.

"'It's not my bug, Commander,' I countered. 'As far as I know, it is nature's bug, discovered by Dr Chris Fadden.'

"'Methane fires are rather nasty and difficult to put out.'

"'All rubbish dumps produce methane,' I shrugged. 'I have seen them spontaneously catch fire in India and Thailand and many other places in south-east Asia, so I can't imagine they would not do so in Bavaria as well. They burn for a while, then go out.'

"'But surprisingly, not this one,' he countered. 'It is too big.'

"He tapped a couple of keys on the laptop keyboard and turned the screen towards me.

"'This is something you won't have seen.'

"I looked at the scene. It showed a stretch of motorway, empty of all traffic except for what looked like police and maintenance crews being busy organising major equipment.

"'It's the M6 south of Lancaster,' he stated. 'Severe cracks appeared in its surface late yesterday, and the southbound carriageway suddenly subsided. Fortunately, no major accident occurred, but the motorway is going to require significant repairs, which will take some time.'

"'Very interesting, Commander,' I sighed. 'But unless you are going to tell me that Chris Fadden's bug has developed an appetite for bitumen as well as plastic I cannot see how it is relevant.'

"An insincere smile flickered across his face disappearing almost as soon as it was born, and suddenly looking at me from across the table were the eyes of someone who was unremittingly hostile. He leaned across and spoke quietly at me.

"'Not bitumen,' he hissed. 'Expanded polystyrene.

"'You mean the same stuff we use to keep our hamburgers warm after we have picked them us from the fast-food outlet?' I whispered back to him.

"'You can drop the pretence,' he snapped. 'I'm sure your academic engineering friends have told you that motorways sometimes have to be built over ground that is soft and liable to subsidence. When that happens, the foundations have to be packed with a material able to spread the load so that the next forty-tonne lorry that passes over it does not punch a hole in it and collapse the whole structure. The material used for that packing is expanded polystyrene.'

"'You mean our motorways are built on foundations of plastic foam?' I snorted.

"I almost laughed out loud. I had no idea it had such engineeringly desirable properties.

"'It is the perfect material,' he replied. 'It can absorb large shocks and carry huge loads and was predicted to last for at least five hundred years, and it would have done had it not been for that nasty little bug that you, Dr Witheney and Dr Fadden created and spread around wherever you went.'

"'Are you saying the foundations under the M6 are being eaten away by *Methylococcus faddenii*?' I queried again.

"I still could not comprehend it.

"'Not just the M6, but also the foundations of roads and transport junctions and even some towns, all the way across

Europe and North America,' he replied. 'But then that is what you designed it for, wasn't it? To make sure everything was brought to a grinding halt and nothing could move?'

"I was shocked at the implications of what he had said, and by the image of all our roads collapsing in sinkholes because they were built on foundations of plastic foam. All I could think was that it was more important than ever for me to find Chris Fadden. Hopefully, he might have some ideas about how this bug of his might be controlled."

Chapter 55

"We were approaching Glasgow, and Anderson's associates were packing away their computers and getting ready to disembark when the female one came forward and whispered something to him. I had forgotten my mobile phone was still lying on the table between us, and he suddenly scooped it up.

"'On second thoughts, you won't be needing this,' he said abruptly. 'When we get off the train follow me. Don't try anything different, I have officers all over the station. You will not be able to spot them and you will not know who they are, but neither will you be able to escape from them. There is a car waiting for us. You will get into it.'

"'Are you arresting me?' I asked.

"'I don't have to,' he replied. 'Under the Antiterrorism Act, I can keep you for twenty-eight days before I even have to think about charging you, and by that time, our American colleagues will probably want to talk to you too. You might like to consider that our American friends are not known to be kind to people who take it in mind to threaten their national security.'

"'Threaten their national security? Me? How do you work that out?'

"I almost laughed at the ludicrousness of what he was saying except that I remembered Chris and the way I had found him two days before. I decided not to laugh at all.

"Anderson leaned towards me, and as he spoke, I could smell the power behind him.

"'It is about time you realised that we know we are not dealing with an amateur group of disaffected individuals who have it in mind to play weekend terrorists,' he hissed. 'A bug has been created which lives quietly in the soil and has been specifically engineered to attack plastic. It gets spread around by assorted individuals and remains undetected while it eats away at the plastic that underpins the structure of our lives, causing rubbish dumps to catch fire, the random electrical circuit to short out, the odd car to crash and the occasional bit of motorway to collapse. It continues making a nuisance of itself until eventually, we realise it has grown into an epidemic. By that time, it is too late because nothing works anymore and every country in the Western hemisphere is now vulnerable to attack. That was the plan, wasn't it?'

"I was transfixed by what he was saying but still could not give him any answers. There were dimensions to his thinking I could not even begin to guess.

"'But the plan sprang a leak, didn't it?' he continued. 'When *Methylococcus faddenii,* which Dr Fadden had just spread around the plastics factories of America, short-circuited the detonators of the contaminated rice flour bombs on the London Glasgow train, we became aware of the existence of a specifically designed, biological weapon. Careless that, because it was also clear in the same instant that its conception, creation and deployment requires more resources than could ever be mustered by a bunch of disillusioned activists with a distorted sense of ideology. We know we are dealing with a hostile action by an enemy state. So, I ask you, who are you working for?'

"The picture he painted was either total lunacy or else frighteningly real, but I had lost the ability to decide which it might be. I looked at him and had no doubts that he was icily certain of the truth of what he was saying. I also knew I could not even begin to imagine Chris Fadden being in the middle of some mad scheme to create global Armageddon.

"'Is this why you are arresting me?' I asked.

"'Detaining, not arresting,' he corrected.

"He sat back and we waited until the train had come to a complete standstill.

"'You asked me why we let Dr Fadden go if we were so certain he was a terrorist,' he continued. 'I will tell you. It was clear he was not going to tell us anything.'

"'You questioned him to the point of collapse,' I answered.

"'He was well shaken but his training held, so we decided on a gamble. We gambled that if we released him, he had been shaken enough for him to seek help from those he was working for. So, we let him go and followed him.'

"'That wouldn't have done you much good,' I dismissed.

"I was thinking of Chris and his famous lack of sense of direction, and the random dance he must have led his shadows as a consequence.

"'On the contrary, it did us a lot of good,' Anderson countered. 'He made no telephone calls nor tried to contact anybody in any other way, and nobody tried to contact him. He made no attempt to go home or to the cheap hotel where he was staying temporarily. Instead, he went to his laboratory at the university, not an obvious place to go if he was looking for help.'

"'I thought that was where you dumped him,' I retorted.

"'We released him nearby,' he replied. 'He found his own way to his laboratory and surprise, surprise, a short while later, you got off a train at Glasgow Central and went straight there.'

"'I was worried about him,' I stated.

"'Undoubtedly,' Anderson smiled. 'But how did you know that is where he would be?'

"'It was a guess,' I answered.

"'A guess? You'll have to do better than that. If I was to guess, I would say it was prearranged. You had prearranged it so that if ever it looked like his usefulness to your operation was at an end, he would go to his laboratory and await rescue, which is why you knew exactly where he would be.'

"'It wasn't prearranged. It was guess on my part,' I insisted.

"'Next, you take him off to what is hardly a premier establishment, then you both go for an apparently random walk all over Glasgow until dawn. What did you talk about all that time, I wonder? Did he tell you he had told us nothing?'

"'Not at all,' I replied.

"'Did you tell him you were going to get him out now that his usefulness to you was finished?'

"'Certainly not.'

"'And did you tell him about the escape route you had used earlier to help Dr Witheney disappear?'

"'You are out of your mind,' I answered, but Anderson was not to be stopped.

"'Finally, you separate,' he continued. 'You take a clear and easily visible route to Glasgow Central station and catch a train back to London. Dr Fadden goes off on a tortuous path through the back streets of Glasgow, and manages to slip out of the sight of my officers for a fraction of a second and lose them. Now, you ask me why I am detaining you. Someone has released a nasty little bug into our community, a bug that can render all the infrastructure and defence of the entire West inoperable prior to a military invasion. We need to know who that someone is and the trail leads to you. I ask you again, who you are working for?'

"'I work for the university,' I replied. 'And as far as I know, Chris' bug is something that nature concocted. As for his wandering around, he does that because he has no sense of direction. A random search pattern is the only way he knows of finding his way to wherever he has to go, and if that strategy left your officers behind, then I would suggest it is they who became confused, not Chris, and you would be better off getting some new ones.'

"A brief, grim smile flickered across Anderson's face again.

"'As I said earlier, you have an instant and plausible answer for everything. Come along, our car is waiting.'"

258

Chapter 56

Gerard paused momentarily, and Aunt Gwendoline moved herself gently in her chair to relieve the stiffness that had crept into her. She did not want to interrupt him. She had been sleeping soundly since her conversation with Anne Blaise and her dream images of Felderby Pit and Iron Works were fading, but he needed to tell his story and there was also the question of the Cleveland Bay that had to be answered.

"I don't know Glasgow well enough to know where I was taken," Gerard continued. "The car had black windows, and I was hemmed in the back seat between two of the biggest bodyguards you could imagine, so I did not have much of a view anyway. All I know is I ended up in a brightly lit, windowless room with only a table and three chairs for company. Belt, shoelaces, contents of pockets were all removed from me and I sat down to wait. It was weird, unreal and very scary and I began to understand how Chris Fadden must have felt when he was first detained by Commander Anderson. I have dealt with corrupt officials in other countries, ones who have the power to harass you, arrest you, inconvenience you and stop you from going about your business. I have known bureaucratic minions in this country who go out of their way to make matters awkward for you for no reason other than to emphasise their own importance. But Anderson was neither of these. He was not corrupt in any sense that you and I would understand. He was totally sincere and unshakeable in what he believed. Neither was he unimportant. He had a huge power that did not leave space for any negotiation. He could make me disappear if he wanted to, render me lost without a trace. I began to think that perhaps he already had and my problem, as I saw it, came down to him being wrong and me having to convince him of it."

After half an hour, he came in accompanied by a female colleague. I wondered if she had been specially selected. She was attractive but unsmiling, projecting an image of power through a business suit and blouse that were tight where it mattered, and wearing a trace of a perfume that promised much but under the circumstances could deliver nothing. She was part of the armoury I assumed, designed to distract, and I remembered Chris' brush with a similar female when he thought he was being stalked by big business after his bug. It seemed an innocent scenario now.

The questions started.

"'Where is Dr Fadden?'

"'I don't know.'

"'But you do know he is in Glasgow?'

"'I assume so. I came up here to find him and I can't think of anywhere else he might be.'

"'What about Dr Witheney, where is she?'

"'I don't know. As far as I know, she doesn't exist.'

"'What's her real name?'

"'Dr Witheney I presume.'

"'When did she first contact you?'

"'When she telephoned my department to tell me she was on her way.'

"'So, she does exist. Why did you say she didn't?'

"'What I meant was that someone called Dr Witheney called my department to say she was on her way but she didn't turn up. I cannot recall her and as far as I know she may not even exist.'

"'So, how did she call you if she doesn't exist?'

"'She may or may not exist. I don't know. That's for you people to find out.'

"'She's not your friend, you know. She has made her exit and left you on your own. She'll not try to contact you to help you.'

"'I have no idea what you're talking about.'

"It went on like that for more than a couple of hours, then Anderson left the room and his partner took over, joined by another male inquisitor. The same questions were repeated *ad nauseam* until I was sick of them.

"'Where were you going to meet Dr Fadden?'

"'I've no idea. I was going to call him when I got to Glasgow.'

"'What number were you going to call him on?'

"'I was going to try his mobile. It's the only number I have.'

"'His mobile phone is switched off. What number were you going to call him on?'

"'I've told you. If you don't know the answer by now, then you never will,' I shouted back at them.

"'So, tell us what we want to hear. What is Dr Witheney's real name?'

"'Dr Witheney.'

"'Who does she work for?'

"'No idea.'

"There was another change of shift and the questions continued. They just went on and on. I lost all track of time and it must have been very late when they finally called it a day. I was escorted to a cell and I slumped on to the bed and was asleep instantly. My last thought was that Chris had been questioned like this for almost three days and they hadn't believed him, and he ended up shattered. I would have to come up with something to counter Anderson's distorted logic if I was not going to end up the same.

"I felt as though I had been asleep for only a couple of minutes when I was woken roughly and taken back for another question-and-answer session.

"'Why did you come to Glasgow?'

"'To see Chris Fadden.'

"'So, where is he?'

"'I don't know.'

"'You came to Glasgow to see him.'

"'I don't know where he is. I just hoped I might be able to find him.'

"The questions went round and around in circles for goodness knows how long before I was taken back to my cell and exactly the same thing happened. I had only just closed my eyes when I was woken up again and taken back for some more questions, or rather the same questions all over again. I'm not sure how many times this was repeated. After the third time, I lost count and in the end, I was too exhausted to care. I was completely disoriented and had no idea what time or day it was. I had not seen daylight since I had got off the train. All I had seen was brightly lit corridors where the lights never went out. I was simply hauled to my feet and dragged to the chair in the interrogation room and after questioning, hauled back again.

"And then I was woken by someone shaking me more gently by the shoulder.

"'Gerry, Gerry,' I heard a voice saying. 'Wake up. Have some tea.'"

Chapter 57

"It was Sergeant Chak. I came to, feeling very dirty, scruffy and unshaven and took the mug of tea from him.

"'Thanks,' I said. 'What on earth are you doing here?'

"'I just called in to see you,' he replied.

"'You'll have to do better than that,' I answered, using a phrase that had been used at me repeatedly over the past few hours.

"He grinned.

"'I was told you were here, and I was told to come and see you,' he admitted. 'How are you holding up?'

"'Considering I'm in the middle of a lunatic asylum and the chief nutter has got the key to the cell, I don't think I'm doing too badly. Nothing I say is believed and whatever I say is interpreted as evidence of some vast international terrorist plot to destroy Western civilisation. If this is the world of top-secret national security you can keep it. They are all mad. Anderson is even talking about World War Three, which is distinctly worrying.'

"'That's the nightmare scenario he's facing,' Sergeant Chak confirmed.

"'You're joking,' I snorted, but I could see he was deadly serious. 'Now you're really beginning to scare me. How do you get to World War Three from Chris Fadden finding a harmless bug in a handful of dirt?'

"'It's not exactly a harmless bug,' he shrugged. 'It eats plastic. We know it eats the plastic insulation around electric cabling so that makes it a fire hazard to every building we live and work in. That alone makes it dangerous, and if it gets into the national power grid then everything stops.'

"I had to agree. I remembered an occasion when we had a total power failure at the university. Nothing worked. There were no lights, no air conditioning, no coffee, and all our computers and other equipment shut down. The only thing we could do was watch a glass bulb thermometer hanging on the wall telling us how hot it was getting, and we could only do that while there was daylight.

"'There's something else you don't know,' he continued. 'There has been a plane crash, a jumbo jet full of passengers coming back from holiday. It turns out that Chris Fadden's bug ate into some plastic in one of the fuel lines, causing it to leak and thereby blowing up the plane.'

"The news shocked me and it took me a few seconds to take it in.

"'Many dead?' I asked.

"'Just short of three hundred,' he replied. 'The whole plane. The worry is that if it can do that to one plane, it can do it to others, and there are an awful lot of planes flying around the world every minute of every day, including the ones that are part of our military air defence.'

"I could say nothing immediately. When Chris first extolled the virtues of his bug as a means of cleaning up the environment, it all sounded so positive. I am sure neither he nor I ever thought it could do damage of such an order.

"'We have to find Chris,' I said at last.

"'At least we agree on that,' he answered.

"I was feeling very tired and must have nodded off for a second.

"'Gerry?'

"I snapped awake.

"'We have to find Chris,' I repeated. 'He has worked with this bug. He has spent his whole life working with bugs so he is bound to have a few ideas on how to control it.'

"'That is the hope, Gerry,' he agreed. 'And let's hope he can come up with something quickly because we don't have much time.'

"'It's still a long jump from him finding *Methylococcus faddenii* in a shovelful of dirt to getting ready for World War Three,' I protested.

"'Not when you consider it is not just this country that is infected,' he countered. 'We know the United States is infected because that is where the bug was found after Dr Fadden's visits. We know we are infected because of our failed train bombers and the collapse of a section of the M6 motorway. We know Germany is infected because of that huge conflagration just north of Munich, and we know Greece is infected because that is where the plane blew up. Other countries in Europe are becoming panicky. The Dutch are sending teams of divers down twice a day to inspect the sea bottom under the Oosterschelde tidal flood barrier. Apparently, when they built it, huge plastic mattresses full of sand and gravel were laid on the seafloor to provide a flat surface for the barriers to seal against. If they fall apart, then half of Holland goes in the next storm surge.'

266

"'So how does arresting me help? I could be out there helping to find Chris unless, like Anderson, you believe I'm some sort of spy.'

"He took his time answering, and when I looked up at him, he simply rolled his eyes upwards and to the right. I looked over his shoulder. I had not noticed it before, but a slight shading in the corner of the ceiling indicated the likely presence of a closed-circuit video camera, no doubt with audio recording as well. He sat down on the bed beside me.

"'The Americans are convinced that this bug is man-made and is a weapon of mass destruction aimed at the West,' he answered. 'They have an international arrest warrant out for Chris Fadden and are on a massive worldwide hunt for Dr Witheney. They are both key to knowing where this bug came from and how it was made, and both have disappeared leaving you as the only identifiable person who knows anything about either it or them. Meanwhile, all of Europe is on the highest state of defence alert expecting an armed attack at any moment. If there is any way in which you can help us, Gerry, then do so and do so quickly, or we really are talking about World War Three.'

"'You're sounding like Anderson,' I answered him. 'You are discounting the idea that *Methylococcus faddenii* might be a completely natural phenomenon. Why shouldn't nature decide that eating plastic is a good thing for a bug to do. There's plenty of it around as you yourself have pointed out. And bugs are very clever little creatures, which is what makes them so fascinating to the likes of Chris Fadden.'

"I realised I had quoted Chris' own words, and the image of his cheeky grin expressing his unbounded enthusiasm for the world of microbes swam in front of me.

"'Quite possibly,' nodded Sergeant Chak. 'But can we afford to take that chance? We know there are countries who hate the West and are jealous of its success. If one of them wanted to attack us, then what better way of doing it than by letting loose an organism that devours plastic. We have to assume that whoever created it did so with malicious intent. We just need to know who it is.'

"'So, you are not looking for Chris because you think he can help collar this bug. You are looking for him because you think he is a terrorist,' I snapped.

He had the grace to look embarrassed.

"'We need to stop this bug before it does any more damage, Gerry. Already we know that replacing all the plastic in the world is going to take years and cost untold billions, assuming we can come up with something non-plastic to replace it with.'

"'And how am I supposed to help you when I am stuck in here?' I shouted at him. 'It is all utter, total lunacy. I know I am not a terrorist or involved in any way with any weapon of mass destruction, and I am as certain as anyone can be that Chris Fadden is not one either. As for Dr Witheney, I have not the first idea who she is. I was not even aware of her existence until my secretary mentioned her name to me.'

"Sergeant Chak put his hand on my shoulder, gave me a friendly shake, but said nothing more. The cell door opened for him to leave, and before he was through it, two of Anderson's people came in and lifted me bodily to my feet. They too said nothing but merely dragged me back to the interrogation room."

Chapter 58

"The questioning was a little more tempered this time, at least at the start.

"'We know quite a lot about Dr Fadden. He's quite an expert,' one of them began.

"'I assume so,' I shrugged. 'I don't know anything about his field of study.'

"'So, when was he recruited?'

"'To my knowledge, he's been at Glasgow University for some years. I don't know whether he was recruited or simply applied for the job.'

"'When did he start working on his bug?'

"'When he brought it back from America. He was quite excited about it. It chewed through the plastic bags the quarantine people insisted he wrap his samples in. That was in Australia.'

"'And is that where you met him?'

"'Yes.'

"'And is that where he met Dr Witheney?'

"'As far as I know, he has never met Dr Witheney.'

"'So, his only contact with her was through you?'

"'I've never met her either. All I got was a note left for me by my secretary.'

"'That was a slip-up, wasn't it?'

"I looked at my questioner through somewhat bleary eyes. The logic of the question escaped me in my tired state.

"'I'm not sure what you mean by a "slip-up". Secretaries often take telephone messages. There's nothing unusual about it. It's part of their job.'

"'Except that this call was not supposed to go through your secretary. It was supposed to go straight through to you, wasn't it?'

"'I wasn't in my office,' I defended, although against what I had no idea.

"'You were supposed to be in your office to receive the call,' he pressed. 'But through oversight, you did not tell Dr Witheney that you decided to spend two extra days in Hong Kong on your way back from Australia. As a result, you were not in your office to take the call, and so your secretary took the message. And like a good secretary, she wrote it down together with the time and the date.'

"'It's just as well she did, otherwise, I would never have got it,' I answered.

"He produced a transparent plastic folder containing my secretary's scribbled note, which presumably he or his friends has retrieved from the wastepaper bin in my office.

"'The mysterious Dr Witheney, who nobody knows and who cannot be traced, calls you with a very brief message from a public telephone at an airport and then disappears. If that message had been delivered directly to you as it was intended, you would have been able to deny it ever happened. But your secretary's note proves Dr Witheney exists. That was a slip-up, wasn't it?'

"We were back in the land of the lunatic asylum.

"'So, who is Dr Witheney and who does she work for?'" he persisted.

"I was too tired to play any more games, and I couldn't think very straight anyway.

"'You know,' I replied, 'If you are going to take that piece of paper to be evidence of anything, and considering we are discussing the rampages of a plastic-devouring bug, I would strongly recommend you keep it in something other than a plastic folder.'

"The interrogation got a bit out of hand after that.

"'Where is Dr Fadden?'

"'No idea.'

"'You know this bug can cause aeroplanes to crash?'

"'You mean by degrading the plastic in them?'

"'Yes. Big passenger aeroplanes full of women and children going on holiday. Do you want them on your conscience?'

"'No, of course not.'

"'So, who funded Dr Fadden to make his bug?'

"'The National Medical Research Council, I presume.'

"'You admit he made it.'

"'No. He found it in a shovelful of dirt and investigated it.'

"'What's Dr Witheney's real name?'

"'Mickey Mouse, sorry, Minnie Mouse.'

"It went on and on with increasing intensity until it just formed part of the background noise. I have read that soldiers have been known to fall asleep in the middle of an artillery barrage simply because the noise of it became so familiar that they were able to filter it out. I know I fell asleep several times during my questioning, only to be sharply woken again by a loud noise or a heavy shake or both. But what really kept me sane through those hours of questioning was thinking about Chris. I pictured his happy, grinning face and his enthusiasm for his bugs. I remembered his good humour as we played our practical jokes on him, and his gentle nature. I saw him as a Cleveland Bay walking beside me, with its big bulk and gentle trust and its wonderfully soft muzzle. I concentrated on those images so I should get through what was happening and not let him down. I didn't want to let him down. I knew that wherever he was, he was in a bad way and I had to get there and find him and try and help him. Meanwhile, I just kept picturing his face, his mischievous, grinning face.

"They were none too gentle when they finally escorted me back to my cell. I was asleep before I hit the floor."

Chapter 59

Aunt Gwendoline watched her grand-nephew as he took another break in his story. His hands were not too steady. 'Shell shock' came to her mind. She had seen it in the old men who had told tales of pert waitresses in French cafes rather than speak of the mud and barbed wire in the sodden fields of Flanders in World War One. She had seen it too in the younger men who had told her about butterflies and monkeys and snow-covered mountain peaks in India, rather than speak of the leeches and fevers in the monsoon lashed jungles of World War Two. The words were always less than the reality, or else they did not speak of it at all.

"I don't know how long it was before I was woken yet again," Gerard resumed. "The shaking wasn't gentle, but neither was it the excessively rough hauling off the bed that had been used previously. I sensed something had changed.

"I was dragged to my feet and back to the interrogation room and was surprised to see Commander Anderson standing by the table. I had not seen him since my first interrogation session. He was tense and business-like but there was also an edge of either excitement or anxiety, or possibly both, about him.

"'Your friend Dr Fadden has revealed himself,' he began immediately.

"I did not answer. I was still gathering my thoughts together.

"'He is in a suite on the seventh floor at the Gold Tower Hotel on George Street. He has been there since Saturday morning, checking in soon after he left you. I thought you would be interested to know.'

"He waited for a response from me. I did not have one to give him, although I woke up a bit at the news.

"'He has made no telephone calls, seen nobody, and has not come out of his room since he arrived,' he continued. 'He has ordered occasional light meals from room service but has insisted they be left outside the door. He has not allowed the maid or cleaning staff into his room. It looks very much like he was trying, in an amateurish way, to keep a low profile while waiting for someone to contact him.'

"I had no idea of the time. There were no windows or clocks where I was, and the cells and corridors were constantly lit. I was tired and had not been allowed to shower or shave.

"'Can I talk to him?' I asked.

"'Absolutely not.'

"He was not in any mood for argument. He gave a single nod to his offsiders and they lifted me bodily from my seat and carried me through a door and into another room that was full of people and activity.

"'Look there,' Anderson instructed and pointed to a television screen on the wall.

"It showed a scene on George Street, looking down from a high vantage point directly opposite a multi-storeyed building which I presumed was the Gold Tower Hotel. It was closed-circuit footage, and I was surprised to see from the date and time display that it was late Wednesday night. Anderson and his pals had been looking after me for three days.

"'At least now you've found him, you can let me talk to him,' I suggested again.

"I could only imagine Chris' mental state. I was not thinking too straight myself, having experienced Anderson's hospitality.

"'Out of the question,' Anderson snapped. 'Dr Fadden's mobile phone is switched off and he is not answering the hotel phone in his room. He remains determinedly incommunicado.'

"I watched the television screen in growing wakefulness. Police cars with flashing lights had sealed off a section of George Street. Armed police officers were clearly visible in large numbers while other officers held pedestrians and shoppers back behind a cordon, reassuring them and telling them that there was no danger and that everything was under control. Curiosity seemed to be the main crowd reaction.

"I looked at another screen. This showed the view from another camera, this time from on top of either the Gold Tower Hotel itself or the one next to it, and clearly visible on the rooftops opposite were the more sinister, black shapes of police snipers. I turned to Anderson, who was watching me like an eagle.

"'What are you doing?' I asked him.

"'That depends entirely on you,' he answered calmly.

"'Me? What am I supposed to do? You've got a frightened academic who is scared out of his wits because you roughed

275

him up and drove him to the edge of his reason, and you won't let me talk to him. He is not armed. He is not a terrorist.'

"'We do not know he is not armed,' he replied.

"'He's scared,' I fired back. 'He is not armed. He has never been armed in his life. You frightened the life out of him.'

"'He is vulnerable,' Anderson agreed. 'Clearly the person who was to come and help him escape did not turn up, and that has left him feeling isolated. So, who was that person? Was it you by any chance? Is that why you caught the train to Glasgow? Tell us the truth and the whole situation will be much easier to deal with both for you and for your friend.'

"'Let me talk to him,' I repeated.

"He ignored me. I looked at the screen, which was still showing the police snipers in their firing positions.

"'You are going to kill him, aren't you?' I challenged. 'Why? Because he happened to find a bug in a handful of dirt?'

"'He will only come to harm if he poses a threat to the lives of the police officers or members of the public,' he replied. 'We need to get him out of his hotel room so we can talk to him. We need to know who he is working for, who recruited him, and who was coming to get him out before we found him. We know you can tell us. To that extent, his life is in your hands.'

"I looked at the television screen showing the scene at the front of the hotel, holding steady on a row of floodlit balconies seven floors above ground level and displaying the windows through which snipers' bullets could crash at any moment.

"'You're mad,' I answered. 'You are totally mad. He is an innocent academic who is more like a schoolboy who has

276

never grown up, moving from school to university and then staying there for the rest of his life. He has never had anything to do with any terrorists.'"

Chapter 60

"Anderson fixed me with a stare that was completely unmovable by any appeal to reason or humanity. To him, the world was divided between those whom he had undertaken to protect and enemies, and I was unquestionably in the category of enemy. It was probably only a couple of seconds that we stared at each other but I knew there was nothing I could do. I had no answers to the questions raised by his view of the world.

"We were interrupted by a hurried knock at the door and another one of Anderson's team rushed in.

"'He's on the 'phone,' he said quickly, and pushed my mobile phone on to the table.

"Anderson changed focus instantly. He thrust the phone towards me.

"'Speak to him,' he hissed.

"'I? You told me I couldn't speak to him.'

"'Speak to him,' he commanded. 'And be careful what you say. You know what we want, and we are listening to every word.'

"I grabbed the phone.

"'Chris? Chris?' I called into it. 'Are you there, Chris? It's me, Gerry.'

"'Gerry, Gerry, thank god.'

"'Yes, Chris, it's Gerry. What's happening?'

"He began crying, sobbing uncontrollably.

"'I don't know,' he wailed. 'I don't know what's happening. I just want it to go away. I haven't done anything. I want it to go away.'

"'It's OK, Chris. Listen to me. I'm here, and I'm going to try and help you. What is it you want to go away?'

"'The police, spies, lights, everything. They are all outside. They are after me. I haven't done anything. Why are they after me?'

"'It's your bug, Chris. They think it's dangerous.'

"There was silence on the phone.

"'Chris? Chris, are you there?'

"'Yes, I'm here,' he sniffed.

"I turned to Anderson.

"'Call your people off. Douse those lights and give him a bit of space.'

"He did not move.

"'Have you been drinking, Chris?' I asked into the phone.

"'I've had a little,' he admitted. 'There was nothing else to do. I didn't know what else to do.'

"It sounded as though he had drunk a bit more than a little, but I was not going to make an argument out of it at that moment.

"'That's fine, Chris, we can sort that out later. We need to get you to somewhere safe. Do you understand me? We need to get you to somewhere safe.'

"'Somewhere safe,' he repeated and sniffed and snuffled some more.

"The camera view of the police snipers on the roof opposite the hotel wrenched at me.

"'Whatever you do, Chris, stay away from the windows. Chris, can you hear me? Stay away from the windows.'

"'The windows,' he repeated, then lapsed back into silence.

"'Chris, Chris,' I called. 'Stay awake, stay with me. Stay with me and I'll get you out of there. Just keep away from the windows.'

"I knew Anderson's people were listening to every word, but I did not care. I had to get Chris to safety before the snipers killed him. It occurred to me that it might already be too late, that the snipers might already have their orders, but I had to try.

"'What's that banging?' I asked.

"'Banging?' he sniffed again. 'It's someone at the door,' he replied after a pause. 'Someone is banging at the door.'

"I covered the mouthpiece and looked over at Anderson.

"'Are they your people?' I demanded.

"He returned my query with a stare which refused to confirm or deny. I went back to my phone.

"'Chris, are you there? Ask them who they are?'

"He did not have to answer. I heard more hammering in the background, followed by the distinct voice of authority. 'Dr Fadden? This is the police. Armed police. Open the door or we will break it down.'

"'It's the police,' Chris answered. 'Why do they want me? I haven't done anything.'

"'It doesn't matter, Chris. They want to come into your room.'

"I was watching the screen on the wall. At least if Chris surrendered to the police it would keep him out of the line of fire of Anderson's snipers.

"'You are going to have to open the door, Chris. Do you hear me? Trust me. Open the door. The police want to come in. Do you understand me? Open the door.'

"'Trust you,' he echoed, then more desperately, I heard him say, 'You are my friend, my only friend. Open the door.'

"Those were the last words Chris ever spoke. I heard his telephone drop on to the hotel carpet and the next instant, there was a crashing and splintering as the door to the room was broken in. Voices shouting 'Armed police, on the floor, stay where you are, don't move' followed. I watched the television screen and to my horror, I saw the glass door to one of the balconies open, and Chris walked out. The floodlights clearly dazzled him, but he kept walking.

"'Target clear,' called out of a speaker three times in three different voices.

"'No, Chris, no,' I yelled down my telephone.

"It was no use. The other end was on the floor in the hotel room where Chris had dropped it. I don't know what happened next. I heard a crash as something fell off the desk beside me, momentarily distracting my attention, and then I could only watch the screen as Dr Chris Fadden, lecturer in microbiology at the University of Glasgow, tipped slowly forward, silently, over the rail of a balcony on the seventh floor of the Gold Tower Hotel and fall headfirst to the ground below.

"It was a second or two before I could react. I turned to Anderson, who was still focussed on me and not on the screen.

"'You've shot him,' I shouted. 'You've killed him. Your snipers…'

"'Did you hear me give the order?' he interrupted.

"For a moment, I saw a flash of emotion in him, but I couldn't decipher it.

"'They are inside,' announced one of his officers relaying information from his earpiece. 'There's no one else. He was on his own.'

"'Of course, he was on his own,' I roared. 'What did you expect? A whole nest of terrorists?'

"I was angry and shocked at what I had just witnessed, almost out of control.

"'You shot him,' I shouted. 'Your snipers killed him.'

"'I wanted him alive,' Anderson replied calmly, but I sensed that something had gone wrong.

"'Bomb squad going in,' relayed the earpiece.

"'Bomb squad? What on earth are they doing there?' I gasped.

"Anderson looked hard at me then nodded to two officers standing behind me. They grabbed me roughly by the arms and bodily dragged me, still shouting and fighting, out through the interview room.

"'You bastards,' I shouted all the way back to my cell. 'You killed him. You scared him so much he didn't know which way to turn. Then you shot him. You killed him.'

"I was blind with rage and not functioning properly, but I do remember the date and time shown on the television display as they dragged me out of the operations room."

"It was just before a quarter past midnight, Wednesday night, early on Thursday morning," Aunt Gwendoline completed for him.

"How do you know?" he asked.

She returned his puzzled gaze and looked hard into her grand-nephew's eyes. The Cleveland Bay that he had rescued from the rockfall was too damaged ever to work again, so there was only one end for it, and a loud noise that could have been a shot had woken her in the dead of Wednesday night. It had frightened her to her core and had left her sitting frozen and frantic with worry for him.

"I think it was mentioned in the newspapers," she replied.

Chapter 61

Gerard sniffed back on the tide of impotence, anger, frustration and sense of injustice that was surging through him. It took him a couple of minutes to recover his breath.

"I was in complete turmoil when I was dumped back in my cell," he resumed. "I was angry that Anderson had created a vast fiction out of some unrelated coincidences of normal human behaviour. I was angry that he had acted on that fiction and had killed Chris. I was angry that he should refuse to acknowledge any responsibility for Chris' death and furious at the thought that he and his people would probably get away with it, all in the name of 'national security'. They may or may not have shot him, in truth I do not know, but I did know that they would avoid all individual and collective accountability for what they had done. I began to despair.

"I wasn't given time to fall asleep. A rattling at my cell door reminded me that although Chris was dead, they still had me. Two minders came in and escorted me back to the interview room where the male and female officers I recognised from previous interrogations were waiting for me. They seemed in no hurry to start, the male especially taking his time reading and rereading two sheets of printed paper on the table between us.

"'Where's Anderson?' I demanded.

"'The Commander is otherwise engaged,' the female replied.

"We sat there a few more minutes while the two sheets of paper were read a couple more times.

"'The official story being given to the press,' began the male quietly. 'It appears that Dr Fadden took his own life by throwing himself off a seventh-floor balcony at the Gold Tower Hotel, George Street, Glasgow. Nobody knows why he did it, but it was known that he had been under considerable stress for some time.'

"'Stress created by you people hounding him for no reason,' I fired back.

"'There are a few additional details,' he continued calmly. 'Dr Fadden had a high blood alcohol at the time, and over the previous two days, his behaviour had become increasingly irrational to the point where it had worried the hotel staff. They had called the police out of concern for his safety.'

"'Is that how you found him?' I asked. 'He checked into a hotel, and the staff were sufficiently concerned about him that they notified the police? Not exactly a glowing tribute to your skills as secret service intelligence sleuths is it?'

"'We both know that is not the real story though, don't we?' he replied.

"'No, it is not the real story,' I agreed angrily. 'But you will never let the real story be known because...'

"I was too tired and exasperated to finish the sentence. There were too many reasons, but all of them came down to Anderson and whatever organisation he worked for being wrong and not being prepared to admit it, and being protected from ever having to do so.

"'So, what is the real story?' my inquisitor asked.

"I could not hide my distaste.

"'You know what it is,' I answered. 'A harmless academic, Dr Christopher Fadden, on a matter of chance, finds a previously unknown microbe in a sample of soil. Interestingly, this bug can degrade plastic. For reasons which only you can explain, you create an imaginary scenario whereby the bug is transformed into a weapon of mass destruction aimed at the Western way of life and something likely to lead to World War Three. On that basis, you hound Dr Fadden until he is unable to feel safe in his own skin. Finally, confused and not knowing where he is, he falls off a seventh-floor balcony of a hotel block, probably with a bullet or two in him fired by your snipers. Hip hooray, you can clock up another success in the war against terrorism and hide yourselves behind a smokescreen labelled 'not in the interests of national security' to avoid revealing any details that might show you to be responsible for the death of an innocent man. Congratulations, I hope you rot.'

"'Why did you order Dr Fadden to kill himself?' he asked.

"I could not believe what I was hearing.

"'I? I was trying to save him. You had snipers lined up to shoot him. You had armed police threatening to break down his door and smash him to pieces. I was the one who told him to open the door and let the police come in so he could surrender to them.'

"He consulted the two typed sheets.

"'What you actually said was, "Trust me. Open the door. The police want to come in. Do you understand me? Open the door." He replied, "Trust you, you are my friend, my only friend. Open the door." He then opened the door to the balcony and threw himself over. That sounds like an order for him to kill himself, which he obeyed.'

"The accusation left me totally nonplussed.

"'You're mad,' I spluttered. 'Chris was a friend. Why should I tell him to kill himself?'

"'We found nothing in his room,' he replied.

"'I'm not surprised. I'd be surprised if he even had a change of clothes with him. There was nothing to find.'

"'You seem very sure of that,' my questioner confirmed.

"I didn't answer.

"'There were no notebooks, files or computer disks in his room at the Gold Tower, but then as a scientist, he would carry everything he needed to know in his head,' he continued. 'You knew that, and he knew it was only a matter of time before we caught up with him again, so he went into hiding. He waited for his contact, the one who was going to get him away to safety, and when you did not turn up...'

"'Only because you people intercepted me on my way to try and find him,' I protested.

"'Precisely,' he agreed. 'We knew you knew where he was and that he had no other way out, and as we expected, when you did not turn up, he knew the game was over. You, his friend, had let him down.'

"'I did not let him down,' I countered. 'I came up to Glasgow to try and save him. It was you who stopped me.'

"The female inquisitor took over.

"'He was desperate,' she continued. 'He broke. He made one last telephone call, to you.'

"'He was my friend,' I stormed. 'Why shouldn't I talk to him?'

"'We misread the situation.'

"'I'll say you did,' I shouted at her. 'He was at the end of his tether. I could have saved him but you wanted him dead. You wanted a scapegoat.'

"'We wanted him alive,' she stated calmly. 'He had the information we need, information in his head and which you have so far managed to protect. You knew he would not be able to preserve that information through another questioning by us, so when we found him, you ordered him to kill himself. It was our mistake to let you talk to him.'

"She referred to the printed sheets again. '"The police want to come in. Do you understand me? Open the door". He replied, "You are my friend, my only friend. Open the door", and he opened the balcony door and threw himself over.'

"I had no credulity left. I stared at her and her impassive faced partner in absolute disbelief.

"'You're trying to sheet the blame for Chris' death on to me, aren't you, to save your own hides?' I gasped.

"'Why do you say he threw himself off the balcony?' the female asked.

"'Probably because he was confused,' I shouted. 'I told you. You had worried him out of his skin and he has no sense of direction. He cannot find his way around, particularly after a couple of drinks. He just opened the first door that came to hand. He didn't know it was the balcony. He just walked through it without realising what it was and was then blinded by the searchlights you had set up. He didn't throw himself off. If your snipers didn't shoot him then he probably just tripped.'

"'Commander Anderson said you always have a plausible answer for everything,' she commented after a pause.

"I think it was at that moment I finally realised I was a dead man. I had no counter to the corrupted logic of their thinking. I was in their hands completely and they had the power and means to make me disappear with never a trace to show that I had ever existed.

"'You are still trying to maintain the fiction that Chris' bug is a terrorist plot, that Chris was an agent in a network aimed at the destruction of the West and that I was his controller. You are not going to allow any other explanation, are you?' I sighed.

"I did not expect an answer and I was surprised when I got one.

"'An impressive performance,' the male interrogator summarised. 'And it might have been quite believable except for one minor detail.'

"I looked up at him wondering what was coming next.

"'Dr Witheney,' he stated.

"For the first time, the calmness in his mask slipped and he leaned across the table and hissed his venom straight into my face.

"'We know that when we look at you and Dr Fadden we are not looking at two inoffensive academics who happen to be jolly good pals and that is all there is to it. Put Dr Witheney in the picture and we know we are looking at a chain of command. So, who is Dr Witheney? What is her real name and who does she work for?'"

Chapter 62

Aunt Gwendoline heard her oak cased clock strike in the hallway but there was no message in its voice, nor had there been for the past week or more. Her Hunter clock had followed the correct time almost to the second for the same period, although she was still watching it in case it decided to misbehave again. She looked deeply at her grand-nephew.

"He will recover," she spoke silently to the sentinel in her hallway and to the aspidistra in its decorated pot on its Edwardian throne. "There is enough of all of us in him for that to happen."

Gerard hauled on a sigh.

"I never saw Anderson again after Chris fell. All the subsequent interrogation was done by relay teams of others, with me being allowed only minimal food, sleep and toilet breaks in between. I don't know how long it went on for. I completely lost track of time.

"They kept asking me about Dr Witheney, who she was and how did I get my instructions from her. Was it she who had ordered me to make contact with Chris Fadden and get him to kill himself, and so on? It was all nonsense and there was nothing I could answer to any of it. They seemed obsessed by her and all I knew was that she had called my department to say she was arriving and then never turned up.

"'You had arranged for her to visit you. Weren't you concerned when she didn't show up?' they asked.

"'Mildly,' I replied.

"'You didn't call the police and report her disappearance?'

"'No.'

"'Why not?'

"'I don't know. It's difficult to get concerned about someone you can't remember you've met.'

"'So, her sudden disappearance after she called you did not bother you?' they pushed.

"'It might have crossed my mind to hope the police didn't find an unidentified female body buried in some spot nearby,' I answered.

"'Are you saying she is dead?'

"'No, not at all.'

"'So why would you be concerned about her body turning up?'

"'That's not what I meant.'

"'Dr Fadden is dead, Dr Witheney is dead and a concerted bioterrorism plot against this country involving all three of you has been neutralised. Aren't you worried you'll be next?'

"The questions came faster and faster, although it was probably just me getting more and more disoriented. And then at some point, there was a change. I seem to recall it was rather abrupt and I don't know when it happened, but suddenly I became aware of the silence.

"I've had a couple of chats with Sergeant Chak over the past few days, and he has helped me put events into some sort of order. I gather that the end to my questioning coincided with the arrival of the news that you, dear Aunt, had discovered the true identity of Dr Witheney. Commander Anderson did not believe it, and he sent a couple of his own people to interview Anne Blaise while he asked the Australian Security Intelligence Organisation to check that she really was nothing more than a displaced Masters graduate in wombatology who had no disruptive political or religious associates. He did not like it when they confirmed it. He interviewed my secretary, and she admitted she habitually adds the title of 'Dr' to anyone who calls the department out of concern she might otherwise insult them. So, Dr Anne 'with an e' was comprehensively revealed not to be a terrorist who was going to start World War Three, and I was rewarded with silence.

"I dimly remember being picked up by my minders and taken back to my cell and thrown on to a bed. The next thing I knew, I was being shaken gently awake by a uniformed police sergeant offering me a cup of tea. He was all proper and official but there was a kindliness in his voice, and as I came to, I began to feel as though I had been allowed to sleep undisturbed for untold hours.

"'I'll let you come around in your own time,' he said. 'Then I'll take you along to the washroom so you can clean yourself up.'

"And that is what he did. He provided me with some soap, a towel and a shaving kit, showed me to some showers and stood discreetly aside while I made myself into a new man again. He handed me back my shoelaces and belt and took me for a meal in the police station canteen, which could have been breakfast or lunch or indeed an anytime meal. I devoured it with second helpings. It was quite tasty and I could not remember when I had last eaten.

"Afterwards he said, 'If you are ready, sir, we can complete the procedures and you can be on your way.'

"I was too bemused to do anything other than follow him.

"'Where's Commander Anderson?' I asked.

"'Commander Anderson?' he repeated. 'No, sir, there's no officer at this station by that name.'

"I looked around me and realised I was in a normal, standard police station with uniformed constables and other staff bustling around going about their duties in police-like ways.

"'What about the people who were questioning me?' I asked.

"'I don't know anything about that, sir,' he replied. 'I've only just come on duty. My chief superintendent told me that you had been in some sort of ruckus, not of your fault or making in case you were wondering, sir, and that I was to look after you until you came around and then see you safely on your way. There are no charges against you. Could you sign here for your belongings?'

"I picked up my wallet, mobile phone, coat and the rest of my pocket contents and signed.

"'Are you feeling all right, sir?' he continued solicitously. 'Would you like me to call you a taxi to wherever you have to go?'

"I assured him I was fine and thanked him and declined the taxi, and I walked out into the dim sunshine of an autumn morning in Glasgow. I was somewhat surprised to find the world was still there and began wondering whether or not I had dreamed the past few days."

Chapter 63

"Was that when you telephoned me?" Aunt Gwendoline asked.

She noted it took him a few moments to order his thoughts.

"Not quite," he replied. "I bought a newspaper and discovered it was Sunday, and I realised I had been in Anderson's hands for almost a week. I found a café and had a couple of cups of coffee and started gathering myself together. I was apparently a free man again, although I did not quite believe it. Commander Anderson would never simply admit he had been wrong and let me go. He had only let Chris Fadden go so he could follow him, hopefully to some supposed evidence to support the bizarre terrorist plot he had imagined.

"I smashed my mobile phone and dumped it in a rubbish bin and withdrew a heap of cash from a teller machine. I didn't want to leave a trail of credit card transactions for Anderson to follow. It is strange how suddenly I began to think of these things, becoming more aware of street surveillance cameras, being extra watchful and observant in case I was being followed or tracked or monitored in some way. I don't suppose my untrained efforts would have fooled any professional, but it is surprising how contact with the Andersons of this world suddenly makes one begin to behave in ways which are not quite normal. I guess that is how Chris started, trying to go about his everyday business while at the same time trying to convince those around him that he was not going mad. I should have been more sympathetic."

He looked across to his aunt.

"It was at that point I called you," he smiled. "I used a public telephone and kept the call short. I was sorry to sound so mysterious, but there was something I had to do and I did not want you to worry. At the same time, I was still anticipating that Anderson would be listening in to everything I said, and I didn't want him to know about it."

He dropped into silence.

"I was pleased to receive your call," Aunt Gwendoline prompted him. "And I did wonder where you had disappeared to."

"I went to the Isle of Skye," he replied. "Chris was proudly Scottish, and somewhere in the hours of happier conversation we had together, he told me that his mother had died when he was young and that late in life his father had remarried. It was a blissfully happy union that produced a daughter, Catriona, a half-sister for him. Because of the age difference between them he became more of an uncle figure to her than a half-brother, and he cared for her very much. I don't doubt that Anderson knew about her, but he seems to have mostly ignored her in his witch hunting, probably because she and Chris rarely saw or telephoned or wrote to each other. The way Chris described it to me they had no need for letters or telephone calls. They seemed to share an almost telepathic connection, so they always knew how the other was feeling. Maybe they did. Anyway, the Scottish newspapers had named Chris in their reports and had dug up the story about him having an argument with the university, of being under stress, of behaving oddly and drinking heavily in the days before falling off the hotel balcony. It was not stated explicitly, but there was a heavy implication that he had committed suicide. Knowing how Chris felt about Catriona, I was determined she should know more the truth about his death than that."

Aunt Gwendoline exchanged glances with Rani, who wagged her tail stump across the carpet.

"I took the train up to Fort William and hired a car," he continued. "I then drove over to Skye and the village of Sconser where I knew Catriona lived, and I pulled up outside a house to ask for directions. As I got out of my car, the front door opened and a woman stepped out."

"'I've been waiting for you,' she smiled at me. 'The kettle is on and I've got your dinner in the oven.'

"I thought she must have made a mistake so I started to introduce myself.

"'I know who you are and why you are here,' she interrupted me. 'And I thank you for coming. I've made up the spare room. You'll be tired after your journey so you'll want to stay the night.'

"It was very strange. She was, of course, Catriona though how I had driven straight to her door, I have no idea. The next few days are a blur. I know we walked a lot of hills, and it seemed as though some days we talked without a break yet never said a word to each other. On other days our hours together were spent in silence yet in those hours we seemed to share so much. I cannot remember all I said to her. I know I cried a lot. We both did.

"I told her about Chris, how I had first met him, how much fun he was and how he had discovered his bug and had dreamed of cleaning up all the plastic pollution in the world. I told her how, through no fault of his own, his dream had become twisted and distorted.

"'Your Commander Anderson sent a couple of his people here to visit me but they got nowhere,' she told me. 'We are an island community and they were more lost than a pair of lowland sheep.'

"Most of all I told her that no matter what else she might hear, and whoever she might hear it from, Chris did not commit suicide. Never in all my hours of talking with him, under all the circumstances we faced together, did he ever voice such a thought. He may have been desperate, but he never for one moment considered ending his own life. I played back to her that last phone call I had with Chris and I tried to be as certain as I could with her, but I had to admit that the moment Chris fell is too confused in my memory for me to be completely sure of everything.

"The only thing I did not tell her about was the police snipers and I still don't know whether that was right or wrong. I got the sense that she knew about them anyway. I don't know whether they shot Chris or not, but if they didn't, I believe it is most likely that, with his absent sense of direction, he simply became confused when the police arrived in his hotel room and he opened the wrong door. He stepped out on to the balcony and tripped.

"'I know you tried to save him,' she said. 'I tried to as well, but I couldn't reach him. You were a lot closer, but by the time you got to him, everything was against you. Don't blame yourself. I know he didn't die because he was drunk or out of his mind, and I can only thank you for being there holding his hand as he fell.'

"As I said, we walked a lot of hills."

Catriona. Aunt Gwendoline exchanged another glance with Rani. Like the old men who came home from World War One and the younger men from World War Two, Gerard had not told her everything. His memories of the past weeks were still too fresh in his mind. It would take time before the clouds they cast across his horizons would disperse enough to give him a clear view again, and that view would be over a landscape that had changed.

"Eventually, I had no more to say," he finished. "A week had gone by, and Catriona came with me to Fort William to see me on my way south and home again. As I was getting on the train, she was crying, and I think I probably was too, and she raised her hand and touched my face.

"'You have the gift, you know,' she said.

"I had no idea what she meant and no answer to give her, but the phrase has stayed with me ever since. She is a lovely girl, and I keep thinking about her, seeing her in my mind's eye whenever I think of Chris."

Chapter 64

"I would love to have seen Commander Anderson's face when you told him that the Dr Witheney he had been chasing all over Europe was nothing more than a transcription error made by my secretary," grinned Gerard as the three of them, four if Rani is included, strolled through the park.

"He wasn't happy about it," Sergeant Chak confirmed, pulling his coat closer around him against the wind. "Of course, he didn't believe me, but every job has its compensations and interviewing the delightful Ms Blaise and those legs of hers was a joy I will remember for the rest of my career."

"They are impressive, aren't they?" Gerard agreed. "She grew up in country Western Australia chasing horses around paddocks, so maybe that is how she ended up with them. She was a good middle-distance runner when she was at school and for a while, she held the junior state record for the high jump."

"And you found her down a wombat's burrow. Lucky you," added Sergeant Chak.

"Do I gather she has gone back to Australia?" Aunt Gwendoline asked.

"She left a couple of days ago," Gerard replied. "I was a bit surprised. I told her she could stay longer but she seemed to want to be away."

They walked on with Rani intermittently emerging from the undergrowth to check on their progress.

"I can't stop thinking about Chris Fadden," Gerard continued. "He died because Commander Anderson, acting in the name of our much protected and highly secretive national security services, got it wrong. He drove Chris to his death, if he didn't shoot him first."

"That is not what the inquest said," countered Sergeant Chak. "According to the coroner, Dr Fadden died through misadventure. At least he was spared the verdict of suicide which is what our secret security friends would have preferred. It is definitely not their fault if somebody kills himself."

"They were prepared to shoot him and may well have done," persisted Gerard. "He died through their actions and after he fell, they tried to blame me for it. There has to be a proper enquiry into how he died. Somebody has to be held responsible."

"There will be no enquiry," Sergeant Chak replied calmly. "Anderson and his people are not answerable to the likes of you and me. I got back to my station to find the last of his crew throwing a final couple of files into an unmarked van before driving off. My Chief Superintendent was more than miffed they didn't have the courtesy to say 'goodbye and thanks for the use of the office' or even announce they were leaving. They left like they arrived, without notice and without explanation, and now everything is back to what it was before."

Rani appeared again, reviewed the trio then turned back to where a thousand interesting smells awaited.

"It can't be back to what it was before," argued Gerard. "Innocent people cannot be killed without there being some sort of accountability."

"Look, Gerry," Sergeant Chak continued. "I'm pleased to be back to my way of policing where a crime is committed, evidence collected and the felon arrested and tried on the basis of evidence. But I have to concede it doesn't work with terrorism, not if we want to stop atrocities happening. Somewhere in the guts of our society, we need people like Commander Anderson, people who are authorised to act on suspicion alone before the crime is committed. And if we accept that, then we also have to accept that occasionally they are going to get it wrong. It's a trade-off, Gerry, and on this occasion, Chris Fadden was the price we paid for that protection."

"Chris Fadden's innocent life is the price we paid for protection against a bunch of non-existent terrorists?" he protested. "I cannot imagine you would expect either Chris or me or Catriona to consider that a good deal. Where do I lodge my official complaint?"

"You would be wasting your time," Sergeant Chak shrugged. "You wouldn't even know who to complain about."

Gerard and Aunt Gwendoline both stopped in mid stride and looked at him, and he smiled back at their bemused expressions.

"You didn't really think his name was 'Anderson', did you?" he asked. "And before you ask, no, I don't know what his real name is either, or even if he has one. In my presence, he was only ever called 'sir' or 'Commander'. Try to find him and you will only be chasing a phantom. Let him go, Gerry."

The two men looked at each other in the bond of their friendship, and Aunt Gwendoline saw her grand-nephew reluctantly sag under the logic of the policeman's advice.

"But how did we get to this?" he asked.

"Nobody sees it at the time," Aunt Gwendoline replied. "One thing simply leads to another. In nineteen thirty, we were all living if not comfortable then at least stable and well-ordered lives when we heard that a few men had lost their jobs. Then one day, the men of Low Felderby arrived at the Works' gates to be told there was no work for them. Shops closed because nobody had any money to spend, allotments were stripped of their produce, rabbits disappeared from the countryside and men scrounged coal from the waste tips to keep a fire burning at home. After that came the hunger marches and the soup kitchens. It was only in retrospect that those desperate months were called the 'Great Depression', and there was never any promise that life would go back to being the way it was after it was all over. And it didn't go back. The landscape had changed."

"I wonder what historians will call our time," Gerard snorted. "The 'Great Suspicion'?"

"I will probably not live to see that," Aunt Gwendoline replied.

Rani emerged from the bushes covered in twigs and leaves. Her coat was damp, her nose was shiny and her eyes were bright. She wagged her tail stump enthusiastically as she spotted her mistress. It was time to be going home.

Chapter 65

The tea was Oolong and Aunt Gwendoline had laid out a selection of chocolate mud cake, chocolate eclairs, some chocolate digestives and some plain shortbread biscuits. She was interested to note that Sergeant Chak was almost as keen a chocoholic as her grand-nephew.

"I see there has still been no public announcement about Dr Fadden's discovery," she commented.

"And there won't be," answered Sergeant Chak. "Largely because nobody can foresee what the effect such an announcement might have on the general public."

"So, are we just to ignore it?" she asked.

"Not quite," he replied. "A lot of new surveillance has been quietly put in place. Banks have received a puzzling request from governments to report any unexpected surge in demand for replacement plastic credit cards that have mysteriously crumpled in automated cash machines, local councils have been asked to track numbers of requests for new, plastic, household rubbish bins to replace those that have fallen apart, and the bottled water industry has been asked to report any problems with their plastic bottles as a matter of public health. Meanwhile, a number of governments are walking on needles because their banknotes are now printed on plastic membrane and not paper, so they are bracing themselves for some very loud complaints when their citizens discover their money is falling apart in their wallets."

"And has this new surveillance told us anything?" asked Gerard.

"Not yet," he shrugged. "The military are reporting that their emergency inspections of all the plastic bits in their tanks, bombers, fighter planes and warships have not shown any unexpected problems. They are even starting to suggest that *Methylococcus faddenii* might have gone away."

"That sounds more like a prayer than a conclusion," dismissed Gerard.

"Perhaps," agreed Sergeant Chak. "But the experts have come up with the theory that whoever manufactured *M. faddenii* could have spliced a suicide gene into it. That way an attacker could use it to disable their target's defences then wait awhile until it mutated itself out of existence, thereby ensuring that they themselves were not similarly disabled when they invaded."

"They are still thinking in terms of Chris' bug being a manufactured biological weapon," snorted Gerard. "I suppose now they have got the idea they will be working on it themselves."

"That's the way military people think," Sergeant Chak replied.

Gerard shook his head. "*Methylococcus faddenii* is nature's creation and it has not disappeared. I've had a letter from Dr Ji in Yangshou, China. A few years ago, the fisherman on the Li River began making their fishing rafts out of plastic polypipes instead of the traditional bamboo because they lasted longer. She tells me they are now going back to using bamboo. Their plastic rafts, which used to last more than five years, are now lasting less than one. Something is causing them to fall apart. I have also had an email from Dr Federovna, who has been working on archaeological digs near Ekerem on the Caspian Sea. It is an area that was amongst the most dead and polluted deserts in the old Soviet Union, largely because of the oil and plastics industries that were established there. She tells me that the landscape around her has suddenly bloomed. Something is breaking down the pollution and making the land fertile again. My guess in both cases would be that *Methylococcus faddenii* or one of its relatives is at work, and I can only think Chris Fadden would be very proud of what it is achieving."

"You could well be right," grinned Sergeant Chak. "Either way, nobody is taking any chances. The United States has quietly announced that all aircraft entering its airspace from overseas will now have to be sprayed inside and out with a particular sterilising disinfectant in their home port before departure. They have not given any specific reason for it other than 'new quarantine requirements' and passenger groups and airports are screaming about the costs and inconvenience, but the Americans are adamant. They do not want aircraft breaking up and falling out of the sky over the United States and putting US citizens' lives at risk. It is likely that Europe and the rest of the world will follow. Are you intending flying anywhere in the near future, Miss Penderrick?"

"I was last in an aeroplane in nineteen forty-three," Aunt Gwendoline replied. "I had a five day leave pass from duty in the Women's Auxiliary Air Force, and a pilot I knew had to fly his Lancaster bomber to an airfield near where my family lived. He offered me a lift."

"And since he was particularly good looking you accepted it," grinned Gerard, buying into a cheeriness they all so badly needed.

"Most certainly," she confirmed. "It saved me a train fare. But I would have to say it was not the most comfortable of journeys. It was very cold and draughty and extremely noisy."

"At least you didn't have to worry about plastic bits falling off," laughed Sergeant Chak.

"All I know is we landed with a big bump, and I needed a couple of gins in the officers' mess to thaw me out afterwards. Other than that, it was rather thrilling."

Gerard laughed too. It was the first time he had ever heard his elderly aunt admit to sampling anything stronger than sherry.

Aunt Gwendoline looked over to the aspidistra. Mother was sitting with her airs and graces beaming at the company as she always used to. The gentle chimes of her grandfather clock in the hallway told her that her dad was also enjoying the banter and nonsense being talked. And Rani, ever patient and watchful at her feet, was wagging her tail stump gleefully, simply because as far as she could see, everyone else was doing the same. Aunt Gwendoline sighed. The jed had gone, the rocks had fallen, the Cleveland Bay had died, and the landscape had changed and would continue to do so for many years to come, but they would all get used to it in time.

CPSIA information can be obtained
at www.ICGtesting.com
Printed in the USA
LVHW050939280621
691317LV00013BA/440

9 781528 972048